The Pig
Comes to Dinner

The Pig
Comes to Dinner

JOSEPH CALDWELL

❧❧

DELPHINIUM BOOKS

HARRISON, NEW YORK • ENCINO, CALIFORNIA

Designed by Jonathan D. Lippincott

Library of Congress Cataloguing-in-Publication Data available on request.

ISBN 978-1-8832-8539-5

10 11 RRD 10 9 8 7 6 5 4 3

To
Wendy Weil,
who inspires

AUTHOR'S NOTE

The reader should assume that the characters in this tale, when speaking among themselves, are speaking Irish, the first language of those living in County Kerry, Ireland, where the action takes place. What is offered here are American equivalents. When someone ignorant of the language is present, the characters resort to English.

The purpose of reality is to show the way to mystery—which is the ultimate reality.

—Sister Mary Sarah, SSND

The Pig
Comes to Dinner

1

Kitty McCloud, hack novelist of global repute, paced the pebbled courtyard of her recently acquired home— one Castle Kissane—on the pretext that she was waiting for her newly acquired husband, Kieran Sweeney, to arrive with his truckload of cows, thereby completing the domestic arrangements that would prove their conjugal claim to be, in the truest sense, a household in the age-old tradition of County Kerry, Ireland.

Although she had not articulated to herself the real reason for the repeated frantic backing and forthing—first in the direction of Crohan Mountain, which bordered their property in the northwest, then to the castle road on the south—she was, in reality, tormenting her imagination, determined to summon from its fertile depths a possible "correction" she planned to write to George Eliot's big mess of a novel, *The Bloody Mill on the Bloody Floss*—the added expletives a measure of Kitty's consternation. The continuation of her career depended on her highly successful ability to pillage novels from the commonly accepted canon and rescue them from the misguided efforts of their celebrated authors.

What she hoped for was a rare insight similar to the one

she had applied to Charlotte Brontë's *Jane Eyre*—in which it is Rochester who throws himself from the attic in despair over Jane's rejection of a bigamous marriage, after which Jane, with her goodness and kindness, tames the Madwoman, and the two of them create for themselves a life of calm contentment fulfilled by weaving, making pottery, and the practice of animal husbandry.

So far, none of the possibilities for *The Mill* provoked her imagination into the state of high excitement and imperative promise without which she could do nothing. For her, only a near-hysterical propulsion would allow her to proceed, and she was, at the moment, grounded in an inertia that refused her every attempt to create even the slightest stir, let alone the volcanic eruption she so desperately craved.

Whether she should curse Ms. Eliot or her heroine, Maggie Tulliver, for this intransigence was not yet decided. (Never did Ms. McCloud consider that the source of the difficulty might lie within herself. Such a consideration lay well beyond even *her* considerable powers.) She raised her gaze to the top of the mounded hill that was Crohan Mountain and saw nothing but heather and gorse and a scattering of oblong stones, whitened with age. She turned to the castle road, praying that the truck would soon arrive and provide some surcease from her torment.

To some degree, her prayer was answered. Indeed, a truck was approaching. But instead of the arrival of the expected cows, as so often happens with prayers the answer came in a form much less welcome. There, moving toward her, *was* a small truck—what in America would be called a pickup—but it was one identifiable as belonging to her American nephew, Aaron McCloud, and his recent bride, Lolly McKeever, now also a McCloud. In itself, their approach could not be considered a cause for concern. They might be coming to help welcome the cows or to invite themselves to supper, or to commit some lesser intrusion.

What roused in Kitty no small suspicion that something more complicated might be involved was the presence, in the bed of the truck, of a pig. A pig all too familiar and not at all welcome. Its snout was raised to take in the castle air, its cloven hooves apparently firmly planted in the bed of the truck to counter the bounce and rattle over the uneven road.

For the first time since Kitty had bought Castle Kissane, she wished it didn't lack the full complement of a moat and the attendant drawbridge, to say nothing of a portcullis that could be lowered in situations such as the arrival of this particular pig. The castle, to be sure, was not without its charms. It could claim a courtyard in which dogs might take the afternoon sun (should there be a sun). There were stables and sheds in arcades from which the healthy stench of manure could find its way into the great hall, where matters of state and strategies of defense had once been argued into incomprehension. At the top of its turret, reachable by a winding stone staircase at the end of a passageway that led past the conjugal bedroom, one could pace in the open air and participate in the life of the Kerry countryside. One could see the snow-dusted summits of Macgillicuddy's Reeks; one could count cows and sheep and search the horizon of the Western Sea for ships of friendly or unfriendly intent. One could smell the salt air, even at this distance, or the fragrant scent of gorse and heather, hawthorn and honeysuckle.

But truth to be told, the castle wasn't all that much. With its two-story crude stone bulk and its four-story turret, it resembled nothing so much as the architectural progenitor of a design that would find its ultimate statement on the central plains of America: the barn and silo—except that this mighty archetype was built for the ages. And, most to be regretted at the moment, it contained no keep into which Kitty could now withdraw, as had the populous of old, to escape unwanted encroachments.

Now, in the bed of the approaching truck, an unwanted intrusion was looking for all the world as if it had just won first prize at the fair and was being given a royal progress throughout the county, accepting with easy indifference the obeisance of those privileged enough to line its path.

So that it wouldn't seem that Kitty had been simply standing there as if waiting to welcome an unwelcome pig, and to let her nephew and his bride know that they were interrupting her at a task of some import, she gave a quick wave and, as best she could, tried to make it appear that she had been, before their arrival, on the way to the farthest of the courtyard sheds. There, in a great heap, was the refuse left behind by the previous tenants of the castle, who happened to be squatters: the stained mattresses, the broken lamps, the computer parts either obsolete or damaged in moments of exasperation; a broken guitar; shoes, boots, and sandals, most without mates; college texts (one in economics), tattered paperbacks (two of them Kitty's inimitable triumphs), magazines, and more than several works written in Irish, not only Peig Sayers, the bane of everyone's schooling, whose Irish writings were force-fed down their gagging throats, but also Sean O'Conaill and Tomás Ó' Criomhthain; and, crowning the pile, a television set with what appeared to be a kicked-in screen.

When the truck pulled to a stop, Kitty's nephew, Aaron, got out of its cab. He was wearing khaki pants, a red sweatshirt emblazoned with the word WISCONSIN, and a pair of muddy sneakers. Lolly dismounted from the passenger side. She was wearing a pair of oversized woolen pants, so large indeed that they could easily have belonged to some former lover who had left them behind on one of his more than several visits to the all-too-accommodating Lolly in the days—and nights—gone by.

Not infrequently did Lolly affect this attire. At times, Kitty considered it a permissibly mocking statement relative to her chosen profession of swineherd. A womanly pig person could surely be allowed to doff her fitted jeans and designer boots and don the obvious castoffs more appropriate to the disgusting chores her calling required.

In less charitable moments—of which there were a considerable number—Kitty convinced herself that Lolly McKeever, now Lolly McCloud, was indeed flaunting, for all to see, some past lover. That she could continue to indulge in this unseemly display even after her marriage to Kitty's nephew was surely an invitation to outrage. But Kitty counseled herself to refrain from a direct challenge during which she would have hurled not accusations but known truths that would shame even Lolly, who was, in most circumstances, almost as impervious as Kitty herself to any assault on her self-assured perfections.

Let her nephew—who, by the idiosyncrasies of Irish procreation, was only two years younger than herself—discover for himself, in the context of his precipitous marriage, the true nature of the hussy he had so ignorantly wed. Kitty would neither do nor say anything that might disturb the pre-

sumed bliss her nephew and her best friend Lolly—the slut—
were inflicting on each other.

That Aaron, himself a writer, had failed to see more accu-
rately the truth about his bride, that his perceptions were so
faulty, Kitty accepted as the reason he was of a renown so distant from her own. Had he possessed his aunt's incomparable
discernments, surely he, too, could have carried his bride
across a castle threshold instead of installing himself in his
wife's house, well within calling distance of the sty that gave
their home its defining distinction. Because competition was
never a consideration, Kitty felt quite free to praise and
encourage him in the exercise of his decidedly inferior gifts.

As Kitty emerged from these reflections, Aaron went to
the truck's tailgate, lowered it, and encouraged the pig to
jump down, which it did with improbable ease. Without so
much as a snort of greeting, it bounded down the slope
toward the stream that flowed along the foot of Crohan
Mountain. As she watched it cavort, Kitty experienced a
growing certainty that some unilateral decision regarding the
pig had already taken place.

Aaron and Lolly now stood before Kitty, smiling, signaling
that Kitty's good nature was about to be taxed.

"We brought you the pig," Lolly said.

"Really?" said Kitty.

"We thought it would be better off here," Aaron added.

"How considerate." Kitty, too, smiled.

At that moment, like a cavalry reinforcement coming to
the rescue at the most needed time, there came around the
turn onto the castle road Kieran and the cows.

The truck pulled up at the far side of the courtyard. Kieran jumped out, slammed the cab door, nodded to Lolly and to Aaron, went to his wife, took her into his arms, and put his mouth against hers—crunching his tawny, well-trimmed beard against her tender cheek, keeping open his blazing blue eyes even when they could see no more than the right side of Kitty's forehead, a strand of sweet black hair, and the upper curve of her lovely ear.

Kieran removed his lips, let his beard spring back into place, and reclaimed his arms, all the while, with still blazing eyes, piercing Kitty to the pit of her stomach with the now familiar warning that she prepare herself for further stirrings yet to come. Kitty, in good wifely fashion, seared his eyes with hers, neither of them blinking—a metaphor, perhaps, for the marriage recently contracted. Kieran turned and strode back toward the truck.

Lolly called to Kieran, "You want some help with the cows?"

"I think I can manage, but thanks."

With an overly casual walk indicating she was trying to make an unnoted departure, Lolly moved toward her own truck. "Maybe we should just go, then," she said airily.

With an overstated indifference all her own, Kitty, not without an undercurrent of resolve, said, "I think you might want first to go fetch your pig."

Kieran caught the word. He paused in his efforts to move the cows. "Pig? What pig?"

"Kieran, sweetheart," said Kitty, "there's only one pig. And it's here."

"What's it doing here?"

"That has yet to be explained."

"First, let me get the herd down to the mire."

The cows, huddled together, seemed reluctant to accept the invitation to go wallow in the bog. Some raised their massive heads and bellowed, convinced that it was to the slaughter they'd been brought and not to the greener ground awaiting at the bottom of the ramp.

Kieran, with the agility of a goat, jumped aboard and, with a nudge here and a slap there, began more of a shifting than a movement toward the incline. The cows stepped daintily, their hooves touching lightly on the weathered planks, proving to one and all that they were ladies of considerable refinement, their swaying udders and a single deposit of cow flop notwithstanding.

Now that the work was mostly done, Sly, Kieran's border collie, entrusted with disciplining the cows, bounded down the hill, having already left territorial claims at the sheds, the foundation stones of the castle, and the rock wall that hedged the apple orchard west of the roadway. Tail wagging, it happily moved among the cows, nipping shanks, barking, and generally making sure that the time for serenity had come to an end.

The pig returned from the stream and presented itself to its old acquaintance, Kieran Sweeney, snout raised as if it detected on the man's person some hidden delectable that would now be surrendered.

"*Faugh a Ballagh!*" "Get out of the way!" Kieran, who was returning to the truck to shovel out manure left behind by an indifferent cow, bent down and clapped his hands close to the pig's ears and repeated the words any Irish pig should understand, "*Faugh a Ballagh!*" He then jumped up onto the truck, shovel in hand.

The pig trotted into the castle courtyard, stopping midway to lower its head and slowly move its snout over the pebbles like a mine detector searching out buried objects. That it refrained from rooting and turning the entire courtyard upside down allowed Kitty to return her attention to Lolly and her nephew. "Should we assume," she said, "that your place has been destroyed by our friend here and now it's our turn?"

Lolly jerked her head back, aghast. "Not at all!"

"It's become quite docile." Aaron weakened his smile to indicate that he was lying.

"It's our present to you. The two of you," Lolly said, expressing a newly arrived thought. "A gift. Since you'll be doing some farming now, surely you should have yourselves a pig."

"All right, then," said Kitty. "Now tell me what's wrong. Why the pig? Why here? Why us?"

"Well . . ." said Lolly.

"Yes. Go on."

"Well . . ." Lolly turned toward her husband and whispered, "You tell her."

"No, it's all right. You're doing fine."

"All right, then." Lolly looked directly at Kitty, raising her head so that her chin and her nose made a show of being loftily indifferent to how her words were to be received. "We can't have it in the herd." She took in a quick breath to strengthen her resolve. "It's a lesbian."

"A lesbian?"

Lolly took in a longer breath. "It—it keeps—well—performing 'proprietary acts' on the females."

Before Kitty could respond, Aaron spoke up. "The females don't seem to mind, but the males, they—well—they get a bit exercised."

"Men!" said Kitty, snorting.

"Then you'll keep it?" Lolly's eyes widened in hope, then deepened into pleading. "I can't find it in my heart to sell it or, well, you know."

"Slaughter it? Is that what you mean?"

Aaron, no longer finding it necessary to whisper, said in a voice first hoarse, then closer to his normal pitch but with tenorial overtone, "Oh, no. We couldn't do that."

"Especially since you're here to dump it."

"Take it," Lolly pleaded. "Save it from a fate worse—"

"For a pig, there's only one fate." Kitty drew her index finger across her throat.

"Oh, don't say that." Aaron was horrified.

"And don't do that." Lolly shuddered.

Kitty, to make manifest the radical changes marriage had wrought in her life, called over to her husband, who had just shoveled the inconvenient flop off the bed of the truck onto the pebbled ground. "Kieran, do we want a pig? It's a lesbian."

"Which pig? That pig?"

"Yes. That pig."

"How can it be a lesbian?"

"Don't ask me. Ask God. She's the one should take full credit."

Lolly exchanged pleading for a lesson in etiquette. "It's a wedding present. You can't return it."

Kieran jumped down and scooped the manure back onto the shovel. "Then we should have had it for the wedding feast. But you'd taken it home with you." He paused. "Of course we could always use a bit of bacon."

"You wouldn't!" cried Lolly.

"If he wouldn't," said Kitty, "I would."

Lolly turned her pitiful gaze toward her husband. "Maybe we could build a separate pen. And maybe put a sow or two in with it from time to time."

"Well." Aaron breathed in and breathed out. "If that's what you prefer."

"It's not what I prefer. It's what I'm being forced to do," Lolly said, as Aaron reached over and put his hand on her shoulder. "Look at it," she added. "Look at how it wants to be here."

Kitty looked in the direction Lolly's out-thrust hand demanded. There was the pig, standing transfixed near the castle terrace, its gaze focused on the second-floor gallery that ran above the great hall. It didn't move, a rare moment for this particular animal.

"See?" said Aaron. "It likes the castle."

Kieran yelled back from the pasture where the flop was being recycled to improve—if such were possible—the planet's greenest grass. "Sure. And I like Dockery's pub, but that doesn't mean they're going to let me live there."

Kitty raised her hand, demanding silence. Aaron was relieved, since he had no answer to what Kieran had said and didn't want to say something stupid in front of his wife. Lolly moved closer to him, a show of solidarity for the verdict about to be handed down. They both looked at Kitty, who was now staring at the castle.

"Who's that in the window the pig's so interested in?" Kitty asked.

"What window?" Aaron squinted to hide his lack of interest.

"I think you mean *which* window," said Kitty.

Aaron didn't flinch. "Which window?"

"There above the great hall, the gallery, the second window from the left. The man standing there."

"What man?"

"The second window. The young man watching us. Brown jacket."

Lolly shook her head. "I don't see any brown jacket."

"Then get the hair out of your eyes. He's there; he's wearing a brown jacket and looking at us, and the pig's looking at him."

"Kitty," Aaron said, "I'm confused. I don't see a man with or without a brown jacket. In the second, third, or fourth window."

"Are the pig and I the only ones not blind, then?"

Lolly stretched her neck outward, Aaron crinkled his nose, each straining for a closer look. Kieran ignored the entire exchange and with noisy emphasis shoved the ramp back onto the bed of the truck.

"There," Kitty said. "Now he's gone, so don't even bother."

The pig clattered onto the terrace and began snuffling among the uneven stones.

Kitty gave a short laugh. "He must be one of the squatters come back for something left behind. We threw out all the bottles and filthy mattresses littered all over the place. They're in a heap in the far shed. But still inside is a loom. Up in the turret. And a harp with no strings. Would you believe the like? And a Ping-Pong table with paddles and Ping-Pong balls." She raised her head and yelled, "Don't take the Ping-Pong table. Or the loom or the harp. We'll buy them from you." She stopped. "There he is again, at the other window, at the end. Now can you see him?"

Again Lolly and Aaron looked.

"I still can't see him," said Lolly.

"Kitty," said Aaron, "there's no one there. You're seeing shadows, or maybe a mist is coming up."

"I'm seeing one of the squatters. And I'm going to go bargain with him."

Kieran busied himself with securing the back of the truck. "Do you want me to go with?"

"No need. If he's not as skinny as he looked, maybe he'd like a job. Help with the repairs they never finished. Like thatching the sheds."

Kieran gave the tailgate a good rattle. "I don't need any help. If I can't take care of a castle and a few cows and do a bit of roofing—with slate—"

"With thatch!" Kitty inserted, reviving a previously stated preference.

"To be discussed another time," Kieran concluded. "For now, don't expect me to train an apprentice in work you have to learn from the day you were born."

How fine he is, thought Kitty. Just like me: stubborn. Her impulse was simply to stand and admire her husband, but she knew that would unnerve him. "He's as good as hired," said Kitty. Then, to goad her husband into another point of contention, she added, "And we'll keep the pig. It is, after all, the one being besides myself has eyesight enough to see what's there for anyone to see." She swept past them all, moving with elegant determination toward the castle. Raising her right arm, she waved at the young man in the window. That he failed to wave back distressed her not at all. That he simply vanished gave her only the slightest pause.

She stepped onto the terrace. As she passed through the

heavy doors into the great hall, the pig followed, but stopped in the middle of the vast room and stared into a corner at the far end. There in the shadows was the young man, cap in hand. He wore a brown, crude-weave jacket over a tunic cinched with a cord that looked like rope. His pants legs went just below the knee. His feet were bare. He was looking at the pig, his brown eyes mournful yet expectant, his mouth and his entire face taut as if preparing themselves for whatever might happen.

"There you are." Kitty took a step forward. "I'm Kitty McCloud. I've taken the place, as you probably know. You're one of the squatters. I'm offering you a job, if you'd like."

She spoke to him in Irish, the language the squatters had come from Cork to learn. But he made no response; then ceased to be where he had been. He had simply disappeared. Kitty herself, unmoving, did not take her eyes off the spot where the youth had stood. She blinked twice, then said in a whisper, "Well, then; I guess he doesn't want the job." The pig sent out from behind a parabola of urine to water the flagstone floor. It was then that Kitty remembered where she'd seen the young man before. At her wedding feast.

2

Kitty McCloud had astonished even herself when she realized she had wanted not Aaron's and Lolly's simple marriage ceremony but a lavish event starting with a nuptial mass presided over by Father Colavin—the pastor of St. Brendan's for as long as anyone could remember—and followed by a feast in the great hall of her newly purchased castle.

So profitable were her novels that she felt almost obliged to appropriate this enduring relic of Kerry history, installing herself and her newly acquired husband, both from County families of ancient lineage, within precincts too long desecrated by foreign usurpers bearing the signal name of Shaftoe. The *Lords* Shaftoe, to be exact. These usurpers had occupied Castle Kissane for more than a century, starting with the Cromwellian conquest in the sixteen hundreds. (It is possibly significant that Kitty invariably referred to her book *profits* rather than her *royalties*, eschewing a terminology dating back to the royal percentages exacted from the gold and silver mines operating within the kingly or queenly imperium. It is also possible that in the light of the Shaftoe dominion, in her present circumstance she was even a bit loath to use the term *chatelaine*, insisting that she was no more or less than a "steward" holding the castle in trust during the times she might be its humble and unworthy occupant.)

In any case, it was these same Lords Shaftoe who had been responsible for a horrific curse being laid upon Castle Kissane, which for Kitty was not least among her new home's attractions. She had not yet had an opportunity to give serious consideration to that curse. The great hall, where she had held her postnuptial festivities, had claimed her more immediate attention.

The church ceremony itself had been something less than a complete success. Father Colavin had been persuaded beforehand not to quote St. Paul's incendiary words, "Let women be subject to their husbands as to the Lord," but Kitty's American nephew had wept throughout, possibly because he and his bride had had to content themselves with a civil ceremony. This was Aaron's second marriage, his first having been to a woman named Lucille who had subsequently run off with a baritone from their church choir in New York. Aaron's divorce was the reason they weren't allowed a church ceremony, but Lolly had consoled him with the prospect that the marriage to Lucille could readily be annulled by the Vatican based on the obvious truth that he had been far too emotionally immature at the time to have entered into a binding contract. The proof was his very choice of Lucille. That Aaron, presentable as he might be and amiable besides, might have contributed to Lucille's change of partners was given no consideration. His certainty of his genius and the unassailability of his ego were subtracted from the equation, and Lucille alone was left to bear the blame.

Once the ring was on Kitty's finger, to the relief of some, the chagrin of others, and the astonishment of everyone else, Kitty kissed Kieran, Kieran kissed Kitty, and the liturgy moved forward as a prelude to the reception in the great hall of the castle.

Not that the great hall was all that great. Since the castle had been built more as a fortification than as a seat of splendor, its boasts were limited to the impregnability of its walls and the narrowness of its deep-set windows. In truth, the hall had served, Kitty surmised, probably either as a barracks for the billeted warriors charged with fighting invading forces, or, more likely, a safe haven for the livestock during the cattle raids that provided repeated sport among the native earls and chiefs of earlier Ireland. There were no fireplaces, which suggested that the animal presence was the sole source of heat.

Still, it had its finer features. A gallery ran alongside the outside wall with four mullioned windows looking out over the courtyard. There was a chandelier of heavy pounded iron, five feet in diameter, with two interior rings, all of them outfitted for candles, at least a hundred by Kitty's count. The flooring was dark gray flagstone, aspiring to black, smoothed by the clatter of cattle and the cobbled boots of yeomen, archers, and, later, musketeers committed to the sanctity of their homeland against the invasions of the Danes, the incursions of the Normans, the coming of the Spanish, and, finally, the arrival of the Cromwellians.

But now the hall was to fulfill its higher purpose: a place of revels and song, of dancing and rejoicing, of gluttonies most painful and of drinking most challenging. In the course of the marriage festivities the true purpose of Kitty's and Kieran's largesse would reveal itself. So eager were the guests to avail themselves of each and every opportunity for excess that the bride and groom were left mostly to themselves, with only the most distant of acquaintances or the most obsequious of strangers feeling obliged to thank the hostess and the host and wish them joy in the connubial adventure to which they had committed themselves. This gave Kitty and Kieran the chance—seated off to the side, away from the musicians—to discuss this man's gorging and that woman's drinking, and to agree that the expenditures were well worth it in the distractions they provided and the privacy they insured. There was also time to look, sometimes boldly, sometimes slyly, into each other's eyes, each provoking in the other a longing and a passion that would later spend and replenish itself, then spend and replenish itself again and yet again until the dawn would decree some repose, some small respite in each other's arms before disruptions of daily life would either nourish or destroy their earthly happiness.

There were, of course, interruptions of their extravagantly purchased solitude, one of the more conspicuous being Maude McCloskey, self-proclaimed Seer of the County, a woman with powers descended from—according to legend—the Little People with whom her ancestors had interbred if not intermarried. (It had long been Kitty's habit to think of her as a Hag, a term residing somewhere between an out-and-out Witch and the more acceptable Seer. Meanness had not prompted the choice. Kitty simply found the word more interesting, more evocative.)

Maude, however, was far from the stereotypical crone, and showed in her height and in her fair form that the genetic contributions of the leprechauns and their like had long been absorbed by some highly handsome and sturdy

Kerry folk. The Little People had left behind only their claims to heightened insight and prophetic certainties.

"So Castle Kissane has come into the clutches of the McClouds, has it?" The good woman was cheerful, almost giddy at this consummation, her dark eyes beaming with approval, her full-lipped mouth wide with a near lascivious grin.

Kitty drew the fringe of her bridal veil over her right cheek, shielding at least part of her face from Maude's bright and unsettling gaze. "It would seem so," she said.

"Well, you're the woman for it, if anyone is."

"Why, thank you."

"And you've got Kieran Sweeney now, and that might be a help."

"I don't doubt it." Kitty managed not to visibly bristle at the insinuation that she was in need of a man's assistance.

"Yes, yes," Maude said, letting Kitty know she was fully aware of what she was thinking. "But you might need him all the same."

"Maude," said Kitty, "if you've come to pronounce some waiting doom, make your pronouncement, please, and let me get on with my marriage."

Maude shook her head, still smiling. "If you knew what I know, you wouldn't be so impatient to hear it all."

"Then you mustn't let me keep you from your other pleasures." Kitty turned away and made a point of looking at no one in particular. This gave her a moment yet once more to rehash Castle Kissane's forbidding history. The eponymous Kissane, one of the mightier chiefs of seventeenth century Ireland, a patriot and a descendent son of Kerry going back beyond the time of Saint Brendan himself, had persuaded one and all that opposition to the Cromwellian heretics was use-less. So, rather than shed the blood of men good and brave, he had negotiated a surrender that would leave them all unharmed—and able to fight another day. With that, the indomitable chief had tripped the light fantastic to France, where, rumor had it, he settled in wine country and lived to a besotted old age. His trusting countrymen who had served the castle were put to the sword: warriors and smithies, fisherfolk and farmers, shepherds and bards.

For a time the intruders thrived under the tyrannies of the aforementioned Lords Shaftoe, who had been given the better tracts of Kerry land as a reward for the perfidies oft told, one Shaftoe generation succeeding the other in unop-posed possession, with the exception of a few thrown stones, a maimed cow here, a poisoned well there, followed by a hanging there and an eviction here. Eventually the Shaftoe line wearied of its discomforts and repaired to London, leav-ing in their steads a series of agents, few of whom died in bed.

Then came the curse that so enticed Kitty and forced her expectant hand as it signed the document proclaiming her ownership. In the early eighteen hundreds, the latest Shaftoe in the succession declared himself once more Lord of the Castle, and preparations were made for his return. As he pro-gressed beyond the pale, rumors reached him that among the improvements intended to guarantee his ease in so cold and crude a land was a built-in cache of explosives that would be ignited as the primary manifestation of his welcoming.

This deterred him not at all. Upon his arrival, the gentry were summoned to the great hall and questions put. Where was the gunpowder? Who had provided it? Who was elected to ignite it? No answers were forthcoming. Practiced in the ways of persuasion, his Lordship selected two youths, the handsomest of the young men and the fairest of the young women, both about age seventeen. They were to be detained for twenty-four hours. If, within that time, no answers to his questions had been proffered, the youths would be hanged.

And so the youths were hanged. Soon after, their lithe and lovely bodies were cut down and buried in a far and secret place to deprive the populace of the martyrs' graves that could become a place of pilgrimage and a source of discontent. His Lordship, under cover of night, set sail for Dingle on a voyage that would eventually land him in far Australia, where, as he must have expected, his despotic talents could still be exercised to the full.

Castle Kissane remained unoccupied. Few would even venture near. There the gunpowder waited. No one doubted it. Everyone continued to expect the eruption at any time. But those commissioned to carry out the plot seemed to have vanished. New rumors arose. Perhaps the handsome boy and the fair, fair girl had been, after all, the designated torchbearers. Perhaps his Lordship had been more prescient than he would ever know, which meant that no one living could dispose of the powder and the danger would forever remain until some chance gesture, some random action, would grant its release.

But then, after the nineteenth and twentieth centuries had run their troubled course, a new breed, a group of determined squatters, young women and men from Cork eager to defy augury, had taken over the castle. No one in the countryside objected. The squatters had come into the Gaeltacht, the truer Ireland that fronted the Western Sea where Irish was still the first language, where the Gaelic tongue had never been stilled. They had arrived to reclaim the long-suppressed and abandoned words and sounds that had, in distant times, proclaimed the presence of a people saintly, scholarly, and given greatly to over-rejoicing—and, one might add, a susceptibility to the myths that alone could give measure to their imaginations.

Due to taxes unpaid by the absentee Shaftoes, the castle had passed on to the nation, and no particular bureaucracy took enough interest to evict the newcomers, especially since they repaired some of the pasture stone walls, partly restored the courtyard sheds, and cleared the underbrush from the orchard, using the twigs and bramble to warm the castle hearths. They also made resident again music and laughter, lust and lovemaking, with a feud or two thrown in to prove the Irish presence.

And so it came to pass that, just as the squatters were beginning to decamp for Donegal there to seek added experience, Kitty—rich beyond repair, famous far beyond her deserving—cajoled, badgered, and beguiled enough bureaucrats so that Castle Kissane, curse and horror and history and all, now came into her possession. This seemed only fair, since her own cliffside home, long inhabited by her Kerry ancestors, had been tumbled into the all-devouring sea by the unlikely concatenation of events that had brought Kitty and Kieran to the blissful contentions that were a favored part of their current conjugal happiness.

Maude broke into Kitty's musings. "I could do with a drink, I suppose," she said.

"And welcome to it."

"And may I drink to your rescue—and Kieran's, too— from the curse the castle holds fast in its every stone?"

"Drink. And drink again." Kitty made a low bow.

"And drink as well to your protection when the stones fly heavenward and the tower topples as has been destined from the years long since?"

Now the woman's smile became a benevolent laugh. And, to Kitty's surprise, it seemed that handsome Maude McCloskey was transformed, for just that moment, into one of the more beautiful women the County had ever seen. Her skin was luminous with an inner glow, her eyes deepened with a sympathetic sweetness, her proud chin relaxed to a benign serenity. An almost tender sorrow crept into her voice as she said, "You know the story as well as any. Lord Shaftoe—what was intended for him may well come down to you. We've taken a chance, all of us, to be here now. Who knows when the moment will come? Before I speak another word? Tonight as you wrestle on the nuptial couch? At daybreak? At dusk? Tomorrow? A year from now? Others search for gold. Search, I tell you, for the gunpowder. It's here."

"Nonsense. That was all cleared up years and years ago. They dug from here to there and there to here and found nothing."

"I know. That means it's still here. But don't let that interrupt the festivities." With that, her face reformed itself, and she became a handsome woman again but no longer a Seer transfigured. "But consider yourself warned. Watch you and Kieran both don't go flying sky-high the way was intended for his Lordship."

"Maybe I look forward to the excitement."

"You won't be looking forward. You'll be looking downward—and from a great height and your eyes gone blind and not a limb left to scratch your nose or reach out and hold your husband's hand. Well, at least you'll be halfway to heaven. Whether you'll go the rest of the way is anyone's guess. And I won't tell what mine is."

"No need for that, is there?"

"Oh, Kitty, Kitty, Kitty McCloud. Why do you resist being what you are?"

"And what might that be?"

"A prophet. Come now, admit to it."

"Really, Maude. Such extravagance!"

"And I a prophet, too. As everyone knows."

"I certainly hope not, with your foretelling me gone sky-high and halfway to heaven and Lord Shaftoe quiet in his grave."

"Why do you talk such foolishness? We're prophets, not fortune-tellers."

"And didn't you just now give the notion you could see this place gone up with gunpowder and me along with it?"

"A prophet doesn't tell the future. A prophet tells the truth. A truth no one wants to hear. Or believe. And that's why you're a prophet. You're a truth teller. I've read the books you've written. And there's a truth in all of them."

"Maude, you've gone stark raving. I'm a money monger. And to satisfy my greed I tell more lies than the snake itself."

"And it's a lie you're telling now. You needn't admit it to me. But you've always admitted it to yourself. You know you're a prophet. You know you hold the truth, and I'm the one knows it as well as you."

"I do it for the money. Isn't it obvious?"

"And did you write the truths told in your retelling of

Jane Eyre? Anyone with the slightest sense of justice would have done what you did—given the rage and the talent that's yours. There was Miss Charlotte Brontë trying to tell us it's a great fulfillment for poor Jane to have her Rochester after all, a bit battered though he may be. And how did Miss Brontë manage that? By having Jane step over the broken bones of a dead madwoman. Is that the path to happiness? Has Jane no conscience? You did it right. Rochester throws himself headfirst from the attic because Jane will have none of his bigamous offer. And it's *his* bones broken, and it's over *his* dead body Courtney—" Here she became puzzled. "Is it Courtney or is it Tiffany you call the Jane character?"

"Brianna."

"Ah, yes, Brianna. And it's over his dead body—is it Kyle or Kevin?"

"Kevin."

"And so it's over Kevin's dead body Tiffany—"

"Brianna."

"—Brianna steps over, and she and the madwoman, cured by Brianna's kindness and caring, settle down to a life fulfilled enough, what with the pottery, weaving, and a bit of animal husbandry. Now *that's* the work of a truth teller. A tale told by a prophet. You. Kitty McCloud."

Kitty tried to stop the squirming that no amount of previous doomsaying had been able to accomplish. The Seer was, indeed, making revelations that Kitty, from the beginning of her career, thought she'd been able to keep to herself.

Her motive wasn't really the money. It was her insistence on truth, on justice. Then, too, she had her wrath, a bottomless cauldron from whose roiled depths would surface some of the most deeply honest fiction of her generation.

But none of this must ever be known. If her worldwide readership—yet another by-product of so-called globalization—ever saw in her not the shameless, exploitative hack of unscrupulous ambition and insatiable greed but a prophet inspired by nothing less than principles of the highest order, she would be abandoned by her votaries. Supermarket book racks, airline newsstands, drugstore check-out counters would no longer offer her output. Best-seller lists, hardcover and paperback, would deny her the accustomed listings, their notations of the number of weeks, the months, the years of her prominence. Critics would ignore her, their vilifications no longer applicable. No more miniseries, no more amused condescension from the academics. Her fame, her fortune would dissolve. She would be forgotten, impoverished, bereft. Maude McCloskey's voice must be silenced, her powers nullified.

To achieve this, Kitty simply reached for the most effective weapon she could summon: not denial but agreement swaddled in ridicule. "Oh, yes, Kitty McCloud, the great crusader! The Maude Gonne of the literary world. Writes with a flaming sword handed down by St. Michael himself. An unquenchable thirst for truth, repository of a wrath not seen since Queen Maeve herself. Take a good look, Maude McCloskey. When will you see the like again?"

"Mock me if you will. I'm used to it. But it changes nothing."

"Oh? Until you uttered this last nonsense I was almost ready to consider that the gunpowder might still be lurking somewhere and I could go heavenward at any moment. But now my mind is eased for good and forever. What you speak, my dear, is one absurdity after another—and I thank you for the assurance it gives me that you don't know what you're talking about. Without your gracious idiocies I might have completed my entrance into the married state without this chance to dismiss from my mind all rumors of a curse yet to be fulfilled. This is your gift to me, and I thank you again, and again."

"You lie, Kitty McCloud."

"Oh? And wasn't I just a few moments past the noble truth teller?"

"You are. Except when you lie."

"Now there's logic for you!"

"You're a prophet. Your books are the proof."

"I'm a coarse and pushy money monger who sells long-dead writers for coin. And you know it as well as everyone else, including myself."

"Look me in the left eye and say that again."

Before Kitty could oblige, she realized she'd been watching a young man at the far end of the hall. Sweetly handsome he was, but sad and sorrowful as well. He seemed to be searching for someone he might never find and was already mourning the loss. The more Kitty watched him, the more annoyed she became, almost as annoyed with him as she was with Maude. His skin was tan, a more pallid shade than his clothing, but not so much a tan bestowed by the sun but rather a pallor no sun had seen. He was obviously one of the squatters come to mock her at her wedding feast. He'd costumed himself like a peasant—even his feet were bare—a servant of such low estate that by an old custom he could allow himself but one color for his clothing. If she, Kitty, were to presume to be Lady of the Manor, he would come as corrective to her pretensions, posing as a menial familiar with the tyrannies of the Lords Shaftoe themselves.

Yet the more Kitty observed him, with his gaze moving slowly from one side of the hall to the other, all sorrowful, the more her annoyance gave way first to mild interest, then to increased absorption.

Maude, aware that Kitty had experienced another shift in concentration, followed Kitty's gaze. Kitty herself had dismissed the smile she'd chosen for her interview with the Hag and, without so much as a nod in Maude's direction, said, "That young man all done up in brown, who is he?"

"Where?"

"There, the wall straight across and a little to the right. Dressed himself up like a peasant."

"I don't see him."

"Wearing all brown. Jacket, tunic, pants to just below the knee. Bare feet even."

"I still can't find him."

"Never mind. Just curious. One of the squatters come to make fun of me."

"Knowing you, it's something I'd not advise. But I still can't find him."

"What he needs most is a full plate of food, and a bit of color in his cheeks. And a pair of shoes for his muddy feet. And a pretty girl to cheer him, all sad the way he is. And next time he puts on his costume he should give up the homespun, the way his jacket has rubbed his neck all raw. Serves him right, making a spectacle and a joke the way he is."

Slowly Maude turned back to Kitty and straightened her spine, a sure sign that she was about to deliver some further pronouncement. But before the Seer could have her say, Kitty let out a quick laugh. "No. Wait. It's all right. He's found the girl he was looking for. And she dressed the same as he. No, not the same. But all done up in something quaint, including a great brown cloak and the hood pulled away and her long hair flowing down on her shoulders. A match for him all right. But look: she's just as sad as he. Now there's a pair! And the cloak has had its revenge, all rough wool scratching her neck, too, right down to the blood practically. Small pleasure are they having by the looks of them. She could take in a bit of beef the same as he and show herself more to the sun. Look at them. She taking his hand, he touching her cheek, as wan as any I've ever seen. Now the two of them looking this way, right at me. To see if I appreciate the joke."

Kitty smiled and gave her head an exaggerated nod up and down. "Yes, I see you, the both of you. And a fine pair you are, come to make fun of me and my marriage and my castle." She didn't call out the words; she simply spoke them, more to Maude than to the squatters. "But enjoy yourselves. Welcome you are to the feast. And I thank you for reminding me of what I am. Hardly Lord Shaftoe—may he howl in hell—but keeper of the castle am I, as rightful an heir as anyone with Kerry blood coursing in her veins. You're standing now on Kerry soil and all the Shaftoe days are done. Eat. Dance. Drink. This feast is yours as much as—"

She stopped, gave a quick move of her head, and began searching among the thronged guests. "Well," she said, "I've lost them now. Funny." Still smiling, she looked at Maude expecting her to share her amusement. But the Seer took two steps back and, mouth half open, was staring at Kitty.

"Oh, Maude, sorry. I was supposed to look you in your left eye and swear some kind of oath and now I've forgot. But you needn't look at me quite like that, as if you've dreamed up some even worse prophecy than the last."

When Maude said nothing, Kitty decided she'd best keep talking until the Hag had found her tongue and could again begin wagging it for all to hear. "All right then. I'm looking straight into your left eye. Now tell me what I'm supposed to say so I can say it and be done."

Maude's jaw moved up and down a few times, until she was able to speak, but in a voice low and unsteady. "His name is Taddy," she said. "Her name is Brid."

Kitty gave the snort she often substituted for the laugh she couldn't quite manage. "Taddy and Brid, you say? The names of those hanged for the plot of the gunpowder? Now you've gone completely off with your head, you mocking me as much as they."

Maude swallowed twice and, without saying anything more, turned and headed straight for where the drinking was and knocked back in quick succession two generous draughts of whiskey, of Tullamore Dew.

Before Kitty could scan the crowd to see where the presumed Brid and Taddy had gone off to, Kieran came up and held out a pint. "You ready for this?"

"I'm ready for anything. Otherwise I wouldn't be here."

As if on cue, the fiddler Annie Fitzgerald, the whistle player Jamie Kerwin, along with Cathy Clarke on the bodhran (the Irish drum) and Charlie Dillon with his guitar jumped headfirst into "Johnny Will You Marry Me" and before Kitty could take a first sip, she was dancing the hoppy, all the steps coming back from her girlhood as if her memory were in her feet. Changing partners, weaving in and out, back and forth, slapping her feet on the wooden platform she'd provided for the dancing, unable to show the impassive face the dance demanded, Kitty found herself distracted by the thought that the squatters, whatever their real names, might come on the dance floor and that, sooner or later, she would loop her arm in Taddy's, if only for a few steps, before being returned by the intricacies of the dance to her newly won husband. When it turned out otherwise, she felt no disappointment, too determined was she not to miss a step and thereby reintroduce into the proceedings the unsettling foolishness Maude McCloskey had tried to put into her mind.

The Seer was helping herself to more Tullamore Dew.

3

Kieran had to be careful not to take out his annoyance at Kitty on the cows. They had done him no wrong. They had not paced from room to room, seeming to listen for a sound that only they could hear, searching shadows, darting a glance into one corner, then another. They had not, when questioned about this strange activity, said, as Kitty had, "Oh, was I doing that? Sorry, I guess I get distracted. You can understand that."

The cows suffered no inexplicable distractions. They had come clomping up from the stream at the first encouragement, followed his directions into the great hall, found the flagstones no challenge to their contentment, and had even chosen, one after the other, a place facing the walls.

They were all a man might ask of a cow—and he must never bring into his relationship with them an emotion or a need generated elsewhere. If Kitty McCloud chose to try his patience, if Ms. McCloud—she'd kept her birth name despite the marriage—if Ms. McCloud decided to indulge in erratic behavior, if his darling and dearest found it necessary to shut him out completely, he must not blame these innocent animals.

Kieran knew the source of her agitation. But to under-stand and accept it was something else. Still, he had know-ingly married a writer, a self-absorbed species set apart from all others, beings who exiled themselves from this world and made forced entry into another.

And, he had been given to believe, she had more than reason enough in this current instance for her exasperating conduct. Contrary to the first rule imposed on any writer, his wife had, on their honeymoon to Ballinskelligs and Skellig Michael, divulged some of her secrets. She had had no choice. The distance between her and her computer—an appendage the honeymoon had severed so they could get themselves away—was too great a loss for her to forgo some sharing of her bereavement.

He had reciprocated by confessing his need for his cows. But, he had had to acknowledge, he would be returning home to a world well known and finely ordered. She would return to disorder edging toward chaos. She had, she admit-ted, taken on a challenge that placed her near the abyss. Not without trepidation, she had decided to correct George Eliot's *The Mill on the Floss* (which he had never gotten through though he had tried). Outbursts like "Stupid Maggie! Dumb stupid Maggie, silly dumb bitch!" would intrude on their moments of bliss. "Bloody Tom Tulliver! Prissy prig, I'll get him yet!" once interrupted the serenity of their drive to Ballinskelligs for an evening of dancing at the local pub, Tig Rosie. Defiant curses, fair warnings, moments of near diaboli-cal laughter promising the imposition of her will by whatever means, words like "Justice!" and "Just desserts" were muttered at meal time. "She's going to be happy. I'm going to *make* her happy!"

Now, home at last, here she was, determined to wrestle George Eliot—aka Mary Ann Evans—into submission.

Kieran, not appeased by his reflections, was milking the seventh cow—there were twenty-three in the herd—when he felt a newly familiar ache gathering just beneath his breast-bone. It would, in the next few moments, spread outward, upward, downward, and sideways, an easy flow that would fill his entire chest cavity and part of his stomach besides. It suggested a reach and an urge beyond himself that could only be mollified when he would take his wife into his arms and hold her fast, protected from all hurt. He would then be granted, in return, the completion of himself, a fulfillment that held within it the true definition of all he had been, all he was, and all he was meant to be. Only within this context could he be revealed to himself. Robbed of this, he would remain undefined.

Watching the squirts of warm, sweet milk spurting into the bucket, he was given, as an infusion of grace, the persistence of his exasperation. It had not vanished; it had simply evolved. It had provided the seed out of which his love would grow. For all his life he had felt nothing but wrath at the sight of this woman—and, as he had now come to know, his wrath had made possible his love. Within his rage lay the knowledge of her vulnerability. At the height of his fury there would awaken deep within himself a need to shield her from every harm. He pitied her because she was undefended; he saw her courage in the face of his ferocity, the presence of her defiance. Only *he* could save her, his hand alone could stay the advance of his malevolence. And so she had cracked open his hate-protected heart and had entered in. But, to Kieran's consternation, she had brought with her all that had made possible his love. She was now, as then, enraging. And now it had been revealed to him that this was a necessity. This was a nutrient of his love, and without it his aches and urges would be endangered, possibly to the point of extinction. She must always annoy him. She must always try his patience. And, Kieran was also given to know, she always would. Her sustaining characteristics were ever at the ready, as potent as Cupid's darts. A well-aimed glance, a shrug, a grunt, the lift of the head: each arrow would reach its mark—and in these gestures his love would be renewed.

The milking done, Kieran threw lime and then straw on the hosed flagstones and, passing the cows one by one, felt that he had put his world back in order. This particular satisfaction was unfailing, and to reap the full benefit, he would always pause to regard the ordered universe his labors had created.

The pig had found itself a favored cow and had bedded down in the straw, its belly directly in the line of the cow's breath in order to appropriate the full benefit of the warmth that only a cow can provide. Sly, too, without any further demands to be made upon his inbred border-collie talents, was content to lie quietly on the flagstone floor, waiting without patience or impatience for the summons to follow his master to the scullery—so called here in deference to its inclusion in a castle—where the good man would serve up a fine dinner of his own preparation.

Just as Kieran was throwing one last armful of straw, Kitty came into the hall with an uncharacteristically tentative step. As soon as she was within speaking distance, she said, "I've decided we don't want the pig."

"Oh, for pity's sake, leave it alone."

"It's going back where it belongs."

"Oh? Look there. It seems it belongs here." He leaned his head in the direction where the pig was taking its ease.

"It's a nuisance. It'll tear the place down—or dig it up—and cause who knows what. It's not to be trusted."

"One doesn't trust or not trust a pig."

"One does. And I don't."

"What made you change your mind? Again."

"I don't need a reason to change my mind. I just change it. And it stays changed. And besides, the pig peed all over my study in the turret."

"What was it doing in your study?"

"Peeing."

"I mean, how did it get there?"

"It wandered in. The study has no door."

"Why didn't you send it away?"

"I was working—I—didn't see it—until it peed." (What she did not tell her husband is that the offending act had been preceded by Taddy's passing through her study on his way up the stone stairway.)

"I like the pig."

"And I—I don't."

"Well, then, that settles that."

"Good. The pig goes."

"No. The pig stays."

Kitty cocked her head to the right. "And I have no say?"

"You've had your say. And I've had mine. The pig stays. After all, it did bring us together."

It was true. The pig had proved a decidedly mixed blessing. On the one hand, it had brought about the resolution of the age-old feud between Kitty's family's and her husband's, the McClouds and the Sweeneys. On the other, it had uprooted Kitty's cliff-top land and, in the process, exposed the skeleton of the prized seducer Declan Tovey, buried among her cabbages, the man obviously murdered. This, in turn, had initiated an irreverent Irish wake during which the McCloud ancestral home was tumbled by the winds and the waves down into the sea, taking with it the as-yet-un-reburied skeleton of the legendary Mr. Tovey. The pig, for reasons never to be known, had followed her newly arrived nephew from New York to her doorstep after a roadside mishap several kilometers from her home, involving a scattering of animals of a species similar to the one then brought to her doorstep.

To everyone's relief, the irresistible Declan was now safely interred at the bottom of the sea, and, to Kitty's even greater relief, the obdurate pig had been given hospice by Lolly, who, as heaven would have it, was one of the last thriving independent swineherds in all of modern Ireland. And who, by an even more peculiar set of divine devisings, was now married to Kitty's American cousin, Aaron, also a McCloud.

So on balance the pig had done more good than harm. Kitty had married Kieran and they now lived in the castle. But that was then, this was now, and the pig had aroused Kitty's hostility for reasons known only to her.

It puzzled more than surprised Kieran when Kitty clasped her hands just below her chin. It was as close as he'd ever seen her approach a posture of petition, much less of prayer. Even at their wedding, there at the altar with Father Colavin bestowing more blessings than they could possibly use up in a long, long life, her concession to the sacramental nature of the event was limited to a loose intertwining of her fingers, resting against her stomach. But now the hands were tightly clasped and held perilously near to the heart. "Please," she said, "it can't stay. It—it's bad luck."

"Just because you're having trouble with your writing doesn't mean you have to blame it on the pig."

"It has nothing to do with my writing."

"Oh? And it has nothing to do with your writing when you're staring off into corners or looking behind you as if you're being followed."

"What are you talking about?"

"You. And what you do when you're brooding over those idiotic Tullivers you're trying to write about."

"This has nothing to do with the Tullivers."

Kieran pulled his head and shoulders back a good foot farther away from his wife, as if he wanted a new perspective on what he was seeing. He narrowed his eyes. When he said nothing further, Kitty asked, "Do I really go staring off into the shadows?" She seemed curious, even worried.

Kieran smiled and shook his head slowly from side to side. "Of course you don't know you're doing it. You're that deep into your work. Your book. And then the pig comes along and distracts—"

Kitty interrupted, but quietly. "It doesn't distract me."

"Well, it somethings you. And I wish you'd tell me what it is."

But how could Kitty tell her husband she was seeing ghosts—and that the pig could see them too. It was the pig, with its stare up at the gallery right after it had arrived at the castle, that had led Kitty to see Taddy. And there had been other visions, other visitations. Earlier that afternoon, the pig, with its stare, had let her know that Brid was standing atop the turret looking out toward the sea. It had been transfixed by its sighting of Taddy walking through the sheds that morning. She'd seen it from the window of her study. Even though she'd seen both Taddy and Brid at the wedding, it was only with the pig's recent intrusion into her life that she'd seen them again and again and again. If the pig was gone, maybe they, too, would go.

That this logic could be easily contradicted was given not the least consideration. To counter accusations against the prescient animal, she never allowed herself to be reminded that, when she'd first seen the haunting pair at the wedding feast, the pig was nowhere near. Nor had the pig been present during those more than several instances when, coming to the wide landing of the winding stone stairway on her way to the top of the turret, she had found Taddy strumming an unstrung harp and Brid at the loom, her muddied foot working the treadle with neither thread nor cloth to be seen.

None of this could affect Kitty's insistence that the pig was somehow an active mediator between her and her sightings. She was determined to avoid the troubling truth of the matter: that the mournful ghosts apparently revealed themselves to Kitty for reasons only to do with herself, with or without the pig present.

Quite possibly, it disturbed her that the secret was known by anyone other than herself—even if it was known only by a pig. That this knowledge was not limited to herself was untenable. She knew the pig could hardly disclose her secret, but, then again, she couldn't keep the possibility from her mind. The pig might tell on her. That she was thinking something so impossible that it hinted at madness mattered not at all. The thought was there and not without force. This pig must be returned to Lolly. It knew too much. It saw too

much. But all she could bring herself to say was, "Please. It—
it can't stay. I told you. It's bad luck."

"But it brought us together. Is that bad luck?"

A note of near pleading now came into her voice. "Can't
it just go and that's the end of it?" It unsettled Kieran that his
wife would resort to begging. He forced a quick laugh. "If it's
superstitious you've come to be, you're talking about a black
pig. They're the ones bring bad luck. This is a pink pig."

"Pink, black, blue, it doesn't matter. I only know we don't
want it here. Doesn't the asking of a devoted wife have any
meaning for you?"

Kieran felt a shudder of fear. Something had happened to
his wife. Not that she had become superstitious but that she
now thought herself as "devoted." Love he knew she had—
and passion and other wifely attributes—but *devotion*? He
looked at her. She was trying to smile and trying even harder
to loosen her hands and draw them away from beneath her
chin. Now more than ever he knew he must not give in. The
issue must remain unresolved. It must be a ready point of dispute. This must be the beginning, not the end, of the disagreement. Their repeated attempts to resolve it would be a
form of intimacy. It would keep them joined. If he were to
capitulate, if he were to rob them both of this means of continuing involvement, it would mark the beginning of acquiescence, the loosening of the bond forged from their youth by
the adversarial, the resolute refusal to compromise or to agree.
He wanted no devoted wife. He wanted Kitty McCloud, the
girl, the woman he had loved from the day she was branded
by his mother and his father as an enemy to be scorned for all
his life. Always had he loathed her. Always had he loved her.
But the enmity infused into his blood gave his passion a more

heated yearning—and the familial proscription added further fuel to his need of her. His marriage had freed him from his family, but he must do nothing that might free him from Kitty herself. She was all he had and all he had ever wanted. But she must remain Kitty McCloud—obstinate and unyielding. Kieran was fighting not for the pig but for the marriage.

"The pig goes nowhere," he said, trying with some success to sound neither insistent nor adamant but merely decisive.

Kitty, putting an end to this strange interlude during which she had experimented with the more usual persuasions of a good and amiable wife, put her hand on a cow's hind quarter and pressed the other hand against her right thigh. "Then whatever happens will be all your fault?"

"I'll scrub where it peed."

"So it stays here, in the hall? With the cows?"

A small smile crossed Kieran's face. He gestured to where the pig lay. The cow's nose had moved closer to the pig's belly, the belly itself rising and falling in a rhythm that can be achieved only by the most pacified. "Does it look like it wants to be anywhere else?"

"Don't let me even look at it." She started out, but stopped. Without turning around, she said, "And don't let it look at me."

As she crossed the hall toward the door, her stride more purposeful than when she'd come in, Kieran watched, but now in sorrow. How could he refuse this magnificent woman anything!

Suddenly the pig moved away from the cow, and the cow stood up and stared at the wall not two feet in front of it.

A cow on the far left side began to stomp, another to moo. The pig moved on a few paces and started to root in the straw. Now two more cows were stomping, then a third. Most were whisking their tails back and forth, brushing the air, as if trying to keep something away from them. The pig snorted, trying even harder to find something buried in the straw. More than half the cows had raised their heads, stretching their necks so that their discordant moos could be directed toward the ceiling and the skies beyond. The snorting of the pig grew louder, then stopped, abruptly. As did the stomping. Heads were lowered, the bellowing tapering off to something closer to a sniffle. The pig's cow lay down again. The pig returned and it, too, lay down, its head snuggled against the cow's neck.

Kieran surveyed the room. Peace, it seemed, had been restored. He waited a few seconds to make sure, turned, and started to leave. It was then that he saw the cause of the disturbance. A neighbor woman, a girl really of not more than seventeen, had come into the hall. She had prepared herself for a cooler night with a heavy brown cloak, the hood pulled away from her head. A homespun dress reached almost to her ankles. She was barefoot, the mud of the day caking her toes, the dirt of the road dusting her ankles. Her brown hair fell freely into the hood of her cloak and onto her shoulders. At first she seemed somewhat plain, but when Kieran strained for a closer look he decided she was more than handsome, her skin fair if pale. Her eyes were blue and her lips plump, the upper more than the lower. Her neck had been chaffed by the coarse weave of her dress.

She was staring at Kieran, quietly expectant, if he interpreted correctly the slight parting of her lips and the merest widening of her eyes. He thought he recognized her as one of the wedding guests. She had worn the same clothing. Now she would tell him why she had come. But she said nothing. She simply continued to look at him, her expression unchanging, her slim body upright, her head tilted slightly to the side, her right foot forward of her left.

He waited another moment, then said, "You're probably looking for my wife." The girl took a strand of her hair that had fallen across the left side of her face, put it behind her ear, then resumed her near-stately stance, her mildly expectant look. "Or is there something I can do for you?"

He looked more closely at the girl. Around her neck was what had seemed a rough woven collar, but when he looked harder, he saw that it was not cloth, but flesh. Obviously she'd worn something of so coarse a weave that it had rubbed raw the skin. It could also have been a burn. Perhaps that was why the girl was unable to speak. Kieran would ask her. But before he could decide on which words might be appropriate, the girl moved her right foot backward, even with her left, paused a moment, then disappeared. She didn't dissolve; she didn't fade away; she simply ceased to be where she had been.

Had he blinked? Had he been talking to the shadows in the far corner of the hall? Had she left when he'd been— unknown to himself—looking elsewhere? He went out into the courtyard. No one. Nothing. He peered back into the hall. No one. He stepped back inside. Most of the cows were lying down, their heads angled away from the wall in front of them. The pig had moved, and the cow was resting its chin on the pig's belly.

Kieran peered along the walls, into the corners. He walked the row between the cows. He made a quick turn, trying to surprise anyone who might be behind him. Only a few shadows. He stood at the end of the hall, facing the animals, shifting his eyes from one side to the other. In a voice of practiced command he said, "I don't appreciate foolish games. So let this be the last time you try this. Understand?"

Before any answer could be given, he had gone back out into the courtyard. Determined not to look behind him, he went toward the scullery, where he knew he could be alone. It was while crossing the yard that he added to the list of possibilities of what might have caused the girl's disfigurement, the wound around her neck. It could have been made by a thick rope of coarse fiber. He was unable to prevent himself from continuing on to the next surmise: she could have been hanged.

He knew now who she was. Her name was one he'd heard since he was a boy. Her name was Brid.

But it couldn't have been Brid. Brid was dead—dead for more than two centuries. This girl seemed very much alive.

4

Kitty was at her computer, in her study on the first landing of the winding stair that led to the turret battlements two flights up. Frustrated by her work, stifled by her imagination's refusal to respond to her proddings, desperate to expand her skull so it could accommodate a brain enlarged enough to comprehend what she needed to know, what she needed to see and to hear, she had decided to go— as she often had before—to the top of the tower and present her pleas to the open air.

When she made the turn leading to the landing above, she stopped. She knew she'd see the loom, unthreaded, bare, the worm-eaten wood worn and gone gray, the treadle smoothed by the touch of uncounted feet. She knew she'd see the small unstrung harp, the kind you held against yourself with one hand and plucked the strings with the other. The pegs for the strings were still there, twisted each in a different direction like snaggled teeth. She had often wondered if some alignment could be achieved if ever the harp could be strung again. The instrument rested on a crudely fashioned stool, its wood never having known the touch of paint or sealing of any kind. Worm holes, like those on the frame of the loom, suggested a passage of years beyond knowing.

When first she'd seen the harp and the loom, Kitty's impulse had been to pick up the harp, to try the loom, to see if the treadle would move at the touch of her foot. Her next impulse was to touch nothing. These had not been left behind by the squatters; ancient they were and sacred to this room. And since that time, passing through to the ramparts above, she respected their dust and continued on, as did Kieran when he climbed to the turret.

On this day of particular frustration with her writing, Kitty made the final turning of the stair and stepped onto the landing. Unresponsive to her presence, Brid was working the loom, her muddied bare feet on the treadle, moving it up and down, the rhythm measured and easy, the cloth beam and the warp beam turning, the treadle allowing the girl to move the boat-shaped shuttle between the warp threads—except there were no threads.

No cloth was being woven, but this didn't seem to bother the girl. While over and through the unseen threads the shuttle went, Brid remained calm and unperturbed. Taddy held the harp against his left side, braced under his chin, the bottom frame resting on his thigh. Slowly he brought his right hand toward his body, the fingers twitching ever so lightly, the entire movement all the more graceful since no strings were being plucked, only the unstirring air brushed by the touch of his fingertips.

Kitty saw him in profile, his face immobile, his eyes downcast. He was listening. As was Brid. Whether the song was sad or happy she would never know, but she could tell from the distant look on Taddy's face and Brid's that memories had been awakened.

Kitty knew she must turn around and go back down as

silently as possible. She must return to her computer. She must deny what she had seen, what she was seeing. Or she must review the workings of her psyche and determine whether she was sane or insane. In self-protection, to reach for some accounting of what was happening, she tried to tell herself it was not all that unusual. All her life—with the exception of her time spent in America—things would disappear and reappear in and out of the mists: a tree a few feet away, the islands in the bay, the high ridge of the hills and every sheep and cow in sight, all seen, then unseen, with the sky the least reliable presence of all. Her own house would vanish after she'd taken but three steps from the door. Long had she been prepared for this present phenomenon. And her acceptance of it was not as reticent as it might have been had she been born anywhere but at this farthest reach of the Western world, where the eternal mists offered hints of the proximity of the seen and the unseen. To see ghosts could be a gift given by her Kerry birth. Refusal of the gift was impossible. The sole act of choice was what she would do about it, about these visitations. That had yet to be decided—especially since she had not the least idea why she had been singled out but, it would seem, no one else, not the squatters or anyone in the countryside around. If someone had, it would have been not only mentioned but proclaimed. Most significant, not even her husband had reported any "sightings."

Her next thought was that she could no longer dismiss these appearances as aberrations peculiar to County Kerry and its ever-shifting shadows, to the rise and fall of the mists that could, without warning, nullify the distinctions between the real and the unreal. This was Brid; this was Taddy, as named by the local Hag. There on their necks were the marks of the rasping rope. On their faces showed the loss to which they seemed reconciled, a grief whose source had been taken into their hearts, cherished and protected, until a rite could be found that would reunite them to themselves and give them peace or, perhaps, a respite from the wanderings to which they now seemed consigned.

Kitty decided to continue on her way to the upper air. With land and sea in view she could test her mind; she could think it through, this assault on her lifelong insistence—mist or no mist—that there were no such beings as ghosts, just as there were no Little People, no leprechauns, no netherworld of kingdoms and castles, of stolen children and predators ready to pounce and to snatch, to abduct and to imprison. She would see how Brid and Taddy, if there was a Brid and Taddy, would react to her passage through their private domain. Would they vanish, as seemed their habit? Would they ignore her? Would they, perhaps, seize her, take her to the parapet above, and fling her down for having invaded this world of their betrayal? There was only one way to find out.

Reverting to the pace of her approach—and fueled by her exasperation with Maggie Tulliver and the misguided Mary Ann Evans—Kitty passed through the room as though nothing out of the ordinary was taking place. Brid, and Taddy too went about their business. At the second step, just before the turn that led to the top of the turret, Kitty stole a quick backward glance to see if they were still there. They were, Brid at her loom, Taddy with his harp, each unmindful of her presence.

The trapdoor at the top of the narrow stair was stuck, as usual. Kitty stepped high enough so that her bent head was pressing against the door, the palms of her hands flush against the wood. With a strength summoned by her need to escape she pushed upward, head and hands, spine and legs all commandeered for the task. The trapdoor had no choice but to spring open.

Kitty ascended to the parapet. It was the sea off to the southwest she chose to watch during her ruminations. But Maggie Tulliver and Mary Ann had been superceded by Brid and Taddy. By what she'd just seen. Not only a fleeting glimpse, a quick, almost teasing, appearance, but a prolonged and uninterrupted display, assured and without the least apprehension on their part. Their existence was their own.

And Kitty their only witness. The Hag hadn't seen them, even though she'd known who they were from Kitty's descriptions. They were the young hostages chosen at random for hanging when the gunpowder plot was revealed. That there might have been no plot was accepted by some and dismissed by others. A search, somewhere between compulsive and rabid, had continued for months. Although the castle was practically dismantled, fields and pastures uprooted, border walls demolished and rock boulders overturned, no gunpowder had been discovered. By the time the ruthlessness had come to an end, the hangings had already taken place, the need for evidence having been dispensed with so that justice could be served without impediment. And so some portion of their spirits had been told—or allowed—to stay. But to what purpose? To haunt, to frighten, to turn white the hair and to addle the mind? As far as Kitty could tell, they wreaked no vengeance. Nothing had been destroyed. They were highly selective, to say the least, about when to make their presence known. Kitty McCloud seemed to have exclusive claim to the honor—or to the curse.

The curse. Did it consist only of these bewildered spirits? If so, let the entire land, the whole wide world, be cursed, so fair were they, so fine their presence. More a blessing, surely, than a scourge. But what had they to do with Kitty, and what had Kitty to do with them? That she had been chosen she already knew. But why? She had no powers. She wasn't all that certain she believed in what her eyes had seen. And yet, she *had* seen.

Off in the distance the sea was wild. Again and again the crested waves flung themselves at the shore. Kitty was indifferent to the whole shebang. She had troubles enough without taking on the idiosyncrasies of the deep. And, she realized, she would have to simply accept what she could not understand. Mystery, by its nature, was not subject to explication.

Of course, as a writer, it was her impulse to search for understanding, to expose a motive, to tame the chaos of the human adventure. She was a skilled manipulator, devoted by her calling to trace the movements of the unseen hand, to reassure her readers that events fulfilled themselves and, in the process, revealed truths otherwise unrealized. She was supposed to solve mysteries. To accept them was inimical to her calling. To admit the limits of her gift would be to admit defeat.

But she had no choice. A refusal to live with the reality of these unrealities would make a demand she was not yet prepared to make: to leave the castle. To abandon the curse. To dismiss these bewildered youths and forget their fate, a fate beyond their hangings, a destiny still to be fulfilled. How could she do that? How could she forsake those who had been forsaken by all the world?

Kitty stood at the parapet and watched the waves bash

themselves against the headlands. She had been wrong to consider herself threatened by this presence of mystery. She had been brought beyond the common boundaries. Either she possessed or had been given a special grace. She had been honored, and to refuse it or rebel against it by going mad or abandoning the castle was inconsistent with her nature. She would go back to the landing below, to the loom and the harp; she would, if possible, communicate to Brid and Taddy that she accepted their invitation into their mystery. She would neither ignore nor deny their presence. They were welcome in her castle. She would make no attempt to exorcise them from her home or forbid them what comforts they might find at her hearth. And if there were any particular demands they had come to make, she would do what she could to fulfill them.

Down the stone stair she went, leaving the sea to insanities of its own. When she made the turn onto the landing, she stopped. Brid, who had been busy with her loom, also stopped, as did Taddy with his harp. No one moved. But when the moment had passed, Brid took up her task again, and Taddy—as if there had been only a marked pause in the score of the music he was playing—resumed his silent strumming.

Rather than continue through to the steps on the other side of the room, Kitty waited and watched. Brid continued to be caught up in the rhythms of her weaving, Taddy intent on rhythms of his own, the work-worn fingers delicate in their plucking and strumming. Even the sea seemed to have become silent. For Kitty there was only the throb of her own blood to reassure her that she too had not been taken into the realm of the dead. She wondered if she could—or if she should—speak to them. After pondering this for no more than three seconds, she crossed the landing, looking at neither of them, and continued on down the narrow winding stair to the no-less-mystifying world awaiting at her computer. Before she could confront Maggie Tulliver, however, she would confront her husband.

But what if he said they must leave, that the castle had obviously overheated her brain, already fevered even in its moments of serenity. She reveled in the castle. She drew sustenance from its stones. The rough-hewn rafters raised her spirits. The view of the sea from the turret battlements made possible this remove inland from the cliffs upon which her family home had been built, the cliffs that had betrayed her by letting her house tumble into the sea, taking with it her first forays into the corrections of *The Mill on the Floss,* a loss she could barely sustain.

Here in the castle she had found her talents awaiting her. Her turret room now held captive the characters she'd sought, the imaginings needed to supplant the misguided author's insufficiencies, the proper plot lines the muses had withheld from George Eliot but revealed to Kitty McCloud, if only she could discern them. Also, for her, the castle pastures were indeed greener, the mire muckier, the fields more fertile. The great hall expanded her spirit—even if it had been given over to the cows and to the pig. The dank cellars inspired in her enough gloom to satisfy the most morbid of her Irish sensibilities. Within these precincts she felt she was in possession at last of this emerald isle, this teeming womb of holy saints, this splendor thrust up by the all-creating sea, this seat of royal Maeve, this mystery, this Ireland.

If Kieran insisted they leave, she would, of course, refuse. That was a given well beyond dispute. Even the very thought would not be entertained or considered, much less discussed. It was this realization that resolved the issue: the potential for disagreement. Immediately she relished the idea. A whole new area of contention. What more could she want?

She found him on the plot east of the castle where he'd been preparing the earth for a planting. He was humming a tune and dropping seeds along a furrow he'd dug in the harsh soil.

"Is it cabbage?"

"Cabbage." He continued to let the seeds sift from his hand.

"Will they grow, do you think?" she asked.

"We'll find out."

"Yes, we'll find out."

Kieran stood up straight and dusted the last of the seeds from his hand, letting them fall where they might.

Still reluctant to proceed with her mission, Kitty searched her brain for an acceptable subject that might occupy at least a few more moments before she'd lead her husband into a territory from which there might be no return. Without much difficulty, she found it. "I was going to do the planting, *you* the digging."

"I'm competent in both." He brushed his hands against his thighs.

"I never questioned that—nor will I ever. It was an observation only."

"Of course." With the toe of his boot Kieran slid some earth from one side of the furrow to cover the seed, then some from the other side. "More trouble with your Tullivers?"

"That, always."

"And I'm no help."

"As it has to be."

"But you'll let me know." He looked at her and cocked his head to one side. "But there's something else I can help with? Is that it?"

"Why do you say that?"

"Look at you and ask it again. You, shuffling your shoes like a woman not knowing where she wants to go. Will you tell me now, or should there be more talk of cabbages?" Direct as his question was, there was no trace of accusation or impatience in his voice. There seemed even a note of amusement.

Kitty herself shoved a bit of earth over one of the furrows, but without tamping it down. The time had come. She raised her head and shook it lightly from side to side to make sure her hair fell reasonably straight onto her shoulders. That much she could do to bring order into the world. Kieran, his gaze unchanged, waited for her to speak. What she would say would be pure and unadulterated truth. But first she would take him up to the turret, to confess to what she'd seen and to tell about Brid at the loom and Taddy at the harp. Then let him judge if she was mad.

"Can you come with me? Something I want to show you. Something to tell you." Kieran waited, then nodded.

It was when they were crossing the gallery that led to the stair that they heard from somewhere high above them the sound of a harp. They stopped. Each turned toward the other. Kitty raised her right hand level with her ear as if she were going to cover it. Kieran took in a slow breath and exhaled even more slowly. Neither of them moved. How many moments passed was beyond telling. The harp continued, a plucked melody so plangent it seemed to plead for stillness even as it filled the entire hall with its sorrows. Rising, falling, the harp bespoke a yearning that reached out into the great world in search of some fulfillment of its longing, of the return of something lost and never to be found again.

At that moment, the harp seemed to have summoned the lowering sun from behind a cloud. The hall was flooded with rose-colored gold, making amber the dark stones, burnishing the dull iron of the many-candled chandelier, and transfiguring both Kitty and Kieran, allowing each to see the other made radiant, suggesting that each was being given for just this moment a vision of the other's true self, the world's first glory, a gift no mortal could hope to deserve. The music rose higher, the yearning now an ache beyond bearing but instilled with the promise that it would never cease to be, that its sorrows would be nobly borne beyond the farthest reaches of time, even past the silence where all things die.

Unable to sustain this vision of each other, both Kieran and Kitty turned and looked out over the courtyard. As if in mercy, the song stopped, midchord. And the sun, having done its mischief, retreated. Some remaining rays thrust themselves out above and below, striking the hills, sending one last shaft into the courtyard beneath them.

And there, staring up at them, was the pig, complete with the brass ring passed through its snout to make uprootings impossible now that the garden was being planted.

"The pig," said Kieran.

"Yes," said Kitty. "The pig."

At their words, the animal turned its hams to them and bounded away to its trough. Sounds permitted only to a gorging pig came up to them. "We'll go ahead then," said Kitty.

Up the winding stones they went onto the first landing, continuing past Kitty's desk. She considered giving a preliminary lecture before making the final ascent, giving Kieran some clue as to what he was about to be told, hinting, perhaps, that he must withhold judgments as to her ability to live in a castle and not have her imagination overwhelmed by ancient lore and thrice-told tales. She decided to wait.

He must already have some premonition. The sound of the harp had been too soulful for any returned squatters and too human to suggest the intrusion of angels.

Maybe Brid and Taddy would be there. Maybe Kieran would see them. Were she and he not one? The implications of this thought were too complex and far too troublesome for Kitty to give it further consideration. Just the fleeting suggestion unnerved her. To be of one heart was acceptable. But it surely had to stop there. To be of one mind with *anyone* but herself was not permissible.

Kieran would either see Brid and Taddy or not. That was hardly for her to decide. But if he did see them, would she be jealous? Would this make her not the unique person she believed herself to be? Would she welcome this rival for Brid's and Taddy's manifestations? To avoid further turmoil—a turmoil given about two seconds of conscious awareness—Kitty continued with even more determination up the stairs, Kieran following behind.

The loom was there, the harp set down on the stool. Brid and Taddy must be off somewhere—if they were anywhere at all—doing who knows what. Again Kitty refused to entertain further speculation. She did not consider it part of the arrangement that she know what ghosts did when they were not in view. That was their business, and she had no intention of sticking her nose into matters that would tax even more her already overburdened imagination.

Kieran picked up the harp. "This could hardly be the one we heard. No strings."

"It *was* the harp we heard," said Kitty. "It needs no strings." She paused, swallowed, then said, "It was a ghost played it." She paused again, then went on. "And we *both* heard it. I not the only one. Her name is Brid. His name is Taddy. They were at our wedding feast. And before you think anything, whether I might be making sport—or gone daft—I'm telling you the truth. Brid and Taddy. I've been seeing them. Like here, in this room. Brid there at the loom. Taddy playing the harp. Brid with no thread, Taddy with no strings to his playing. You don't have to believe me. But you have to believe I haven't gone away with my head."

More mournful than fearful, Kieran asked, "Can this be?"

"Who are we to say what can and cannot be?"

"We're rational. We're sane. Or we were until we came to this—this *place*."

"We"—Kitty squirmed a little as if trying to test the fit of her dress—"we have a few adjustments to make."

"The squatters—"

"Ghosts, Kieran. Ghosts. The ghost of Brid. The ghost of Taddy."

Without taking his eyes off Kitty, Kieran lowered himself down onto the stool, still holding the harp. "Ghosts," he said.

"Yes. Ghosts." Kitty's voice was quiet. "They appear. And they disappear. They're here, and then they're not here. You can believe me or not, according to your way. But it's God's truth—and if it isn't His, then it's mine."

Kieran stared toward the window high on the wall. "Then

I've seen them, too," he said quietly. "Even when my own eyes watched them be here, then here no more. Brid in the great hall one evening when the cows first came. Taddy alongside the pig on the slope goes down to the stream. But I couldn't admit who they were, what they are. If I did I'd have to tell you. And how could I do that? Mad, you'd say I was. And—my worst fear of all—you could be right. How could I say anything would make you think you're married to a madman?"

"Are we both gone off with our heads, then?"

"If so, at least we're together." He guffawed. Kitty, too, allowed herself a small bit of laughter, but it was more than mildly nervous.

"The old tales tell they were innocent," he said, "and knew nothing of the gunpowder. So if they're here, is the gunpowder here as well?"

"It's something let's hope never to know."

"And no one sees them but us? Or does everyone see them and not say, for the same fear as ours—that they'd be branded as gone off?"

"Taddy and Brid—I told you, they were at our wedding feast. I saw them. And probably you did, too. But Maude McCloskey didn't. I described them, what they wore, how handsome they were. It disturbed her, that much I know, and nothing disturbs Maude McCloskey. There was something she wanted to say, but she couldn't say it. And Maude never shuts up. If she didn't see them, no one sees them. Except us."

"But why . . . ?"

"When you have the answer to that one, will you let me know?"

"And you the same: you'll tell me, won't you?"

Kitty's eyes softened as she looked at her husband. "I'm a woman with no secrets left. Since I've told you what I've told you now, I'll tell you anything." She paused and raised her right eyebrow. "Unless, of course, I decide not to."

"Good. Then I needn't feel bad if I do the same."

"You wouldn't. Hold back, I mean."

Kieran shrugged, got up from the stool, and reverently put the harp back where he'd found it. Before he had withdrawn his hands completely, still bending, he looked up at Kitty and said, "Are they always with us whether we see them or not?"

Kitty, who'd been running her right hand over the frame of the loom, gave a quick glance to her right, then to her left, then looked down at her hand. "I—I don't know. I never considered it."

"Could they be here now? In this room!" He made a particular effort not to look around.

"No. I don't think so."

"But you aren't sure."

"I'm not sure of anything anymore."

"May I ask a delicate question?"

"Ask it and I'll tell you if you can or not."

"When you and I—when we're together—just the two of us—are they—do they—in our room at night and in the morning?"

Kitty pulled her shoulders, her head, and part of her upper torso a full foot back as if withdrawing from the subject itself. "I hadn't thought of that."

"Well, think about it now."

"But surely they wouldn't—I mean, why would they—there—at a time like that! No. Of course they're not there!"

"You're sure."

"It's a terrible thing to think."

"Yes. Terrible."

"Shouldn't we just ignore—"

"Maybe you can. But can I?"

"But why would the two of them be spying on us? They're not here for that. Are they?"

"Then why *are* they here?"

Kitty sat down at the loom, unable to answer. With her foot, she worked the treadle up and down. She said nothing. She looked only at her hand on the breast beam, the treadle sending it back and forth. Finally she spoke, but continued the motion. Her speech was hesitant, as if she were giving voice to confusing thoughts as they came to her from some distant region within herself. "They have their being else-where. In eternity. Love is theirs. But joy and peace are yet to come. Some part of themselves separates itself from who and what they have become—and stays here, in this place, within these walls, through these fields and pastures, searching for what will make them complete for all time to come. Some task has been left undone. It agitates their souls. It harries their spirits. They are beyond time, where everything that ever was is now and everything that is to come is now as well. It is one moment—and it is forever without change. But sometimes they return to the world of time, where change is still possible. And it is within time that they will fulfill them-selves. They will complete their task. And the moment for it is yet to be revealed. And maybe they are here—shown to us alone—to ask our help." She turned toward Kieran. He was holding the harp again and had just raised his right hand as if to strum his fingers across the nonexistent strings. "They're here," Kitty whispered.

She turned again to the loom. There were the threads not seen before—coarse and brown—worked through the machine. Spread out before her was a cloth, heavy and woven of the same brown thread. She raised her hands away from the loom and took her feet from the treadle. She heard, in the instant, the sound of the harp, touched more it seemed by a soft breeze than the thick fingers of Kieran Sweeney. Metal strings, brass it seemed, were strung in place. Kieran was gripping the harp more tightly, afraid he might let it fall. Both Kieran and Kitty had their mouths slightly open, their breaths held. First Kitty turned toward the stone steps where they opened onto the landing. Then Kieran shifted his gaze to follow hers.

There, just to the left of the stair, stood Brid and Taddy, he slightly forward, she staying closer to the stones behind her. They were bewildered as always, but now it was as if they knew even less the reason they were there or what path would lead them away to a place of peace.

Taddy's hair, light brown, fell to just above his broad, straight shoulders. His body tapered down to the waist. His hands were hard and calloused, but the long fingers still retained a delicacy that could only come from the practice of a great tenderness. But it was his brown, almost black, eyes that defined him as a being most present.

It was as if they were being given more than a single vision, forced to see not only this room and the objects and the people in it, but also some other place, some other time altogether, and they grieved the loss of one, and were perplexed by the sight of the other. Taddy's mouth, small but well formed, was open more in quiet surprise than in preparation for speech. He took a half step backward, so his arm could touch Brid's, and let the side of his mud-caked foot touch what would have been the soft flesh of Brid's right heel.

Brid, too, was filled with wonderment—and sorrow, too—

but seemed more frightened than surprised. Her black hair and blue eyes—a blue deep enough to be the purple long allowed only to royalty or to the gods—were in contrast to her pale skin, a color too suggestive of fresh cream to be considered pallid. Her lips were red and moist as if she'd been eating berries picked from the hedges along the castle road. She was slender, and the erect hold of her head and the steady gaze of her eyes, sorrowful as they were, let it be known that there was no weakness in her. The homespun of her dress fell close to her body, forming itself over the small breasts, the compact thighs, and the calfs that narrowed to the trim ankles showing below the hem. She shifted her left foot so it covered the toes of Taddy's right foot. Both their necks were circled with the raw burn of their hangings.

The earth-brown threads in the loom and the cloth now vanished. Kitty stood and moved away from the treadle. Kieran set down the harp. The strings dissolved even as a few last vibrations of his single strumming still lingered in the air. As if to demonstrate a solidarity with his wife—as Taddy had moved closer to Brid—Kieran stepped quietly toward Kitty and let his upper arm press against hers. Together they faced the ghosts.

Kitty didn't know what to say, but said it anyway, the words catching in her throat, resisting, but finally forced out in a half-swallowed sound. "Why are you here?" she asked them.

The question seemed only to deepen their perplexity. Brid made a slight turn toward Taddy, and Taddy drew higher his head. "We are your friends," Kitty said—but before she could find some ending to her sentence, both Brid and Taddy pulled themselves closer to each other and the fear in Brid's eyes made them widen to a look bordering on terror. She leaned even closer to Taddy.

"Are you Brid and Taddy?"

At the mention of their names, in panic they vanished. Gone. Nowhere to be seen. Kitty and Kieran continued to stare for more than a moment. Then Kitty looked around the landing, at the darkened stones, at the floor and up toward the beams of the ceiling. She touched the loom. "They're gone?" she asked in a near whisper.

"Yes. Gone."

"I scared them off. They didn't seem to understand a word I—" She stopped, took in a slow breath, and slapped her right hand onto the frame of the loom. "Of course they didn't understand. I spoke in English. How would they know English? I was supposed to talk Irish. But because they're strangers—How stupid can I—"

"In Irish," Kieran said. "Say the words again. See if they can hear. If they'll come back."

Tentatively, in Irish Kitty called, "Are you here?" No answer came, no stirring of the air, no manifestation suggesting their return.

In Irish Kieran said, "Tell them we didn't mean to frighten them. Tell them we're from Kerry, the same as themselves. Only say it in Irish."

"I don't have to," Kitty said. "You just did."

But still there was no reply, no movement in the shadows. They waited. Kieran reached down to pick up the harp again, but stopped himself before he'd touched it.

Quickly he straightened. "Our problem is solved," he said in English.

"Talk Irish."

"No," he continued, still in English. "We don't have that—that 'thing' to worry about."

"What 'thing'?"

"When we're together—I mean when we're alone at night—if we do it in English we'll know they won't be anywhere near. They'll be frightened off."

"Make love in English?"

"To preserve our privacy."

"How can we make love in English?"

"Why can't we?"

"You can't make love in English. English doesn't have the right sounds. It doesn't have the right words. *You* can't and *I* can't—and we shouldn't even try."

"But if it guarantees we're alone?"

"It won't work. I can't do it. It wouldn't be love."

"Then you want them spying on us?"

"No. But if I have to make a choice—"

Kieran lowered himself onto the bench at the loom. "You're right. We can't do it any other way that I can think of."

Kitty shrugged. "Maybe they'll learn a thing or two."

Kieran reached over and took his wife's hand. "Instruction is not what I usually have in mind." A smile that can only be described as a leer spread across his face, bringing his beard close to his eyes. "Shall we show them now?" he whispered in Irish. "Here? See if they show up?"

"Here?" Kitty pulled her hand away, then after a pause during which she held it modestly near her right breast, she quickly grabbed her husband's hand and brushed it against her cheek. Reverting to her native Irish she said, "Well, we could give it a try. But what if they interrupt us?"

"Spiritus interruptus?"

Kitty groaned. "Now you've ruined everything."

Kieran stood up. "I'll make amends."

"Irish only. Right?"

"There's no other way," Kieran answered. After he took his lips away from hers, she said, "And no stopping if someone starts playing the harp."

And so their Irish splendors began—in the presence of the harp and the loom.

5

The merry month of August had arrived and with it the near lifelong requirement that both Kitty McCloud and Kieran Sweeney see and, more important, *be* seen, at the famed Dingle Races. This would be the first time they would be there together. In days past, before their miraculous marriage, their avoidance of each other, and the exchange of invective when they did meet, had provided added sport to the running of the horses. Everyone, of course, had taken sides. Were not the McClouds and the Sweeneys both progeny of familiar if not always respected lineages? No one knew exactly what the ancient quarrel was about, allowing as many certainties of the cause as there were people in County Kerry. Some spoke of a stolen cow, others of a boundary dispute; more than a few assumed the seduction of a wife, the elopement of a daughter. Most subscribed, however, to the charges and countercharges of a Sweeney priest betrayed by a McCloud informant—or, depending on one's familial allegiance, McCloud clergyman's secret escape passage to the sea exposed by a greedy Sweeney, the man captured and hanged. Since these accusations were for crimes beyond forgiveness and redemption, no one could be neutral on the subject. It could not be ignored.

Long years ago, divisions within the community threatened to become permanent, to be passed on from generation
to generation, like the Guelphs and the Ghibellines, the
Montagues and the Capulets, the Hatfields and the McCoys,
rending the community, unraveling the weave of the social
fabric, disfiguring the body politic, and distracting the populous from the common cause that required the employment of
all their energies and all their resources: everyday survival.

To restore the needed unity, one Father Fitzsimmons,
now many years gone, a man of Solomonic bent, spread a
series of false rumors, declaring in whispered confidence the
truth of each, contending that the story of priests betrayed
was a cover-up for a far lesser cause of contention, one that
lacked heroics, a more domesticated source that, in their
pride, the Sweeneys and McClouds discounted. The good cit-
izens, however, eager to accept any diminishment of a friend
or neighbor, took up the priest's rumors and elevated them to
gospel status, mocking the Sweeney-McCloud pretensions. In
time, the feud became more a cause for amusements than
contention—except, of course, between the Sweeneys and
McClouds themselves—a local topic that could be called
into service should a conversation lag or a television set go
out of commission.

The walk from the town of Dingle to the field where the race
course had been set up was less than a half kilometer. The
morning rain had moved on toward Tralee, and Kitty and
Kieran climbed without effort the slow rise of the road, managing not to be killed by those foolish or lazy enough to drive
their cars. Intent on provoking comment, they held hands.

Today was the last of the four days the races ran. Kitty had argued to go the first day. It was more festive, and the horses would be in better shape, since most of them would be required to run each day, sometimes in more than one race. Kieran, more melancholy by nature, preferred the closing event with its intimation of the end of things. In support of his preference he became an out-and-out Darwinian. Only the surviving horses would run. The spent and the disabled would have been eliminated, leaving for his and Kitty's pleasure only the fittest.

Kitty, after a moment of thought, had accepted his reasoning. She had other points of contention, far more serious. She was convinced that Kieran Sweeney had fallen in love with Brid. How could this man, whose passion and affection had proved to be inexhaustible—even gaining strength and momentum as their days and nights progressed—how could this most stable and honest of men be falling in love not just with another woman but with the ghost of another woman?

To have allowed the thought to even enter her brain was enough for Kitty to question her own stability. Common sense, to say nothing of overwhelming evidence, argued against such nonsense. Yet there her suspicions were. From whence they had come she knew not. When she presented to her oppressed head a lengthy list in her husband's defense, itemizing his show of ardor, his deference to her more stupid whims, his exuberance in her company, his offering of small joys and intimate pleasures, she would find comfort, even assurance, that her imagination was being overactive—as was its wont.

But within seconds she would come to a more sophisticated understanding of these attributes. He was, no more, no less, covering up for his growing delinquency. The increase of ardor was a measure of his infidelity.

The intimations had begun innocently enough. When Kitty and Kieran were planting an herb and spice garden, Kieran had mentioned that Brid would sometimes come when he was preparing their meals. She would sit on a stool in the scullery corner and watch, expectant more than bewildered, yet clearly appreciative of the wonders he would produce. Kitty found this of minimum interest. At first.

Another time, playing their evening game of Ping-Pong—they took full advantage of this particular artifact donated by the squatters—Kieran spoke of finding Brid near the stream, her face mournful even as she smiled sadly at the cows ruthlessly tearing up and munching the reeds nearby. He went on to note that he had paused and watched, not wanting to disturb her. Kitty's subconscious made a note of it.

As they were pruning the orchard, probably too late for a fair yield that year but hopeful for the next, Kieran expanded on the sweet solemnity of Brid's blue eyes during that morning's milking, her stately posture as she sat on a stool, observing the duties she herself had probably done, her muddied feet bare on the flagstone floor. Kitty listened to his words and said, "Ummm."

Then, as they had burned the pruned branches in an evening bonfire behind the castle, Kieran talked of his pity for the bewildered Brid. Kitty was attentive. He next spoke of the quiet pleasure it gave him to see her obvious affection for the cows, to see her wandering among the animals as they came up the hill from the mire, admitting with a sly smile he was less regretful than before that solutions had yet to be found to effect her departure. Kitty kicked a wayward branch closer into the fire, then plucked an already burning firebrand from the flames, flung it to the top of the pyre, and watched it intently as it was consumed by the flames.

Kieran noticed.

After that, there was no word about Brid. Nothing. It was the silence that gave Kitty full possession of the topic. Dismissive at first, then allowing herself to entertain a slight possibility and then a growing suspicion, she was finally filled with an absolute certainty that her husband was in love with Brid.

Insatiable, what she craved most was still more proof. His silence on the subject was one. Why this sudden avoidance of Brid's name? Another bit of evidence was his increased passion during their lovemaking. This was a manipulated distraction, pure and simple. And there was the time when Kitty had blithely asked, "Do you never see Brid anymore?" And he answered with a word borrowed from Kitty's own vocabulary: "Ummm."

The Dingle racecourse consisted of a dirt (or mud) track the width of a single lane road and fenced with white wooden rails nailed to white wooden posts. It was situated in a field that sloped gently upward, with the starting point at the top and off to the left of the grandstand, a fair distance but near enough to require the horses more often than not to pass the grandstand twice before reaching the finish. The grandstand itself was raucous and snug at the same time. Its limited seating made it seem like a fairly large but overpopulated opera box filled with a celebratory rabble that had come to exercise a determined joy and, in the process, raise as much ruction as possible.

Kitty and Kieran preferred the grassy infield, where they

could wander among the horses, the trailers, and the jockeys—boys of about fourteen, thin as sticks, with a ferocity made endearing by a sweetness even their more ruthless need to win could not disguise. For food, the Travelers—people descended from gypsies still in thrall to their ancient wanderlust—had brought their carts and stalls, offering hot dogs, potato chips, beer, and whatever else might satisfy the spectators' appetites.

Most important were the bookies: men wearing woolen pants, ill-fitting sweaters, scuffed shoes, and, for most, a stained fedora pushed to the back of the head the better to display a face so creased with knowledge and weathered with intuition that it could afford a look of disdainful indifference at the entire proceeding. Standing on his crate, his chalkboard with the next races' odds at his left, each called out his encouragements, suggesting by the tone of voice, by the casual loftiness of manner, that he and he alone had a direct line if not to the horse's mouth, then at least to those unseen, unsung arbiters who might or might not exercise an influence one would do well to consider.

(For the event, Kitty was wearing a Mets baseball cap and Kieran a floppy hat, the brim of which tickled the tops of his ears—which is why he wore it.)

After they had placed their bets for the third race—Kitty putting two euros on Rory's Boy at seven-to-one, Kieran five euros on Quodlibet at three-to-one—it was time for a hot dog and a beer. As they made their way through the crowd that ambled aimlessly around the infield, some scrutinizing the scheduled horses, others clustered to compare notes, more than a few enjoying a welcome visit in the afternoon air, first Kitty, then Kieran became aware that they were being stared at, mostly by women in their middle years, even though no comments were made beyond a wickedly smiled greeting. When Kieran reached for Kitty's hand, she drew it away. "Why not let's have a row, just to make them *really* happy."

"Fine with me. Any idea what about?"

Before Kitty could answer, Kieran had slowed and was looking intently toward one of the horse trailers. When Kitty followed his gaze she saw what he was looking at. There, talking to one of the jockeys—a boy in blue and white silks—was a girl, with creamy white skin and hair so black it suggested ancestral association with the raven. She was wearing what hinted at the return of the miniskirt, made of black leather and making a joyful display of legs so perfectly formed that to cover them could be deemed a crime. Her tank top lacked style—which tank top does not?—and the color beige helped not at all. (Kitty herself would, in similar circumstances and with similar figure, have chosen red, forgetting that this particular young woman required no such extravagance to attract the world's attention.) Most striking, however, was the slender neck rising unblemished in a natural flow from the delicately boned shoulders to a head composed of a highly successful merger among geometric shapes that had contended for the honor of crowning so pleasing a proof of what God could do given the right genes to work with.

To add to the obvious perfections was, at the moment, a laughter so animating that the jockey, in self-defense, could only grin sheepishly and try not to look at her too directly. He also kept striking his riding crop against his right leg, the inflicted pain intended no doubt as penance for the thoughts and urges rushing through his young libido.

"It's Brid," whispered Kieran.

After Kitty had made a chuckling sound, she said, with a light laugh, "It's not at all Brid."

"But the face. How often have we seen it? Just look at her."

"Why? You seem to be looking hard enough for both of us."

Too distracted by the girl to detect any emotional content in his wife's words, Kieran continued, "Listen to her laugh. She's not sad anymore. She's come alive."

"Have you never heard of recurring genetic traits? Maybe Brid died, but didn't her brothers and sisters carry into the next generation the same ingredients, and didn't their children pass them on so they could be passed on again and again until now?"

"But I want it to be Brid. Alive. Happy."

"Well, it ain't Brid. So get over it."

Now the girl was walking away from the jockey toward the bookies, bumping into one person, then another in the crowd, neither of them aware of the honor. The boy's grin had transformed itself into a leer of such lasciviousness that Kitty wanted few things more than to go up and give him a smack. He was punishing his right leg with an intensified whipping and had begun to pull on his left earlobe with the thumb and forefinger of his free hand, the equivalent of a pinch to convince himself he wasn't dreaming.

Kieran's eyes were following her. He shook his head in disbelief. "Why don't we go see which horse she's going to bet on? Maybe it's good luck."

Kitty took hold of his upper arm, squeezing into the muscle. "And you tell me I'm the one superstitious."

Kieran looked down at the ground.

He spoke quietly. "She was once as happy as this. At the castle I see her all mournful and wondering where she is and where everyone and everything's gone off to. And she has only the sight of the cows to comfort her and the sad move of the loom and Taddy with his harp playing whatever tune she might hear. Have you never seen her just sitting there, her muddy feet touching the stones? And patience she had for all the bafflement. And a sweetness to match how lovely is her face and her hands not meant for so much work as she'd had to do. Have you ever really watched her?"

"Yes. I've watched her." Kitty loosened her grip and let her hand fall to her side. She was looking at the girl move more deeply into the crowd, the sway of her hips avoiding obstacles, shifting her entire behind with unconscious agility rather than adjust her step or make the slightest change in the course she'd chosen.

For lunch, Kieran had two hot dogs with ketchup and onions, Kitty three with mustard and sauerkraut. Kieran had one beer, Kitty two. When the little girl tending the stand—a child of about ten—shortchanged Kieran, he offered no correction. When she asked if he wanted his palm read, he smiled and said no. Kitty considered encouraging him to change his mind but thought better of it and set down on the counter her plastic cup, her second beer only half finished. That the child had shown no interest in reading *her* palm puzzled Kitty—until she decided (wrongly) that the girl wanted only to hold her husband's hand.

There were no further sightings of the girl who reminded Kieran of Brid but soon it would be Kitty's turn. Three lead horses had made the turn into the homestretch. Kitty and Kieran were at the rail just down from the grandstand. Kieran had five euros on Jackeen at three-to-one, the jockey in blue and white, the one Brid's descendant had favored with her torments. Kitty had one euro on—unavoidably—Pig-O'-My-Heart, twenty-to-one, the jockey in silks featuring huge pink polka dots on a field of pastel green, making the boy—the single chubby jockey in the entire pack—look like an anemic ladybug. Jackeen had yet to make the far turn, but Pig-O'-My-Heart was still in contention in third. Now the horse was making its move, challenging Fisherman's Folly. Kitty crushed her fists into her cheeks. Kieran, ever the sport, called out, "Pig! Pig! Pig!"

As the horses galloped toward the finish, Kitty prepared herself to scream, the sound already rising toward her glottis, when the chubby boy in the saddle slipped sideways, not falling, but hanging on as best he could, jerking the horse's head up and giving the signal that the animal could ease its efforts, that the race was over. As for Kitty, as for Pig-O'-My-Heart, as for the chubby boy, it was over indeed. Who came in first was no longer of any interest. When Pig crossed the line, seventh but well ahead of Jackeen, the boy's torso was parallel to the ground, his head held slightly higher, his right leg raised as if in rude salute to the grandstand spectators who responded with the wildest cheering of the day.

Across the track, in the shadow of the grandstand, looking angrily down at the ticket in his hand, was Taddy. Not Taddy exactly, but nonetheless wearing mostly brown: brown corduroy pants, a brown sweater, and, in concession to the era in which he was living, white sneakers. The hair was only a bit shorter, but the shoulders, straight and broad, were readily recognizable, the torso tapering to the narrow waist. The hands had experienced no evolution. As they tore up the ticket and let the tatters sift onto the grass, Kitty could see that they were unwashed and calloused by some harsh task not different from those performed by his antecedent. When he looked up, his brown-eyed gaze went just beyond Kitty, to her left. Mournful he was and again there was the bewilderment. He, too, must have bet on Pig-O'-My-Heart, and if he didn't know the origin of this prompting, Kitty did.

Taddy at the castle had been chosen by the pig as a favored companion. And Taddy seemed to have accepted the honor. From the narrow turret window of her study she had seen more than several times the pig running, its snout down into the grass, hoping against hope that the ring with which it had been pierced would not prevent it from visiting the usual devastations upon Kerry's green and pleasant land. Taddy, meanwhile, would stand aside and watch, his head bowed for the first few thrusts of the snout. Small jerky movements would he make, pausing, then swinging his head to another point on his one-hundred-and-eighty-degree range as if on guard against anyone who might ridicule the pig's bootless efforts. When no one would appear, Taddy would bow his head again, reassured that no one was aware of the pig's humiliation, that he, Taddy, every faithful, was on guard and would allow no amusement at the pig's expense.

Then, at other times, he and the pig would simply wander the field, Taddy ahead, the pig following, more a dog and master than pig and ghost. For these excursions Taddy walked slowly, not looking down, gazing off somewhere. An exile, he was having perhaps some vision of the world taken from him long, long ago. So needful was he in his bewilderment, so forlorn in his loss, yet innocent and manly in his every movement, that Kitty had experienced, over the days and weeks and months, first a sympathy, then a grieving of her own, and, finally, a yearning, a need to hold and to cherish, to comfort and to—

Here she would invariably stop. She was indulging herself. There was work to be done. Maggie Tulliver still had not been successfully redirected along the plot lines that would correct Mary Ann's ineptitude. Kitty's agent, her publisher, and, of course, her ravenous public were all waiting with aroused appetites and money at the ready. She would return to her computer and stare at the wall in front of her desk. She would tell herself not to budge until the needed corrections came to her, until one word, then another, then another appeared on her screen. She would remain planted despite a desperate urge to rise up, to go to the window and see again the brown-clothed form brushing through the pasture grass, with the sturdy legs, the slender waist, and the large calloused hands, their corded veins pulsing surely with Kerry blood even though he was no more than a wandering shade lost this side of the River Styx with no one to make the offering to the ferryman who might see him safely across to the Elysian shore.

Kitty would return to her computer. How could Maggie be so inane as to allow her rising id to direct itself toward a man so impossible to her happiness as Stephen Guest? Of course love should make its claims, but impossibility was still impossibility, and any woman worthy of her gender would surely check her impulses and take control of her heart before disaster could strike. Thank God, she, Kitty McCloud, would never be capable of such insanities. Never. Not she. Not Kitty McCloud. Never. Et cetera.

She would stare at the blank screen; she would stare at the wall. It had been around this time that she began to suspect that her husband had fallen in love with Brid. There was evidence enough—if only she knew where to look for it.

The young man on the other side of the racetrack was kicking the scattered pieces of the torn ticket at his feet. Kitty considered directing her husband's attention to the youth by saying something like, "Oh look! There's Taddy!" But she decided not to. It was of no interest. And the young man didn't really look that much like Taddy. Taddy was far more handsome, more manly, less sullen. He certainly wouldn't have littered the ground with the remains of a losing ticket. Then, too, there were the sneakers. Without the sight of bare feet, mud-crusted and calloused, the Taddy across the track was much diminished.

Kieran said, "Oh look! There's Taddy!"

Kitty looked sideways at her husband. Had she been staring at the young man? Was that what had prompted Kieran to look over and see him standing there? Had she been observed in her ruminations? She was relieved to see that her husband was nothing more than mildly pleased at this apparition of an apparition. It meant little to him, if anything at all.

"Where?" Kitty asked.

"Can't you see him? Right there. Kicking the ground."

"Oh. Him." She gave her head a bit of a shake. "Well, yes, I can see some resemblance. The county is probably overrun with Taddys if we wanted to take time for a census. You want to see the horses for the next race?"

"He doesn't interest you?"

"Maybe. As a genealogical phenomenon. The gene pool of Kerry is, as you said, easily able to avoid mutation and replicas do occur from time to time." She took three steps toward the paddock area reserved for the horses scheduled for the next run. "You coming?"

"I thought you'd be more interested. After all, it *is* Taddy."

"It isn't Taddy. And even if it were, don't we already see more of him than we might want?"

Kieran shrugged. "If you say so." She took three more strides away, then waited for Kieran to catch up. When he did, she said, "We've seen Taddy. We've seen Brid. Now can we concentrate on the horses."

"No. Wait." Kieran stopped. He let out a guffaw. "There's Brid again."

"Where?"

"You missed her. She was right over there, by the trailer."

"Our Brid or another one? There seem to be no end of Brids around."

"The one from before. With the tank top."

Kitty took mental note of which part of Brid's anatomy he most readily referred to. The tank top. The breasts. The unblemished flesh. The slender arms. The delicate hands. She was ready to accuse him outright of infidelity, a breach of troth—whatever a "troth" might be. He was in love with Brid. She had all the proof she needed. Her wrath demanded a confrontation: just what was expected of them by their friends and neighbors. The populous was not to be disappointed. Her gathered accusations, her accumulated invectives, her hurt, her cries for vengeance—all were to be unloaded now. At the Dingle Races. For the benefit of strangers and Travelers, too. In front of the jockeys and their trainers, the owners and the bookies. She and Kieran were still close enough to the grandstand to be assured of a worthy audience. Would she strike him? Would she weep? A quick image of throwing herself onto the turf passed through her mind, but she didn't want to get that far into character.

Now she was ready to begin. She would start with a repeat of his phrase, "With the tank top!" but spoken with a sarcasm that would alert him to imminent danger. The words were already on her tongue. She had only to open her mouth and set them loose upon the world. Killer bees. Outraged wasps. Nettle-tongued midges.

Then another thought came to her. The time had come to rid the castle of its ghosts. They had to go. Means could be found—and she would find them. Where they would be sent off to she did not know nor did she care. They would take their bereavements with them, their sorrows and their perplexities. Her marriage would be saved, her savage breast tamed again to the ways of conjugality. No more would Brid and Taddy wander at will—if wills they had. No more would they appear at whim, then dematerialize when it suited their fancy or purposes. They would be free to wander where they would, the two of them, off to whatever haven was reserved for marriage-wrecking ghosts.

Somehow the thought of their wanderings—together— gave her pause. Why should Taddy be included in the expulsion? He was blameless. He was hardly a threat to her connubial expectations. He was content to be in the castle. The pig would miss him. Yes, Taddy could remain. But Brid must go.

Calmed by her rational self, Kitty walked alongside her husband, now taking his hand in hers. A fat man in a black suit, worn to a shine, with a white shirt gone gray with use and a tie marked with evidence of the meals that had contributed to his corpulence, smiled and nodded his approval as they went by. Old Mrs. Fitzgerald with the bright blue eyes said softly as they passed, "God be with you." Both Kitty and Kieran responded as their upbringing required: "God and Mary be with you."

Without breaking stride, Kitty, in a voice so lilting that it shamed the birds, said, "Wearing a tank top, was she? I'd forgotten. Didn't she have on a black miniskirt?"

"Did she? I hadn't noticed."

Oh, the hypocrisy! Kitty was about to return to plan A but restrained herself. Soon all would be well. All would be wonderfully well.

6

As was his custom when expecting a parishioner of some affluence, Father Colavin had managed, when Kitty arrived, to be poring over the parish ledger. As was also his habit, he invited her to sit down while he finished one little matter in which he had been deeply involved. He then traced a pen down the columns of the ledger, emitting little gasps and a few groans, but no words. Kitty was treated to this familiar rubric until the good priest sighed, pushed his chair away from the dining room table where they were both seated—he on one side, she on the other, in keeping with procedural etiquette prescribed back in his days in the seminary: when alone with a woman always keep some barrier between the two of you. The reasons were obvious: no vow could survive the lures emanating from the female of the species, or, worse, the woman herself was, by nature, a temptress not to be trusted.

Father Colavin's dining room table was covered with what looked like a large shawl—his mother's?—a relic from his boyhood or even beyond, when his ancestors had come down from Ulster five generations ago. They had since become more the people of Kerry than the people of Kerry themselves. The shawl, with broad strips of brown and maroon and a fringe of gray yarn like thick but exhausted hair, provided some sense of decoration. At the table's center an empty glass bowl intended for fruit completed the attempt at bourgeois display.

What had fascinated Kitty from childhood were the table legs. Thick to begin with, they swelled halfway down to the floor, then diminished to their original circumference, suggesting to Kitty that each had swallowed a melon and been unable to complete the transaction. The chairs had cushioned seats, the embroidered fabric worn down on only one at the head of the table: Father Colavin's. The rest had simply faded, the red of the roses a pale tan and the green of the leaves close enough to this same tan color, hinting that both foliage and blossom were among time's indifferent achievements. The chairs also testified to the priest's solitary life, his loss of that most civilized human ritual, a shared meal. Perhaps the Eucharist—the ultimate meal shared with the Savior himself—was sufficient, even superior, and he felt no deprivation.

There was a sideboard, a repository for the place settings seldom used and the bottle of Jameson whiskey called into service for visiting dignitaries and applicants for weddings, funerals, and baptisms. (Kitty and Kieran had been given generous sips during their nuptial arrangements, a foretaste of what lay ahead when the baptisms and the funerals would be required.) The Cross of Saint Patrick, the Celtic cross with a shortened horizontal beam, was centered above the sideboard, the rest of the wall bare out of deference to this symbol more Irish than the shamrock itself.

Near the door leading to the pantry were the expected pictures of the Sacred Heart aflame with love and the Blessed

Mother, her exposed heart pierced with the daggers of her seven sorrows.

On the other side of the doorway were framed photographs, yellow brown by now, of the priest's parents, the man uncomfortable in a high stiff collar, the woman, born Fitzgibbons, looking rather pleased with the lace around her neck and the brooch worn at her throat. The windows opposite the sideboard were curtained with a sheer gauzy cloth; the drapes were velvet, a plush amber, held back by braided cords that might have done previous service as the belting for a bathrobe. The rug underfoot was so thin and the weave so worn that it was constantly being crumpled by the least movement of anyone's foot.

Father Colavin folded his hands on the table top, looked wearily at Kitty, and said, "You'll have to forgive me. There's the roof and none but the devil to mend it."

Kitty had learned from experience that the priest was not coercing her into making a contribution but offering her a bargaining chip. She was there to ask a favor. Few came to see him for reasons other than to complain about the music, the homily, the behavior of fellow congregants, the altar boys and girls scratching themselves in forbidden places. Unfailingly, Father Colavin would greet such "suggestions" with awed gratitude for the information, offer a hint that heresies, liturgical abominations, and public sinning would soon become the object of his full attention, then go about his business with an equanimity available only to those capable of ignoring the presumptions of upstarts.

More often than not, Kitty was grateful for his barricades. Given any proximity she would have been unable to resist the urge to reach out and plant a kiss on the dear man's time-furrowed brow. She didn't doubt that the impulse would recur during this present session, especially since the opening moments—ledger, groans, despair—indicated that all would go according to plan, ending with Kitty pledging a sizeable sum to repair the very roof that she had already paid to fix after her previous intrusions concerning the wedding.

Also, Kitty was particularly grateful that this was the day set aside for her appointment. She'd just returned from Cork and a session with her lawyer, one Debra McAlevey. Ms. McAlevey had summoned her after Kitty had ignored a series of e-mails informing her that the current Lord Shaftoe, George Noel Gordon Lord Shaftoe no less, had hired solicitors in London to represent his charge that he alone, and neither the Crown nor the Republic of Ireland, was claimant to ownership of Castle Kissane. Kitty had dismissed the previous e-mails and their content as unworthy of her attention—until Ms. McAlevey had threatened to resign as her advocate should she persist in her silence.

That very morning Kitty had been told that his Lordship's case was far from negligible. Documents had been presented that might possibly contradict previous assurances that the castle had, through a longtime failure to pay taxes, come finally into the possession of the Republic from which Kitty had made the purchase. She must respond. There were papers for her to sign, affidavits to which she must subscribe and, in general, she must be more attentive to her predicament.

All of this, she told herself, was no more than an annoyance. Her right of purchase had been thoroughly researched and duly processed. Her claim was as solid as the walls of the castle itself; no one could announce himself after an absence of two centuries and presume to lay a bloodied hand on a single inch of Irish ground. Although she had signed on every dotted line Ms. McAlevey had placed before her, she had drawn on her inexhaustible fund of displeasure, allowing herself the certainty that these proceedings were meant to do no more than offer a feeble and temporary diversion from the real difficulties with which she was currently besieged—difficulties that had brought her to Father Colavin's rectory, to her side of the table.

Father Colavin was again shaking his head, staring down at the intractable ledgers before him. "First," he said, "the Son of God had no place to lay his head, and now He's to have no roof over it either. But that's hardly your concern. You've no doubt come on more urgent business." Kitty considered, by way of experimentation, making a pledge now and getting on with her purposes for being there. But then Father Colavin, in his wisdom, might interpret her opening offer as an invitation to bargain once her needs were made known. No outright increase would be asked, merely repeated interruptions of her cause, Father Colavin noting sadly the challenges to his concentration occasioned by the imminent collapse of his roof. To relieve his worries and focus his concentration, she might consider upping the pledge just a wee bit.

Kitty decided to stick to the old ways: plead her case now, bargain later. She was fully aware that, before this meeting would be brought to its conclusion, not only the roof but also a stained glass window or two, plus a new bell for the belfry, might be put on the table as bargaining chips in the sought-for resolution of her requirement that the castle be relieved of one ghost but not the other. She was prepared to include the bell but not the windows. Some things must be kept in reserve for future emergencies.

"Now then, Caitlin"—Father addressed her with the name he had bestowed on her at the font—"tell me what I can do for you and rest assured I'll do it if it's within my feeble powers."

"What I have to say, Father, isn't very easy."

"Oh, don't tell me! Not you and Kieran. Not trouble so soon!"

"Oh, no, Father. Not that. Or—no—not really—"

"Then praise be! You gave me a fright I haven't had since the reforms of Vatican Two."

The good priest had been horrified by the conciliar changes: the idea of the Pope acting in concert with the bishops instead of ruling by fiat from the Chair of Peter had unsettled him completely. Fortunately for the aging priest, succeeding Popes—men of insufficient faith to trust in the workings of the Holy Spirit, as Pope John XXIII had done— had, with the craven acquiescence of those same bishops the council had meant to empower, nullified the reform. In doing so, they safely placed the children of God back into the grip of a mortal man too uneasy to expand the bounds of the universal church to include the Third Person of the Holy Trinity.

The reform they retained—the liturgy in the language of the congregants—was, however, much to Father Colavin's liking. That he should celebrate the divine mysteries and expound the good news of salvation in Irish seemed to him the just reversion of an ancient wrong that had been inflicted long centuries ago—against all common sense—to retain Rome as the Seat of Peter rather than transfer it to the one place on earth untouched by the barbarian rampage that had imposed illiteracy on an entire continent. It was an article of faith for Father Colavin to believe that it had been an Irish monk, schooled in an Irish abbey, who had journeyed to the land of the Franks to teach Charlemagne how to read. It was only too apparent that Dublin should have been declared the heart and head of Christendom, surrounded as it was by saints and scholars obviously able to rekindle the civilization of an extinguished continent. The suppression of this inspiration had been a torment to the priest, but still, he did have the consolation that it was now Gaelic words that summoned into the sacrifice of the mass the very presence of God himself. Of course, that this bit of Irish speaking in the liturgy was confined to a small patch of the planet along the coastlands of the Western Sea did, at times, disquiet him, but then he would celebrate yet another mass in the Church's rightful tongue—Irish—and feel the triumphant swell within his breast available only to those who had waited patiently for this remediation of history.

Kitty looked down at the shawl covering the table. "It's not about Kieran I've come."

"Ah—answered prayers. I must remember to give thanks."

"Yes. Please do." Kitty then, like Father Colavin, folded her hands on the tabletop. She was ready to begin. Or, if she was not ready, she would begin anyway. "There are ghosts in the castle," she blurted.

"Ghosts in the castle," Father Colavin repeated, nodding his head in ready belief. "Ah, yes. I'm not surprised. Interesting."

"You believe me?"

"Brid and Taddy. Are they the ones?"

"You know their names?"

"Doesn't everyone? And anyway, one of the few disadvantages of a long life is that so much knowledge is heaped upon my head that I sometimes worry my poor skull is going to crack under the weight and my brain drip down onto the floor like puffin droppings."

So surprised was Kitty by this easy acceptance that she wasn't prepared to move on to the next phase of her mission: the actual request for an exorcism or whatever might be required to rid her marriage of this impermissible threat, the ghost of Brid. She had expected a lengthy discourse complete with Father Colavin's disbelief, followed by Kitty insistences, then *his* demands for common sense, then *her* reiterated assurance that the supernatural was at work in her castle, then *his* attempt to cajole her by offering counsel often needed by newlyweds that some susceptibility to the extraordinary had to be expected, *her* growing anger and anguish, and, finally, *his* pretended acceptance—a condescension meant to prevent her agitations from evolving into hysterics.

But this hadn't happened, and she was stuck with the need for adjustment with no time left for the summoning of her craft, the invocation of her cunning, powers derived from her presumed female helplessness, which would make its appeal to the immensity of the spiritual powers bestowed on her pastor.

She, being Kitty McCloud, effected her recovery in so short a time that her bafflement remained imperceptible to Father Colavin and was, to Kitty, only a momentary hiccup in the ongoing presentation, not requiring further consideration.

Father Colavin cleared his throat. "But surely you knew about Brid and Taddy before you bought the castle."

"Well, yes. In a way. There are always the old stories—"

"I remember only too well," Father Colavin interrupted. " 'Be home before dark, or Taddy'll take you and lock you in the tower.' "

Kitty tried to tell the priest that her parents, her entire family, were too concentrated on the blood feud with the Sweeneys—"The Sweeneys will get you!" or "I'm going to give you to the Sweeneys!"—to need recourse to the ghost threats of Brid and Taddy, but the man was too deep into his subject for possible extrication.

" 'Brid and Taddy are wanting a little boy answers to the name of Colavin, and I've a mind to tell them where you sleep and they're welcome to you. . . .' Ah, how can I forget? My mother—" Here he stopped, his eyes gone into the distant past, a sad smile on his face, his mother, his care-worn mother, not raising her head from her sewing while persuading him to stop tormenting the cat and to bring in more turf for the fire as he'd been told. Or to do his studies instead of making mischief with his sister's pigtails. "Taddy and Brid, Brid and Taddy. Ah, yes—" And then he said no more.

Kitty waited to make sure his reverie had ended. "You saw them then?"

"Oh, no. I did as I was told and they were never sent for."

"If you want to chance it, come to the castle."

"And I'd see them?"

"Maybe." Kitty knew there were no guarantees, and she hardly wanted to make claims she couldn't honor, so she added, "Only Kieran and I have. So far. But you're welcome to give it a go."

The priest shook his head. "I know you mean to be generous, but they're the last ghosts I'd want to see. Terror is what I'd feel. From birth I was taught they were evil spirits, staying behind their time so they could roam the roads and the hills, appearing in and out of the mists, grabbing up wicked boys and bold girls and doing to them things beyond what can be imagined by anyone still in possession of his own soul."

"But you imagined anyway."

"Of course. How could I not?"

"And what did you think might happen?"

Father Colavin lowered his head and put his right hand to his chest. "I was afraid they would hurt my mother and I not there to protect her." Again he shook his head, bidding the memory to release him and let him go. He looked up at Kitty and put his hands again on the ledger, his voice now an eager whisper. "What do they look like?"

This is not how Kitty had expected the interview to go. She had come to rid herself of ghosts and now she was having to summon them—even if it was only in her mind—and make them present to the priest whose aid she would ask in banishing them.

"They have bare feet," she said, not looking up. "And around their necks, each of them, the flesh raw from their hangings."

"No," interrupted the priest. "No more. I don't want to hear." He then added quickly, "But I do want to hear. Tell me."

"Their eyes are so sad, so very sad, and they seem not to know why they're there, in the castle still. They wear brown, Brid a plain dress to just above her ankles. Black hair. High cheeks. Young lips. They both look to be seventeen."

"And so they were. And so they are." He paused and Kitty had a strong sense that he was breathing a prayer. She waited until he was ready to speak again. "And Taddy?" he finally said.

"A tunic tied at the waist. Brown jacket, brown home-spun pants to just below the knees. Brown hair. Dark brown eyes. Calluses on his hands, mended cracks where the work was too much. He plays the harp. She works the loom."

"They do that? And you see them doing it?" He was almost breathless with wonder.

"Sometimes. Just before the sun goes down. She spends most of her time with the cows, going where they go, just being with them. And he wanders around with a pig we have. They're lost. They don't know where to go."

"But they don't frighten you?" He asked this as if not quite sure he was prepared to believe any answer other than yes.

"No. Why would they frighten me? My mother never said anything about them. I was never—threatened."

"But still. They *are* ghosts."

"Yes. I know."

"And you aren't afraid of ghosts?"

"Should I be?"

"I don't know. I've never seen one. And I hope never to see one. It would be the death of me, I'm sure."

"You've nothing to fear. Not from them."

"Just the sight of them—No! I couldn't. I'd be destroyed."

"No, you wouldn't. It would break your heart. And it would make you want to rise up again against those who did the hanging."

"Those days are gone. And we must thank God for it. And I've no need of having my heart broken. Not again."

"Oh?"

"Never mind. Nothing more than we all suffer, living in the world."

Kitty waited to see if he would elaborate. He did, but only in his thoughts, his inward gaze off now to the curtained windows as if ghosts of his own were appearing through the scrim. He waited for them to vanish, his closed lips pressing one against the other, trying to keep any sound, any word, from escaping. His mouth relaxed. His gaze was diverted to his hands. He took in a breath and let it fill his lungs and expand to what degree they could in his frail and sunken chest. "Is there more you want to tell me?"

"Is there some way they can be made to go?"

"You want them to leave?"

"Of course. You said yourself you wouldn't want ghosts wandering about."

"That's because it's a mystery my faith can't comprehend."

"People have visions all the time, I thought. All over the place."

"These aren't visions. They're ghosts."

"What's the difference?"

"Visions appear by the grace of God. And for his purposes. Ghosts—who knows what they're up to."

"They are up to nothing. They're just there."

"Precisely. But how can I know they have no purpose?"

"What purpose could they have other than to wander around and work the loom and play the harp?"

"They can do that?"

"Yes. I told you I've seen Brid at the loom. No threads, but she works it with the treadle and moves the shuttle as if she were actually weaving. And—and Taddy plucks at the harp—but no strings are there. Except one time we heard music. Another time we saw the cloth being woven."

"God have mercy." Again Father Colavin shook his head. "I don't know. Except I need them to have a purpose. The same as everything and everyone else."

"Maybe they do, but you don't have to know any more than I do about what it might be. Which is nothing."

"But if I don't—"

"Yes?"

"If I don't, well, it's something I want to go nowhere near."

"Then you won't do anything to help me?"

"Exactly what do you have in mind?"

"Don't we still have exorcism?"

"Yes."

"Well, then—"

"No. Absolutely not."

"Why not?"

"For me to confront evil so directly—to become intimately involved with it—"

"But they're not evil. They're good. They—they're martyrs."

For more than a few moments the priest considered this, took it to himself, and let it take hold. Finally he could find no reaction other than to shake his head—again—but only slightly this time. "There are ways to rid ourselves of devils, of evil spirits. But what has been devised to rid us of the good? You yourself have said they're not evil; they're good and that makes me more helpless than ever."

"But they're not at peace. Or part of them isn't." She then blurted it out, "And besides, my husband has fallen in love with Brid. There. I've said it."

"But you told me none of this was about you and Kieran."

"All right. I lied. I hadn't intended to mention that part of—of the—of the—"

"Difficulty?"

"Yes. The difficulty."

"And the difficulty is that your husband, Kieran Sweeney, is in love with a ghost?"

"Yes. In love." She took in a breath through her nose, then added, "She's young. She—she's very beautiful." She paused again, then repeated one last word: "Very."

"He's said as much?"

"He doesn't have to."

"Then how do you know?"

"I just know."

"But there must be some indication—some evidence— something said, something done—"

"It's the way he talks about her."

"How?"

"That she's beautiful. That he sees her with the cows. And sometimes when he's milking. She's there with him. She watches him. Doing the milking."

Kitty then went on to explain, step by step, the evening that led to her conviction that her husband had gone astray, in his thoughts and in his heart. Father Colavin kept nodding, apparently the physical means by which information entered into his consciousness. Kitty went on: how Kieran no longer mentioned Brid. How his lovemaking with her had become more ardent. How he was obviously intent on contradicting what she knew to be the truth. The sordid truth.

Father Colavin had stopped nodding about two-thirds of the way through her recitation. Perhaps he had been given as much information as he could process at one sitting. Perhaps he had begun to have thoughts of his own, responses to what was being said, but was reluctant to interrupt. Kitty had been telling the priest about Kieran as he had watched Brid at the loom, then went on to tell him about Taddy at the harp.

"There he sat, Taddy did, the harp held against him, so mournful his eyes, cast down as they were, and they as deep as wells. So straight he sat and his feet light on the floor and his toes muddy and no one to wash them. An angel he must be, but more a man than an angel. No angel could be so sad yet never weep. And no ordinary man is he, even for the ghost of one. No ordinary man could be strong and still so gentle. You'd have to see him the way I've seen him. The poor man, so lost, and I'm the only woman alive knows his sorrow. Not even Brid. Of that I'm sure. It's Brid must go. It's Taddy can stay."

What thoughts, what images came after, she had no words for. She held them, silently, with her eyes veiled so Father Colavin couldn't see there what she was seeing. The priest waited, shuffling his feet under the table but making no move with his head or his hands. When Kitty stirred slightly on the seat of her chair and coughed a needless cough, Father Colavin said softly, "I see."

And see he did. What he saw made clear to him the reason Caitlin McCloud had come to call. But what he must do now had not yet been vouchsafed to him. It would do no good to intensify his concentration. That would only clamp everything closer together, making the situation that much more impenetrable. He must clear his mind, not knot it further. But rescue was near at hand. He untwined his fingers, parted his palms, and reached out past the ledger. Slowly he drew it closer to himself. He could give his mind a few moments of relief, applying it completely and without distraction to another matter quite foreign to the truths he had just been given.

"Forgive me, Caitlin," he said. "Forgive me for the interruption, but I suddenly remembered—" Without obligating himself to name specifically what that remembrance might be, he pulled the heavy book toward himself and sighed, as if the sound secured the transfer of his consciousness from Kitty to his accounts. Perhaps during this interval the needed solutions would come to him.

With effort he lifted the cover and with further sighs and shakes of his snowy head, he turned page upon page with a licked finger, giving Kitty a full display of all the figures, all the orderly columns, one upon another, that gave some measure to the burdens of his ministry. After the search of more than several pages and more than several columns, his head moving up and down, emphasizing the labor needed to accommodate his scrutiny, he sighed yet again and placed his right hand on a column of figures, holding them in place lest they juggle themselves before he'd be given the opportunity to resign himself anew to their inadequacy.

Kitty's stirring elevated to a squirm. She feared—as well she might—that she had said things she hadn't meant to say. But her fear was quickly dissolved when she considered that Father Colavin had probably heard nothing, or very little, of what she'd been saying. He had gone back to his columns and his figures, his roof, his windows, and his belfry bell. So grateful was she that even with the prescribed barrier between them she wanted desperately to kiss his brow, his white hair, the back of his freckle-splotched hand.

But she restrained herself, eager to be told the amount to be levied against her for the session now drawing to its close. That nothing had been resolved, nothing determined, was, at this point, fine with her. She'd been told—without it being said in just so many words—that the priest could do nothing for her. Evil spirits were his business. Good ones were on their own. She should have known he could offer nothing. But, Catholic that she was, she'd had to try. Her obligation to give the Church first dibs at her problem had been fulfilled. She'd need tarry no longer, except to be given the bill for services that had been, in their fashion, rendered close to her satisfaction.

Father Colavin was scribbling some figures on a paper pad just to the right of the ledger. He was, she didn't doubt, adding up the check. Still doodling, he said, "You're convinced that your husband is in love with Brid. Her ghost."

"Yes."

"Have you ever asked him if he is?"

"Why—no."

"And why not?"

"Because—because I don't have to. I know."

"I see." He drew his finger down a column of figures, stopped, and noted three sets of numbers on his pad. He added them up, then looked at the bottom of the column, but without much interest. He turned a page and doodled some more. "And Taddy is no problem?"

"You mean does Taddy suspect about Kieran? I mean, I assume Taddy and Brid, I assume they are—well—they were—lovers. Brid and Taddy. But I'm afraid the two of them are beyond reach. They have their own—existence. I almost said lives, but I guess *existence* is the better word."

The inward gaze had come again into her eyes. "Neither of them cares anything for us. About me. About how I feel."

"Then any feelings toward them are hopeless?"

"Yes," she said quietly. "Hopeless." She let the full meaning of the word pass through her. During its passage she repeated the word. "Hopeless."

"Then what you have in mind is saving someone from an involvement that is hopeless. Is that it?"

With a long-suffering resignation new to her repertoire,

she said, "Yes. That's it precisely. I—I don't want him hurt. I can't bear to see him suffer."

"We're talking about your husband."

"Why—why, yes. Of course."

"And have you observed anything like that? His suffering?"

"Well, no. Not yet. But—but it's coming. I'm sure of that. One can't feel so deeply—and know there's nothing ever to come of it—that no matter how much you love—how much you keep longing and wanting—" She stopped, recomposed her features, and said, "As you can see, I get carried away. I'm that concerned. About my husband."

"Yes. That I can tell." Father Colavin put down the pen and folded his hands on the open ledger. "Have you anything else you want to tell me?"

"I—I don't think so. There really isn't that much more to tell, if anything at all. You know the situation. And, if I understand correctly, there's not much you can do."

"May I ask you something, Caitlin?"

"Why, yes. Of course, Father."

"Do you, does Kieran, do you pray for these young people? For their souls? For their eternal rest?"

The impulse to squirm returned, but Kitty was determined to suppress any and all movement. "Well—no. I never thought in those terms. I just accepted their being there, and that there was nothing much I—or Kieran either—nothing we could do about it."

"I understand." He bowed his head, then lifted it, but said nothing.

"We should, I suppose." Kitty began to squirm after all.

Father Colavin sent his puckered lips forward and puffed up his cheeks a bit. He shrugged. "It wouldn't hurt."

"I'm rather ashamed I hadn't thought of it."

"You have other things on your mind."

"That's true enough."

"But allow me to ask one thing more."

"Of course, Father."

"You seem to feel only Brid should go. To spare you husband. But should the two be separated? From what you say, they seem a comfort to each other. Shouldn't they both be—released?"

The squirming increased. "Well, yes. But, of course, if Taddy wants to stay—"

"Why would he want to stay?"

Kitty straightened in her chair, then managed a quick laugh. "How would—how could I know? I don't even know why he's there to begin with."

Father Colavin was looking at her more directly than she liked. She should never have come here. It was all getting more stupid by the minute. What she had wanted was some means to deal with Brid, some ritual to send her packing. But now she was being expected to pray for the wench. But then, if Brid did find eternal rest, then she wouldn't be around all moony, and with Kieran watching.

It was too complicated. She didn't want to think about it anymore. At least not here, with Father Colavin looking at her as if he knew more than he was letting on, and was daring her to know what it was. To get both of them back into more comfortable territory, where each knew what the other was up to and what the world was all about, she said, "Not to change the subject, Father, but a thought. Didn't you mention some time or other, something about the belfry, about repairs so the bell doesn't go flying out onto the street the next time it's rung?"

"Oh. That's been taken care of. But thank you for thinking about it."

"And the windows. Which ones did you say they were? The ones behind the altar?"

"All mended. But thank you."

"Oh." She shifted in her chair. "But the roof—"

"Ah, Caitlin, Caitlin. I can hardly ask you about that. You've paid for it twice. Surely I won't ask you again."

"But—but maybe I could—"

"No, no, no. You've done more than your share—long since." He closed the ledger.

"But if there's anything else—"

"I'll come to the castle next Tuesday and say my mass there. In the room with the harp and the weaver's loom. It'll be for Taddy and for Brid. That they find their rest. And maybe that will be the end of it."

"Oh, Father, I wouldn't want to inconvenience you."

"What you want is of no concern to me. Tuesday. Seven o'clock. You needn't attend. Nor Taddy nor Brid nor Kieran nor anyone. And if I fall in a faint into a heap on the floor at the sight of them, I'll get up soon enough, so don't bother yourselves about it. But that's where I'll say my mass. Is that understood?"

Kitty, rather than hit herself on the side of the head and let loose a few shrieking screams and grind her teeth to dust, nodded her head yes.

7

There had been five days without rain, and rumors of a drought spread throughout the county. Even the mists that shrouded the tops of the hills had dissolved and, exposed to the continuing glare of undisrupted sunshine, the citizenry began to feel a slight unease, as if their privacy was somehow being invaded. Good weather had always been looked upon as a blessing, but now the sense of blessing was being withdrawn. They'd been given in its stead a string of days one so like the other that much of the variety and surprise had been removed from their lives. The gorse and the heather on the slopes of the mountains looked the same on Wednesday as they had on Monday and Tuesday. And the peaks of the high hills were always there, easily seen, never disappearing, always present.

Predictability had been introduced, a phenomenon no one could get used to. Unreliability had been the norm, but now one must cope with the threat of certainty: change had been repealed and a succession of days, one like the other, might in time encourage a conformity in the people themselves, a likeness one to the other, a characteristic unknown in their race. Of course, it was only the fifth day and the general unease had yet to heighten itself to fear, but the tension was there.

And, to add to it, Father Colavin—to no effect—had come as promised and said his mass alongside the loom, in the presence of the harp, with Kitty and Kieran in attendance. When told about the impending liturgical celebration, Kieran had responded immediately with approval, wondering why neither he nor his wife had thought of it sooner as a means of bringing peace to the mournful pair.

His want of objection, his instant acceptance, Kitty saw as further proof of his infidelity. He'd been afraid to challenge the event. It would raise questions he wouldn't want to answer, knowing full well he'd have to confess his anguish over the possible loss of Brid.

Of course, Kitty would have had no way to express her worry that Taddy too might be swept away, balancing her loss for his—but this she hadn't really articulated to herself, for the simple reason that she had yet to admit that her suspicions of Kieran's infraction had its source in feelings of her own. Which is why she never thought of it. She couldn't afford to.

There was some disappointment that the ghosts absented themselves from the holy sacrifice. Father Colavin had prepared himself for their presence; Kitty and Kieran hoped for conclusive evidence of their claims. After a full breakfast of oatmeal, eggs, sausages, muffins, potatoes, and coffee, Father Colavin departed, asking only that he be kept informed if any changes had been effected by his efforts. They hadn't. Brid turned up for the late milking, and Taddy had been seen taking the sunshine in the company of the pig.

The following day, it was Kieran who came up with the

most plausible explanation for the absence at the mass. It had been said in Irish and not the Latin liturgy so familiar to Brid and Taddy. Unknowing of this remaining shred of conciliar reform, they had no doubt assumed the event was under the aegis of the protestant Church of Ireland—which had, from its inception centuries before, realized it made no sense to keep the liturgy at a remove from its participants and that God was conversant in any language, even Irish. Kieran suggested Father Colavin should return and say a Latin mass, but Kitty contended that the efficacy of the mass was not contingent on who was there and who was not there. Grace was unconfined. They had faithfully participated in their priest's efforts and could now search for other means to bring peace to those in need—whomever that might prove to be.

Another manifestation of the aberrant weather—the constant surveillance by the sun—was, for Kitty at least, an impatience with her work. It could also have been Brid's continuing residence, a possibility that never occurred to her. In any event, she was ready to drown Maggie Tulliver, Tom, and Stephen Guest in the flood waters of the Floss and be done with the uncooperative wretches. But before she could indulge in so reckless an act, she was rescued first by the arrival of Lord Shaftoe and second by a deluge arriving out of nowhere, nearly drowning a cow in the stream and exciting the pig to ecstasy in the courtyard mud.

Lord Shaftoe's entrance on the fifth of the sunshine days was a bit unexpected. Yet there he was, the man descended from the same Lord Shaftoe who had been given the castle as a gift from Cromwell, a reward for his highly efficient slaughters in the days of old. He was descended as well from the Lord Shaftoe who, when he'd been told of the plot to blow the castle heaven high had had the two young people hanged. That particular lordship had then left somewhat precipitously, fearful that the gunpowder was still in place, and encouraged his agents to be pitiless in rent collections, tithings, floggings, and evictions.

A succession of dutiful agents occupied the grounds, but not the castle itself, which remained empty for fear of the promised explosion. They lived high on the hog, with a full complement of henchmen available for the humiliations and whippings known to be a source of imperial enjoyments. The lordly line, over time, became confused by several bastard claims, and the ownership of the castle passed into a maze of litigations from which a single survivor had only now emerged to make his case. One issue, however, had yet to be resolved. Thanks to the unyielding ruthlessness of Kitty McCloud and the machinations (which she preferred to negotiations) of her even more ruthless solicitor, Debra McAlevey, the deed of ownership had devolved into the sure hand of Ms. McCloud, who took proud possession, curse or no curse, gunpowder or no gunpowder. She considered it a return of stolen property, since she'd been told from infancy that she was descended on her mother's side from a kingly line, dispossessed and long since dispersed to lands ignorant of their nobility and indifferent to the calamities. Here in this castle would she flourish, here would she indulge her impulse for intimacy in the company of her beloved husband, Kieran Sweeney, himself descended from kings of equally obscure origin.

But now, under a cloudless sky the color of Our Lady's mantle, the present Lord Shaftoe—George Noel Gordon Lord Shaftoe—drove up in his whale-sized SUV, emerged, and unloosed from the vehicle's capacious rear compartment an evil looking Rottweiler. While the hound, drawn by the scent of the cows, went howling down the hill toward the stream, Lord Shaftoe crossed the drive, opened unaided and unwelcomed the massive door, entered the great hall, and shouted in a voice fully supported by a native arrogance and disdain, "Miss McCloud? I've come to see a Miss McCloud! Hello? Miss McCloud?"

Kitty, having wrested herself from her computer before the summons could be repeated—or Maggie and Tom and Stephen drowned—appeared at the railing of the gallery and said, "If that's your dog, I suggest you fetch it before I start shooting."

"Miss McCloud!" Lord Shaftoe raised his right hand in limp salute. He was wearing tan slacks of the kind Kitty gave to male characters she would eventually reveal to be inordinately vain, and the obligatory expensive tweed jacket complete with sleeves patched with the unneeded leather. "I'm Lord Shaftoe. No doubt you've heard of me. George Noel Gordon Lord Shaftoe."

"Do you call your dog or do I get my gun?"

"Don't be alarmed. He's harmless. And allow me to say I've looked forward to this moment, to meeting you. I've read your books."

"Who hasn't?"

"*My Dream of You.* Lovely."

"*My Dream of You* was written by Nuala O'Faolain."

"You're sure?"

"Reasonably. And we were talking about your dog."

"I repeat: harmless. Unless you have chickens or a cat. Or maybe another dog. She tends to be territorial."

His Lordship was tall and graying, with what could have been a craggy face had not gravity pulled it earthward. The entire man seemed to sag and droop as if the effort to keep the skin attached securely to the bone had proved beyond his interest. Even his eyes slanted downward and his near lipless mouth had curved itself into a perpetual frown, relieving him of the need to rearrange his features when displeasure was being expressed.

Kitty didn't doubt that, beneath his well-cut clothing, the pectorals and the abs, the belly and the buttocks were all descending in a flow similar to the meltings of a waxen effigy. His ears were small, even tiny, well on their way to becoming vestigial, an evolutionary phenomenon possibly influenced by a longtime disdain for listening to whatever was being said. His Lordship did, however, possess sufficient wisdom to surrender himself to a first-rate tailor—the first refuge of the hopelessly unappealing—who had provided a tasteful sartorial display to distract the viewer from the unprepossessing anatomy mercifully hidden from sight. Kitty came resolutely down the stone stair, walked past his lordship, out the door, around the side of the castle and down the slope toward the mire. The complaints of the cows could be heard over the barking, a cacophony announcing the arrival of the dog. Kitty was relieved to remember that Sly was with Kieran in Tralee for the afternoon. So determined was her stride that George Noel had to half run to catch up, then hop a little between steps to keep himself at her side. "May I assume you didn't get the letter from your solicitor—or from mine? Or perhaps an e-mail? Or even a phone call? A message on your machine?"

"I accept no communications when I'm working. And I work all the time."

"You weren't expecting me?"

"Call your dog."

"Then you know nothing of what's to become of you?"

"I know of what's to become of your dog if you don't call it off."

"This is most awkward."

Three panicked cows came crashing through the brush that hedged the bog, the dog nipping and snarling at one, then another. Kitty quickly turned, grabbed the front of this lordship's tweed and twisted the cloth clockwise to bring his face closer to hers. "Listen," she said, "I'm a woman of infinite patience, but infinity has just run out. You're trespassing. Your dog is menacing my cows, and if you aren't gone by the count of one I'll sue the shirt right off your back."

"I think you might want to let go of me."

A great squeal and a shriek sounded from the brush, and the dog, pig in pursuit, came galloping up the hill, then off to the side, then down, then up again. Now the pig charged the dog directly, and, stunned by the audacity of the challenge, the animal stopped dead in its tracks, silenced itself for what could have been two seconds, then retreated behind his lordship's leg. Up the hill came the pig, straight toward both dog and master. Without pause it forced itself in between the legs of the tan slacks and the denim of the jeans Kitty was wearing. The dog made one thrust toward the pig, teeth bared, snout twitching. Kitty twisted the jacket lapels still tighter until her nose and the nose of his lordship were near to touching. She, George Noel Gordon, the dog, and the pig froze each in his, her, or its separate attitude.

His lordship, speaking into Kitty's clenched lips, said calmly, "Could you call off your pig? It's soiling my trousers."

And so the episode ended. Kitty released his lordship's tweeds, allowing both of them to step back from the rubbings of the pig against their legs. The dog was returned to the SUV. The pig disturbed the grass.

"I hadn't," said his lordship, smoothing his jacket against his hollow chest, "I hadn't expected anything so unseemly."

"Well," said Kitty, "now you know. I seldom entertain in the afternoon."

"But I was hoping—as was said in the e-mail and the phone message—that we could discuss arrangements." He was scratching a bit of still damp pig saliva from the left knee of his slacks.

"Arrangements?"

"But you've heard of what's happened."

"I think enough has happened for one day."

"I own the castle."

Their eyes met. His were pale blue. Hers, she knew, were blue as well, but deeper, darker. She also knew—immediately—that she and this man were met in combat, that a contest had begun and that one would win and the other lose.

Not for a moment did she doubt the outcome. It was determined by the color of their eyes. His were too pale, too watery. Hers were just the right shade, just the right depth. The poor man would be bested, about that there could be no mistake. There remained only the deployment of forces, the strategies, all cunning and clever, the feints and parries and, in the end, Kitty's triumph, while George Noel Gordon was left feasting on dust. That having been decided to Kitty's satisfaction, she became willing to apply condescensions appropriate to the occasion. "Maybe I don't entertain in the

afternoons, but that doesn't mean I'm unwilling to be entertained myself. Suppose you come inside and tell me what this
might be about."

"Willingly. If you'll pardon my appearance. Somehow my
tie is far from presentable."

"For a lord, one always makes allowances."

And with that, Lord Shaftoe followed Kitty into the great
hall. Too restless to merely sit and listen, Kitty suggested a
stroll through some of the castle while his lordship spoke his
piece. Presented here is Kitty's version as she would always
remember it.

His lordship's grandfather, great-grandson of the first Lord
Shaftoe to have expected to take up residence in Castle
Kissane after generations of absentee landholders, had, in his
Majesty's service, been sent to Australia with the distinct
command that he school the transported felons colonizing
the continent in disciplines duplicating the family's Irish
experiments. The Crown considered Ireland the prime training ground for a more perfect form of tyranny and felt
compelled to draw upon the Shaftoe expertise so famously
evolved in the complete subjection of that portion of County
Kerry the Cromwellian marauder had committed to the
Shaftoe family's care.

Apparently it was an accepted fact that greed and blood-
lust were genetically transmitted, that cruelty and arrogance
were properties of primogeniture and would, in nature's
course, be passed from generation to generation in the male
line. True, his grandfather had been murdered in his garden
outhouse; true, he had, previous to the event, sired several
bastards by the wantons sent to Australia from Mother
England in that country's failed attempts at moral cleansing.

True, the bastards made claims, no doubt at their wanton mothers' instigations. True, at least two of the wantons had produced marriage certificates. True, Lady Shaftoe was long considered the outhouse murderer, but the blood on her clothing was repeatedly declared by all the authorities to be spatterings from a sheep she'd slaughtered that morning, even though the same knife was found in his lordship's left ventricle.

Primogeniture, however, still prevailed, as proved by the court proceedings that were soon initiated, when the legitimate George Noel Gordon Lord Shaftoe, father of the present lord, was recognized as the long-lost inheritor of Castle Kissane and all the territories not yet returned to the families from which they had been so rudely appropriated long centuries since. And now the son had come to claim his inheritance.

All this had been clarified in letters not yet read by Ms. McCloud. But his lordship was now on the premises to arrange an amiable transfer, whereupon Ms. McCloud would be removed and his lordship installed in the family seat left unwarmed from the time of the thwarted gunpowder plot.

The recital was, in its course, interspersed with amused asides from his lordship such as "You can imagine my surprise . . . ," and "You can imagine my concern for your disappointment . . . ," and "You can imagine my relief when told that you'd be fully compensated—after, of course, the legal fees have been paid."

For her part, Kitty imagined nothing. As far as she was concerned, she was indulging the man in his absurdities, allowing these moments of presumption, encouraging him even to expand and expatiate on his expectations. She herself would say next to nothing. She would be attentive, in the same way she would—out of pity—be all ears to the babblings of a demented tinker. What *did* amuse Kitty, however, was his lordship's blithe wanderings through parts of the castle during the delivery of his revisionist histories. Not content with his survey of the great hall, he opened doors leading into a storage room converted to a washroom and into the dining room complete with Ping-Pong table; then he strode up the spiral stair to the gallery, onto and into uninhabited spaces, looking up chimneys and testing the solidity of the stone work as he went.

When they reached the bedroom Kitty shared with her husband, she simply closed the door she'd left open, allowing his lordship only the slightest glimpse of the massive bed with the tangled sheets and thrown blankets, the tossed pillows, all suggesting a riot recently not so much quelled as recessed until its forces could regroup for further rambunctions. Raising only one eyebrow in recognition of what he'd seen, his lordship felt free to open and close the rest of the doors along the hallway, expressing with a stifled "ah!" his surprise and his approval of the newly renovated bathroom, where he took the time to congratulate Kitty on the cleanliness he'd observed. Kitty, a few paces behind, responded by sticking out her tongue.

"I think," said Kitty, "that you've persuaded yourself that all is in order here and that further inspection at this time is unnecessary."

His lordship put his right foot onto the bottom step of the stair. "This leads to the top of the tower?"

Kitty figured she'd practiced enough condescension for one day. "The room where I work, where I write, is up there," she said. "No one passes this point but me. I'm sure you understand." What she was really protecting, however, was not her sacred space but what she referred to in her mind as the Loom Room. To her, that space was more sacred even than where she plied her trade. That this man might defile her work space with his mere presence, or his simple passage through the turret room, was something from which she and her artistry could recover. But the very thought of his setting foot into the high sanctuary where Brid worked her unthreaded loom, weaving eternally the mysteries into which she and Taddy had been so unjustly condemned, engendered throughout Kitty's being a rage that could find no boundary.

That a Shaftoe might pass them by, unseeing—without knowledge or without horror of the Shaftoe crimes committed against their youthful persons—was more than Kitty was willing to endure.

But before the gorge could rise to the point where it would take possession of her words, she had another thought. Perhaps he *would* see them. He would step into the room. Brid and Taddy would turn and look at him, their sorrow, their bewilderments there for him to see. She would tell him who they were and who they are and why they were there, their necks unhealed from the rude rope, their souls far off—they knew not where—waiting for some act of justice or mercy that would reunite them to themselves, whether in heaven or in hell. Now George Noel Gordon Lord Shaftoe would see them with his own bleared eyes. And the sight would summon from the mists of time the Furies of old that would seize him and send him to torments beyond naming. Kitty lusted for the event.

"But then, of course," she said, continuing almost without

pause her previous phrase, "you've been so kind as to have read my books. So I really shouldn't be so selfish. Yes, please, go right ahead. But careful. Some of the stones might be loose. I certainly wouldn't want you to break your neck." She was unable not to laugh at the thought, a laugh she hoped didn't sound to him as it did to her: like a witch's cackle, infused with an evil glee.

"I'm honored." Naturally enough he was nothing of the kind. He was being granted no less than his due. He was descended from Shaftoes. He was himself a Shaftoe. And being a Shaftoe was not, as an irreverent acquaintance once put it, a stack of shit. What door could remain unopened at the sound of that name? And so his lordship began the ascent.

"So here is where you perform your miracles." This he said with a smug smile.

"You're too kind," said Kitty.

His lordship allowed his nose and lips to emit a humming sound, indicating to Kitty that he was in complete agreement. "I suppose I'm not allowed to ask what you're working on now."

"A book," Kitty said.

"Well, I won't complain about that." He went quickly to the narrower stair that would lead to Brid and Taddy.

Before beginning to mount, he asked, "Will the book be as good as your *In the Forest*?"

Her face frozen, Kitty answered, "*In the Forest* is by Edna O'Brien."

"Really? Fancy that." He started up the stair. "Does this take us to the top of the tower? I want to observe the view. I'm sure you understand."

Kitty did. He wanted to stand at the parapet and proclaim himself master of all he surveyed. This, she felt, should be permitted, to prepare him for every disappointment possible when it would be revealed that, Shaftoe though he might be, the castle was Kitty's and would be Kitty's until she would consign her spent remains to the soil from which she'd sprung. Yes, he must take in the full view. But first, Taddy and Brid.

Kitty should have known. There they were, he with the harp, she at the loom. But only she and Kieran were to be granted the dispensation to see with mortal eyes the corporeal spirits that hovered and had their being. And clearly she had wronged her ghostly friends. By the time Kitty had fully entered the room, both Brid and Taddy had left their stations and were huddled in the far corner, Taddy's arm around a trembling Brid, whose hands were covering her neck as if to shield her wounds from the man passing through. They seemed helpless, unable to find refuge in shadow or in a mist.

"Forgive me," Kitty said in Irish, intending her words for the ghosts. "I thought this would be different."

"What did you say?"

"Nothing," she said, in English. "I mean—don't bother. I usually speak in my native tongue. Rude, of course, in the presence of the unschooled."

His lordship raised *both* eyebrows and made the humming sound, accepting her admission of incivility if not her insult, and went with a newly determined step toward the stones that would lead him to the parapet.

Brid had stopped her trembling and Taddy had released his hold. Side by side they stood, with all the dignity of their sufferings stiffening their shadowed selves as the man passed them by, as unseeing as had been his ancestors whenever no service was needed or humiliations required.

Kitty considered herself monumentally stupid to have hoped that some susceptibility to guilt or remorse or even fear was possible for George Noel Gordon. Instead of guilt, the remorse, the fear were hers—and with some justice. New sufferings had she inflicted. Ancient wrongs had been made present again through an act of hers, but with no effect whatsoever on the man most deserving of their infliction, the Lord of the Castle, the Lord of the Land. The Landlord. Only Kitty and Brid and Taddy, descended from kings deposed, rightful heirs of lords and laborers, of those who had worked the land and fished the sea, only they were made to feel the ancient pain. And it was ever so.

His lordship had a bit of trouble lifting away the old wooden trapdoor that closed off the sky. Kitty offered to give it a shove, but he insisted. This was, after all, to be his castle. Its components must be made to submit.

They gained the battlements.

Off to the north the hills rose and fell, the modest mountains worn down by the inexorable ages, by wind and by rain, by every scourge the heavens had to offer, but rising still with a comforting solemnity against the sky. Green they were with low walls built stone by stone wrested one at a time from the earth, the walls parceling off one man's field from another man's pasture, giving way to commonage on the higher slopes that led to the summit. Massive white rocks lay easily in the sun, awaiting the next upheaval. Sheep, too, were placed without discernable pattern against the land, the herds moving at a glacial pace to fields considered yet more green. One glint, then another, flashed from the stream. The gray roads, bordered by riots of fuchsia and honeysuckle, threaded through. The slate roofs of the cottages were allowed to seem blue in the afternoon sun. A pickup truck and a bus were on their way to town, which consisted of a huddling of houses not visible even from this height.

Lord Shaftoe, standing at the battlement, negligible chin raised, took in the view, satisfied with what he saw. A slight breeze tried without success to lift the crumpled silk of his tie. As Kitty watched, he turned to the west, toward the sea. Two curraghs bobbed in the waters off Dunquin, and a ferry from Dingle was headed toward the Great Blasket, the island's slow upsweep a final mute thrust toward the mysteries of the sea itself.

Again Lord Shaftoe seemed approving of what lay before him. Or, it seemed to Kitty, he stood motionless as if he were a monarch accepting the homage and obeisance of his realm.

It came to Kitty then that she would come from behind and, with one great heave, lift and shove him down from the battlements onto the stones below. Dispatching him at this moment of high pride all the more ensured that his descent would not end at the foot of the tower but continue on into the netherworld.

The strength was growing in Kitty's back and in her arms. She could feel the roused muscles of her legs, the firming of her stomach. Her lungs, too, assured her of their ready assistance. All her being was summoned for the event. And look there! His lordship's chest was expanding. He was appropriating the air itself. A great wealth of purpose rose in Kitty's soul. The time was now.

But before she could make the fateful lunge, another

prompting, Hamlet-like, presented itself. If she were to dispatch him now she would be robbing herself of the great moment that had been promised when his lordship would be, in the truer sense, cast down. When he would be told in terms irrefutable and beyond appeal that he had been misinformed, that he had indulged in illusions and encouraged imaginings. The castle was not to be his after all. It belonged in perpetuity to Kitty McCloud and Kieran Sweeney. Every word and gesture of this afternoon would return to him revised and vivified by this devastation. Could Kitty possibly deny herself the sight of his lordship divested of all his presumptions, denied all his delusions? The words written by her fellow Irish writer came quickly to mind: "Absent thee from felicity a while—"

Surrendering to the certainty of this greater satisfaction, Kitty dismissed the reinforcement that had brought her the added strength needed for her now abandoned purpose. From her back and legs she released the taut muscles. Her stomach was told to hang loose. And, while she was at it, she might as well unclench her teeth and allow the heated blood to drain from her cheeks.

When, however, his lordship turned toward her—but looking past rather than directly at her—and said, "Yes, this will all do very nicely," Kitty found her strength returning and her blood rising all over again. Down he must go—and with not another minute permitted to pass.

But then, an interception: far, far out along the horizon, coming up out of the sea, was an empurpled cloud stretching from one end of the ocean to the other. The needed storm was on its way, the rumored drought was not to plague them after all. Rescue was at hand, advancing toward them over the waters of the deep. The curraghs were nosed toward Dunquin. The Dingle Ferry was on its own. She was returned to her second resolve. She'd wait. She'd savor. All in expectation of the tardy arrival of justice.

Kitty told the poor man to go ahead down the narrow stair, she would replace the trapdoor in its own idiosyncratic way now that the storm was coming. She was reasonably sure Brid and Taddy would not be at their tasks, and she was proved right. But, unnoticed by his lordship, the harp had been set on the stool and the shuttle placed safely on the frame of the loom. Whether she and Taddy were there in the growing shadows she could not tell, but when a quick flash of lightning flared in the room she thought she saw, off in the corner, Brid sitting on the other stool, her head bowed into her hands, her black, black hair falling over her knees. But in the great crash of thunder all was obliterated as a sudden dark filled the room.

Kitty, leading now, helped his lordship down into her workroom, having—at his request—to hold his fine-fingered hand as they descended. Just before they reached the final flight that would lead to the long hallway, the man said, "*Scarlet Feather?*"

Tonelessly Kitty said, "Maeve Binchy."

"Oh yes. Of course. Very good it was, too."

Through growing glooms Kitty led him along the gallery and into the great hall. By now the storm was in full flood, the thunder and lightning reveling in the mayhem.

"I don't suppose you have an extra umbrella?" his lordship asked.

Rather than tell a lie, Kitty simply said, "If you get wet, you'll get dry."

With a small smile, indicating he had not the least idea what she meant, his lordship stepped out into the storm. As Kitty was closing the door she saw him raise his right hand, palm opened upward, to confirm the fact that it had indeed begun to rain on his lordly and unprotected head.

8

Maude McCloskey, the Seer—or, to Kitty's preferred thinking, the Hag—had four children, the eldest away in Cork, the remaining at home when Kitty came to call. Two girls and one boy, they seemed to be aged five to nine for the girls with the boy stuck somewhere in between at about seven. They were sitting on the floor, a gray-green wall-to-wall carpet, playing cards. The turned-on television was close enough to suggest that the sports commentators going about their business could, if they chose, peer over the shoulder of the boy and the older girl, and read their cards.

At first Kitty guessed they were playing poker—cards were being dealt, discarded, laid out before them—but closer scrutiny informed her that those laid out had no recognizable relationship one to the other. It would have to be a game with which she was unfamiliar. But then it seemed possible that they'd made up the game themselves—perhaps improvising as they went along. Her next guess was that they were simply aping with their movements and comments what they had observed when their elders had played. But even that had to be revised when, from time to time, their mother would lean forward and direct the youngest, Ellen, to play a particular card, which she would then do, much to her advantage—and, rather surprising—to the amusement of her brother and sister.

They apparently accepted this as evidence of the girl's prowess, ignoring completely their mother's intervention. The older girl was called Margaret and the boy Peter—not because it was his name, but because his baptismal name was Stanislaus, the same as his father's, and the household could accommodate only one Stanislaus at a time. So the name Peter was brought in as substitute.

Kitty had come to ask the Hag how she might get rid of Brid. Kieran was, to Kitty's thinking, too far gone for rational measures to be of any use. Brid must therefore be dispatched as soon as possible. Kitty knew that great wrongs had been done to the girl, and that quiescence was impossible until some modicum of justice had been realized. But what act or actions might restore the needed moral balance was beyond Kitty's present powers. The miscreant, the Lord Shaftoe who had ordered the hangings, was long gone and, presumably, already judged by a power even higher than Kitty McCloud. To reach back into history and pluck him into the present seemed an unlikely achievement. What was required was nothing less than some reconciliation of things of earth with the things of heaven. Somewhere along the line, by whatever mixed signals, some earthly incompletion was let stand, or, quite possibly, ignored by the Eternal Conciliator Himself for reasons of His own. Or could it be that the present predicament had not yet come to the attention of the Supreme Arbiter? Or, worst of all, had everything long since been known by the Almighty but been dismissed as of no interest?

Had it been decreed that, at some point, the lesser beings inhabiting a not very prominent planet should, on occasion, be required to figure things out for themselves? More intellectual equipment had been given to them than had been put to use. Divine inspiration shouldn't have to do all the work. Kitty should be able to discover the formula suited to her present needs. Her situation, after all, had not been imposed upon her. No one had told her to buy Castle Kissane. Nothing but her inborn recklessness, her overevolved urge toward risk, had suggested that she, Francis and Helen McCloud's little girl Caitlin, should install herself as chatelaine—and now she must pay the price beyond the euros already paid.

That, Kitty had no objection to doing. She'd been doing it since her wedding day, when Brid and Taddy announced their residency. But now human frailty, in the form of a husband, had intervened. Kitty had no fear of rivals—unless, of course, the rival was not only young and supremely beautiful but also predestined by the nature of the predicament to remain so while Kitty, with all her admitted advantages of looks and intelligence and talent, was subject nevertheless to the claims of time.

Brid must go. She, Kitty, would be doing her a favor. Brid deserved better than her current situation allowed. And Kitty, with characteristic kindness, would see to her release, as soon as truths as yet unvouchsafed were placed into her resolute hands. It was the Hag who must provide her with whatever clues she might possess, which accounted for Kitty's present visit.

"It's been a full week," Mrs. McCloskey was saying, "since Peter's wet the bed, and we're crossing our fingers for another week. Ellen sleeping next to him is particularly pleased, since he would be wetting her as much as the bed. Are you sure you wouldn't like a bit of something else in your tea?" She began tipping a bottle of Tullamore Dew in the direction of Kitty's cup.

"No, this is fine. The tea's really quite good as it is."

"Ah, yes. If there's one thing I know it's how to make a good cup of tea." Hearing this, Kitty thought it impolite to mention that Peter had made the tea. And besides, Mrs. McCloskey was far advanced in the one topic she considered suitable entertainment: her children. "Now Margaret," the woman went on, "Margaret there seems to be developing asthma like her aunt, but I've warned her it'd better be a chest cold because she could die of asthma with the next attack. Her aunt went just like"—she snapped her fingers—"same age as Margaret is now. So she's been duly warned." She reached down, studied Ellen's cards, pulled one out, and placed it on the rug. Again Peter's and Margaret's pleasure at this stunning move was immediately apparent.

"Ellen's going to win!" Peter laughed at the inevitability. Margaret, too, rejoiced. "She's going to beat."

Mrs. McCloskey smoothed Ellen's hair, then, sitting back in her chair—overstuffed, a darker green than the carpet—whispered to Kitty, "Peter's the one to watch. And to think I was furious the day I found out he was on his way inside my belly. I could have killed Stanislaus. But I decided to send the dear man off to work in Cork instead, where he can send the better part of his wages and we can get ourselves organized around here. But look at Peter now. He's the one to watch." Mrs. McCloskey looked toward the television, where the inevitable soccer game was being played, this one on some foreign field where there seemed to be more dust than grass underfoot. The commentators were discussing one of the athletes—someone with an unpronounceable name—which suggested that he was a foreign import on the Irish team. Satisfied with what she saw and heard, Maude tipped a few more drops of whiskey into her teacup, possibly in celebration, then gave her attention to the cards in Peter's hand.

Not always a beauty, Mrs. McCloskey was now having a time of revenge. She had, over the years of her marriage and childbearing, become "handsome" in the extreme. Her figure had become more ample, but in perfect proportion one feature to the other. Without resorting to measurements, Kitty could tell that the ratio of her bosom to her waist, to her hips, and to her buttocks was more than presentable. Her hair had calmed itself after several torturings she'd executed during her youth and was now a thick, straight black, pulled strongly together and gathered in a becoming bun. Her lips had filled rather than thinned, her teeth—her own, Kitty was fairly sure—were even, white, and could come close to a dazzle when she smiled, which was often, the woman having a near-demented ability to be joyful at the least provocation. And, in contrast to the animated mouth, the eyes, dark brown, managed to remain serene at all times, reflecting perhaps an inner being quietly pleased with herself and all her works. A woman could do worse, Kitty thought, than advance in the direction so successfully traveled by Maude McCloskey, Hag or no Hag.

Raising her teacup with one hand, handsome Maude tapped the seven of diamonds Peter was holding and directed Ellen to take it. "This one," she said. When Ellen drew the card from her brother's hand, Peter let out a half laugh, half holler. "No, not that one!" he cried, giving full expression to his delight at so masterful a coup on his sister's part.

Kitty's one hope was that the game would end and the children sent out to play or do chores or get kidnapped. She must question Mrs. McCloskey about disposing of Brid.

As if to let Kitty know that she rather enjoyed having her children about, Maude next began extolling the virtues of Ellen, which consisted mainly of her no longer eating from the dog's dish. She held out the Tullamore Dew and pantomimed tipping some into Kitty's cup. Kitty shook her head no and, so as not to waste the gesture, Mrs. McCloskey let a few more drops fall into her own cup.

"Of course, Joey—that's the dog—Joey helped. Can you see the little scab on Ellen's nose? That's from the last bite she got. Mostly Joey went for her chin, and once her ear, but apparently the nose was what was needed to make its point. But don't give Joey all the credit; Ellen promised she wouldn't do it again—and she's kept her promise, the way she always does."

A roar was raised on the television and three players—Irish as far as Kitty could tell from their uniforms—were threatening an official. "That's it, boys!" Mrs. McCloskey called out to the set. "We're out to win and let no man take it from us!" On her way to bringing her attention back to Kitty, she gave a cursory glance at Margaret's cards, took a three of spades and put it in on the rug. Peter quickly grabbed it up and added it to his hand, discarding a four of hearts. Pleased with her accomplishment, Mrs. McCloskey whispered again, "I told you. Peter's the one to watch."

Desperate, Kitty considered bringing up the subject in front of the children, since it was obvious they were going to be in attendance throughout her visit. But she was afraid to open herself to ridicule, or to questions—to which she would have answers she would just as soon not give. She could, of course, tell them to mind their own business and get on with their game, but then Mrs. McCloskey, offended by this affront to her cherished children, might clam up and refuse Kitty the knowledge she'd come to seek.

An alternative could be an invitation to Mrs. McCloskey to come some day soon to the castle, but there could be no doubt that she'd turn up with her precious children in tow, and Joey as well. A guided tour would be required. The children would run rampant through the halls, screaming in search of echoes, grabbing at each other and saying, "Boo," and wanting to use the bathroom. There would have to be biscuits and cake. There would have to be Coca-Cola. Joey would harass the cows. The pig would harass Joey. Sly would slink off and hide for the next two days. The loom would be broken, the harp destroyed. Worst of all, the children might see Brid and Taddy and laugh at the way they were clothed, then scream with delight when they vanished right before their very eyes and insist that the poor apparitions do it again. Kitty could, of course, inadvertently lock them in the dungeon.

For one of the few times in her life, Kitty was at a loss. Perplexed by an experience so rare, she smiled at Mrs. McCloskey and said, "Maybe I will have a drop after all."

"That's my girl." Kitty had to steady the woman's hand after far more than a few drops had been poured into her cup. "Too kind," Kitty said, trying unsuccessfully to part her upper teeth from her lower.

Now Mrs. McCloskey was giving her full attention to the

television, kneading her knee, closing and opening her fist. "Thieves! Thieves!" For not more than a second, the three children turned toward the television. Their expectations were quickly disappointed—no outright thievery was apparent, merely a group of grown men rushing in more than several directions at once—so they returned their concentration to their cards, with Peter putting down a jack of hearts and neither Margaret nor Ellen the least bit impressed.

After a fortifying gulp of tea, Kitty said, "Do you think we might talk in private?"

Surprised and bewildered, Mrs. McCloskey, for the first time since Kitty had entered the cottage, focused her gaze on her guest. "But this is private," she said. "No one here but family."

"I mean, perhaps just the two of us."

Mrs. McCloskey's laugh was perhaps a bit more derisive than she had intended, since there was genuine joy in it as well, but Kitty nevertheless had to check an impulse to give her a smack. "There's no need," the good woman said. "The children have no interest I'm sure in anything you might want to say. May I assume it's about you-know-whom you saw at the wedding?"

"It is, I'm afraid."

Mrs. McCloskey patted Kitty's knee. "Then let's hear it." The Hag then tugged a card from Margaret's hand and placed it in front of Peter, who picked it up. "Just so you know I don't play favorites," she whispered. She took a few more sips of tea, then, with a small bit of ostentation, leaned back in her chair, letting Kitty know she was open for business.

Kitty drained her cup, set it on its saucer, and wiped her lips with the back of her little finger. She stood up. "Perhaps another time."

"But we're having tea. I made it special."

"And I thank you. But I must be going." Kitty could hardly believe how polite she was being.

"Well, if you have nothing you want to talk about, then I won't keep you."

"Most kind."

"I do my best." Mrs. McCloskey, too, was on her feet. "Peter, I'll take over your hand. You walk Mrs. Sweeney—"

"Ms. McCloud," Kitty corrected.

"Yes. Of course. I'd heard that but preferred not to believe it when Sweeney's such a fine Kerry name."

"No more than McCloud."

"If you insist."

"I do."

Mrs. McCloskey heaved a sigh underscoring the one word she had to meet the occasion. "Well—" she said.

Peter gave his mother his cards, tugged up his pants by the belt loops, let them fall immediately back into place, and started for the door.

"It's not necessary," Kitty said. "It's not that far, even though I decided the walk would do me good. And I surely know the way."

"But Peter would be so disappointed. And he's been such a good boy." Kitty took this to mean that a castle tour would be the only acceptable reward for the boy's gallantry. Peter, holding open the door, had on his face—a face so open and cheerful—a look of proud anticipation.

"But I mustn't take you away from your game," Kitty said to him.

"Ellen can win without me. Can't you, Ellen?"

Ellen's answer was limited to a muted, "Ssshh."

"See?" Peter, so pleased with his commission, wore a look

of such pathetic expectation that Kitty had no choice but to say, "Okay, then. Let's go."

A backward glance told her that farewells were not needed or even wanted, so intent were the players on their game. She was already forgotten and felt obliged to be gone without further ceremony.

Outside they walked the path to the road, passed through an opening of the hedge and made the turn that would take them up the hills to the castle. (Kieran, measuring the distance, said it was one kilometer down and two kilometers up. Kitty agreed, as did anyone who had ever made the journey on foot.) Peter chose to half skip, half bounce as he took his place next to Kitty, an escort obviously energized by the honor.

Late afternoon was about to become early evening. Soon the sun would be past the crest of the hill and long shadows sent out across the fields. The hill, some of it already dissolved in the mists, rose up to their right. Its downslope to their left, almost clifflike, was abundantly strewn with huge white boulders. At times the rocks seemed to Kitty like fossilized sheep.

As the road turned to the right, then to the left, the scattered cottages down below were silent in the cooling air. To the west, not far off, was the sea, calm, with three curraghs and what could be a kayak making their way slowly, confidently, toward the island to the north. The clouds had not yet come, and it was the sea now and not the hills that would take the setting sun.

Without consultation, as if responding to some ancient prompting born in the blood, both Kitty and Peter moved to the rock wall that hedged the road and looked out over the darkening water and the glistening narrow path, a silver ladder that could, if legend spoke true, take one from the sea to the sun.

It was Peter who spoke first, but quietly. He had picked from his nose a tiny bit of dried mucus and was examining it as if it were a computer chip holding within itself, like the contemporary equivalent of a crystal ball, a knowledge available nowhere else. He turned the chip held between his thumb and forefinger, curious as to what secrets it might impart when viewed from different perspectives. "My mother says you see Taddy and Brid. Is it so?"

Kitty's impulse was to turn to the boy and express her annoyance that his mother had opened her big fat trap. What right or reason had she to tell a child about something as intimate as her seeing ghosts? It was no one's business. Now the word would spread, and she'd be regarded as some kind of nutty woman given to visions and other forms of superstition. But as soon as the thought came she dismissed it. What did she care who thought what? Never had she concerned herself with the opinions and judgments of others, and she saw no reason to begin now. Almost defiantly she said, "Yes. Of course I see them. They come with the castle."

"My mother thinks not."

"Not what?"

"They don't come with the castle. I mean—other people come to the castle, they don't see them, do they?"

"How would I know?"

"They'd tell you, the other people would. Or they'd tell someone, who'd tell someone else. Who'd tell you."

Kitty did not like being contradicted, especially by a boy small for his age, with freckles across his nose and—from the evidence she'd observed—who didn't wash his neck when he washed his face. Still, she didn't want to be rude. Or even interfere with his interest—an interest obviously informed by what Kitty herself had wanted to find out from his mother.

And then it struck Kitty that Mrs. McCloskey had purposely sent this surrogate, unbeknownst even to himself, to deliver the message Kitty had come to their cottage to collect. The boy would tell her all she wanted to know. Or at least all that Maude McCloskey knew from her divinations, or, more likely, what she had collected from stories, from lore, from the legends that had been passed from generation to generation. The boy, quite likely, had, for whatever reason, been elected the new repository of hidden knowledge, and it flattered Kitty to believe that she herself was, in turn, elected the first beneficiary of this initiate's recently consecrated calling. Much had been entrusted to him and great must be his mother's faith in his gifts. "Peter's the one to watch." How Maude might have discerned these gifts Kitty would never know, nor did she require that she should. All that was demanded of her now was a show of respect, and perhaps a bit of sympathy for the burdens of truth placed on the boy's scrawny shoulders. His would be the prophet's knowledge, refused or avoided or denied by other mortals; upon him would be heaped the scorn and ridicule, the awe and fear his seerlike propensities would earn for him. He was set apart, and difficult would be his way: to speak the truth and be disbelieved. But Kitty would try to believe him now. Whatever he might prescribe she would, if possible, obey.

As if fully aware of her resolve, the boy, scratching his left calf with the toe of his right shoe, still staring with considerable intent at the mucus he had retrieved from his nose, said, "Your husband sees them. But he's the only other one."

A compact was being offered, an agreement that he would speak and she would answer with no less truth than he. Kitty had no choice but to say, "Yes. He sees them too."

The boy nodded, acknowledging her acceptance of the covenant now formed between them. "And that's only natural."

"Natural? Why?"

The boy let out more a snicker than a laugh and jerked his head upward a little as if the subject embarrassed him. "My mother says when two people get married they become as one. And you know what else she says?"

"No. But I'd like to hear."

"She says since you saw Brid and Taddy and now your husband sees them, too, she knows which of the two of you you're likely to become. You. Because you saw them first. She seemed to like the idea. What do you think?"

"I can hardly contradict your mother, can I?"

"Best not."

"And she laughed?"

"She was very proud of herself for thinking it."

"Umm. Yes."

"But she said you shouldn't worry. He'll never know it. About which one he's to become. Unless you choose to tell him."

"I don't believe that would be—necessary."

"That's what my mother said. Except she said it wouldn't be wise to tell him."

"Thanks." Kitty kept her voice as uninflected as possible. She would prefer if at all possible not to have the boy know *everything*, particularly some intimate thoughts not intended for communications to anyone, especially her husband, two-as-one or no two-as-one. Or to anyone else for that matter, prophet or no prophet, seer or no seer.

Confirming immediately Kitty's worst fears, the boy without pause said, "But you should know that this is just what my mother thinks, not what she really knows. She says she's not sure yet about what I just told you. It might be the truth—and it might not." He paused, then said, "She's still working on it."

"Oh?"

Before she could ask for elaboration and before he could give it, Joey came wagging up to them and put his nose between them. The boy moved quickly away. "Joey! You're not to be here. You're to be at home. You've got chores and you know it." Joey, a breed of border collie with brown and black splotches on its white fur, wagged its tail even more enthusiastically at the admonition, then looked from Peter to Kitty, then Peter again. "Now I have to take him home," he said. "He's to help with the cows."

"But you were coming up to the castle, I thought."

"Oh, no. I couldn't do that."

"Oh?"

He'd been tickling Joey behind the ears. Joey wagged the back half of his body in appreciation. "I don't want to be there if now is when it blows up."

"The castle is not going to blow up."

"Oh, but it's supposed to. My mother says so."

"Oh?" Kitty did not approve of her newly acquired habit of speaking in monosyllables, but there seemed to be nothing she could do about it.

"I have to get Joey back home."

"But if your mother is so sure the castle is supposed to blow up, surely she can say when."

"She can't."

"And you. Can you?"

"I have to get Joey home. Or he'll get a beating."

"But wait. You have to tell me what else you know. Or what your mother knows."

Peter stopped tickling Joey and stood up. He looked down at his sneakers and wiggled the toes of his right foot. When he'd finished, he said, "You say my mother is a Hag."

"I never said that!"

"To yourself you say it all the time. You said it three times: when my mother was helping Ellen with her cards, when she was watching the football, and when she told you about Margaret's asthma."

Kitty thought it best that they part now. Whatever the boy might have to tell her she would do without. Such incursions into her innermost thoughts should never be allowed. Not when employed against her. He must also know she'd commented to herself about his unwashed neck. But she must stop thinking now. Not one more thought. Not until a safe distance could be put between herself and this—this—

"I'm peculiar," the boy said, providing her with the wanted word. "And my mother is peculiar. But in the way my mother told me peculiar means. It doesn't mean crazy or even strange. It means distinct. Set apart. Not like everyone else. And you're peculiar, too."

"I?"

"You're a writer. Maybe that's why you can see Brid and Taddy. Because you're a writer. At least that's what my mother thinks it could be."

"Oh?" Then, to break the hold the word had on her, she added, "Why because I'm a writer?"

"Because you live with ghosts all the time. People no one else can see. You're used to it."

"But—"

"I have to get Joey home." He stepped back onto the road. Kitty placed herself in front of him, blocking his path. Peter looked from Kitty to Joey, then back to Kitty. Joey moved back, away from Kitty, Peter at his side.

"You mean," Kitty continued, "You mean that if I invite any of my writer friends to the castle—"

"You have no writer friends."

"All right then. But in the unlikely event that I did have one and invited her—make that him—invited him over—"

"He wouldn't see them unless he's as good a writer as you."

"I'm a very bad writer. Everyone knows that."

"Maybe Brid and Taddy don't."

"That's because they can't read. At least not English."

"Oh, no. They recognize that you see things no one else sees."

"Me?"

"You. And they know you look for the truth. When you're writing, I mean. You don't always find it, but when you don't, you accept it not like it's a failure but because you believe in mystery. You accept it. You're not afraid of it. You don't feel as if you have to explain everything. You've got not very many talents. As you said, you're a bad writer. But you don't put a rock wall around your imagination. You don't go running back to your brain, as if the truth can be figured out by the mind. It can't. The truth comes only through the imagination. If you were smarter, if you had more intelligence, you might be tempted not to use your imagination the way you always do now. That's what my mother says. And she's not a Hag."

"You're making this up. Or I mean your mother is. The same as she made up the reasons my husband and I both see the ghosts."

The boy and the dog skirted around her, Joey keeping an eye on Kitty, the two of them starting down the road. Kitty caught up. Peter, continuing on, said, "And if you don't believe what I say you won't be peculiar anymore. You'll be like all the others. They don't believe us either. Which doesn't bother me. I mean it doesn't bother my mother. She says—"

"Can't you tell me what *you* say?"

"My mother, she says it means what we say and what we see is the truth. But if everybody believed what we said, we'd know it couldn't be true. But you've believed it. Because you're not like them. I told you. You're peculiar."

"Can't you think of another word?"

"A writer?"

"All right, then. Make it peculiar."

"Joey, come on." He moved faster, Joey at his heel. Kitty waited, not sure what she should do. Too confused, too agitated by so many unanswered questions to go on her way, she went after them. When she'd caught up, the boy snapped his fingers.

"Joey, over here." Joey stopped looking up at Kitty and obeyed.

Kitty walked sideways, the better to see the expression on the boy's face. He was angry. "All right, then," Kitty said. "Your mother is not a Hag. And even if she were, what's wrong with that? Doesn't a Hag know what no one else knows? Think of it. If your mother's a Hag, from what she thinks of me, I'm a Hag, too." Kitty was supremely pleased with herself. "That's it. I'm a Hag. Look at me. I'm a Hag."

"A Hag has no soul. A Hag can't die. My mother can die," he said quietly. "And so can you." He paused. "And so can I."

So determined was his step, so quiet his voice as he said these words, that Kitty considered abandoning her quest for knowledge. In this, as in most cases, maybe ignorance was preferable. She must turn around and go up the hill, to her castle, to her ghosts. To her husband.

Peter had stopped and was picking his nose again, this time extracting an even tinier bit of dried snot. He regarded it with keen and concentrated interest. "If you want Taddy and Brid to go, blow up the castle. They'll go."

Kitty wanted to stop, but the boy kept on walking. "How can I blow up the castle?"

"The gunpowder."

"I don't mean *how*. I mean *why* would I want to blow it up?"

"So Taddy and Brid would go. If you want them to go, that's the only way."

"I go out and buy some dynamite—"

"No need. I told you. The gunpowder. It's there."

"Where?"

"There."

"Where's there?"

"My mother says details are sometimes left missing."

"Oh, thanks. You tell me I'm sitting on a keg of gunpowder and then you won't tell me where it is."

"Not even Brid and Taddy know."

"How can they not know?"

"They know nothing. They knew nothing then. They know nothing now. They don't even know why they're there or what's happening to them. They only know they're supposed to be someplace else. But they're supposed to be in the castle, too. As long as there is a castle."

"And blowing up the castle will send them there—wherever that might be?"

"The castle is where they were hanged and didn't know anything about anything. The castle was supposed to die. Not them. Until it does, they have to stay."

"And that's the only way? Blow up the castle?"

"My mother says it is. And this she doesn't just think. She knows."

A new thought came into Kitty's head. Maude McCloskey *was* a Hag. A Witch. A Sorceress. It was Mrs. McCloskey who had summoned the shades of the grieving Brid and the bewildered Taddy. Hers was the witchcraft that had brought them there for the sole purpose of getting Kitty McCloud out of the castle. She was envious of Kitty's success and wealth, of her beauty and her capture of the best man on the face of the earth. Kitty had made herself an object of the world's envy— but given her gifts, had she any choice? What the boy had said about her imagination, her so-called peculiarity, was crafty and cunning, a form of flattery to which she was, for those moments only, susceptible. But her susceptibility had come to an end. She would free herself from the thrall of the resident Seer. She would dismiss all that had been said. She would certainly not blow up her castle. *Her* castle. She would get Father Colavin to come again and this time rid the premises of unwanted spirits. There would be no more nonsense. With the right words, the right blessings, he'd dispatch—

Here she stopped. Suddenly, she realized she could never do that—terrorize them with bell, book, and candle. Drive them off—*evict* them as if she herself were the Anglo Ascendancy returned to do unfinished work.

Let Kieran love the lovely Brid. She was a ghost, a shadow, a wandering shade. Surely Kitty had charms, all palpable and present, that should without too much difficulty distract a man as needful as her husband, heaping upon his splendid person prizes only she could provide. She had already proved she had no fear of ghosts. What she must do now is extend even further this admirable trait; she must encompass this latest intrusion to include the natural order— a natural order in which it was decreed that she would experience no competition for the full and undistracted devotion of her husband—she must embrace it, accept, and ignore it.

How she would do this, given the wrath that had arisen even as she was thinking these extravagant thoughts, she had not the least idea. But if it had to be done, she would do it. Her inborn competence would rescue her. It would more than rescue her. It would, as it so often did, make her triumphant.

Kitty felt herself nudged toward exultation, but, alas, before she could effect her arrival to that blessed state, there came to her one final thought. Keats's Grecian Urn came crashing down right on top of her incomparable head: the youth pursuing the maid, the two of them stuck for all eternity on a piece of pottery, but bearing the news that threatened now to send poor embattled Kitty into a swoon. "Though winning near the goal," Keats says to the youth, "forever wilt thou love, and she be fair!" *And she be fair! Forever!* Kitty, a child of unrelenting time, destined to age, to grow fat perhaps, then to wither. And *she* be fair!

Had she the means at hand, the castle would be blown up by sunset. Or, better, let Father Colavin come. Let the dastardly Brid be driven Eve-like into the savage unknown, with or without the requisite fig leaf. Let her howl and shriek. And let her take Taddy with her.

Mournful, bewildered Taddy. Exiled. Away from Kitty's sorrowing eyes. Gone. To be seen no more in the shadowed halls. Never again to play the plangent tunes that only he could summon. To lay down the harp one final time, and be gone forever.

If Kitty McCloud could be given an action commensurate with her feelings, she would—no gunpowder needed—blow herself up into a thousand pieces, scattering over the Kerry countryside and out over the sea itself bits of flesh and hair and bone, remnants of her spleen, gobs of her overburdened brain, slivers of skull, and, more far flung than any, the exploded heart into which she had implanted more confusion than it was meant to bear.

But so simple a resolution to the contradictions battering her about the head and heart was not available. Instead, she must turn away and walk a fairly straight line up the narrow and increasingly steep incline that would take her home. To the castle. To the bloody castle. Blood. Blood. Blood was what she wanted. But whose? No one's. Not Kieran's. Not hers. Not even—were it possible—the blood of Brid or Taddy. Only one thought was permitted to her now. The curse had descended. The curse of confusion and contradiction. And it had come down like a shroud over good, sweet, blameless Kitty McCloud.

Without Kitty noticing, Peter had stopped and the dog with him, five paces ahead. It was only when he called out to her that she became aware of her solitude. "I'm taking Joey back. He's got chores."

Kitty turned around completely to face the boy. He crinkled his nose, sending a few of the freckles onto his cheeks until they almost touched his eyes. The dog sat, tongue out, still looking at him, awaiting a command. "My mother says come have tea any time. She likes it you live in the castle. She says she's glad it's you and not us."

Calmer now, Kitty had one more question. "Before, you said there's a difference between what your mother thinks and what she knows. Then the dog came and you didn't get back to it. Can you tell me again which is which? I'm a bit confused and I—"

"I don't know," Peter interrupted.

"But you said it just a few minutes ago."

"Maybe. I don't know. I don't remember saying that."

"But you very distinctly said—"

"I don't remember that either. I say things and then I don't remember."

"You said your mother said—"

"I keep forgetting what my mother said. But don't tell her."

"You remember nothing that you—"

"I've got to get home. And Joey, too. Or we'll both get beat."

Kitty considered asking him to pick his nose again, but decided instead to let him go. He had earned his surcease. She went up to him and looked into his eyes. They were a soft brown and the whites as white as porcelain. He seemed puzzled by her being there, next to him. She was reminded a bit of Taddy. "You're a good boy," she said. "And I thank you."

She reached out and touched his cheek. At that, the dog, responding to an ungiven command, sank his teeth into her left thigh. "Ahhh!" she screamed, swatting her hand at the little beast. The dog wagged its tail and, Kitty was sure, smiled at its handiwork.

"Oh," said the boy. "Sorry about that. But don't worry. He's harmless."

"Harmless! He just bit me!"

"I know. I'm skinny at school so he does that when anybody touches me."

"You could have warned me."

"I didn't think he'd do it, not to you."

"Oh?"

"You live in the castle. I didn't think anybody lived in a castle ever got bit."

"Well, now you know."

"Huh. Strange, isn't it?"

Kitty did not respond. This was one more confusion she could do without. The boy turned and started again down the road, pausing only to scratch his left calf. The dog watched, then trotted alongside, looking up, tongue out, smiling, eager. Kitty watched until a bend in the road took the boy and the dog from view, leaving the way empty.

Coming to the rock wall where the boy had dispensed his peculiarities, Kitty was tempted to stop, to gaze out again at the wide world spread there before her, land, sea, sky, rock, sheep, gorse, but she, like the boy, like the dog, had chores to do. And she must do them. Whatever they might prove to be.

9

If Lord Shaftoe had left the castle in a downpour, it was in a torrent that he returned. The sea was enraged and had persuaded the sky to join in its frenzy. The seething waves broke over the land, sending walls of water down upon the defenseless countryside; the clouds, rent by lightning and clamoring with thunder, had opened wide and emptied their full allowance of rain without discipline on the hills and steeples, the cottages, and, perforce, the castles. The water seemed to be responding to more than a gravitational pull; more than merely falling, it was hurling itself, as if shot from the exploding clouds that were doing battle among themselves for domination of the sky.

As ruthlessly as all of nature had turned upon itself, it was nothing to the devastation recently slammed down upon Kitty's unready head. To her aghast amazement, the courts had ruled in favor of George Noel Gordon Lord Shaftoe— and against Caitlin McCloud and Kieran Sweeney. Proofs had been presented that the Shaftoes, from far Australia, had indeed paid their taxes faithfully and promptly, which meant that the title to Castle Kissane had never passed to the Crown, much less to the Republic, and least of all to Caitlin

McCloud, despite her generous outlay in cash. Against this Shaftoe triumph, she had no appeal. Her clamorings could go forth to the gate of heaven itself, but they would achieve no more than desperate prayers sent in the same direction all those years ago when the county was being ravaged and the innocent strung up from the nearest height.

Having troubled deaf heaven with her bootless cries, she'd had to listen to her less impressionable husband when he pointed out that he lacked the means and the know-how to blow up the castle, as she'd threatened to do. Besides, since the castle was no longer hers to destroy, all the time she would spend in prison for its destruction might provide an uninterrupted opportunity to finish her correction of *The Mill on the Floss* and, possibly, depending on the judge, time to get busy with yet another correction or two.

That she would simply go mad was considered yet one more possibility. Kitty in her near derangement felt she was left with no recourse from this outrage but to do what any self-respecting free citizen of the Republic would do in the face of eviction: throw a great and festive feast, and everyone invited. As for Brid and Taddy, she would concern herself with their fate another day. Her mind could accommodate only so much, and it was already crowded with enough competing claims to suggest madness as a means of saving that very same mind.

But once the feast had been decided upon, she was given a purpose in life that not only mocked her reversals of fortune but also distracted her from all and any actions that might land her in jail or in the madhouse.

For the moment, she had to deal only with the raging tempest, whose obvious goal was the total obliteration of the civilized world, a not uncommon happening in these parts. With Kieran gone off to Caherciveen in search of shallots for the dinner he'd planned for that evening, Kitty had to make her way up the side of Crohan Mountain to the commonage at its summit and, with language foul and unseemly, with threats and with soothings, bring the near drowned cows safely not only down the pasture slope but into the great hall of the castle itself.

Brid had accompanied her, but other than an encouragement communicated by her very presence, she was not of much practical use. Wandering among the confused and frightened beasts, she did, however, seem to bring some degree of calm to counter Kitty's slaps and shoves.

Before Kitty could secure the massive doors of the great hall after the entry of the last drenched cow, in came the pig, its squeals and screams at the indignities of lightning, thunder, water, and wind more than a formidable competitor to the storm's howling. Again Kitty made an attempt to best the wind and close the doors against the elements' wrath, but this time there entered not just the pig but Lord Shaftoe himself, conjured by the tempest as yet one more scourge sent to blight the earth and all the people on it.

Unlike that other apparition in the great hall—Brid, who had been exempt from water and wind and had made her way up and down the mountain and into the castle as dry and as composed as was possible, given her uncertain status among the living—his lordship, not having learned from his previous visit that an umbrella was a useful implement when touring the county, was more ghostly than Brid or Taddy had ever been. From the depths of the sea had he risen, shrouded in a mist of his own secretion, bedraggled, and bringing with him into the confines made sweet by the presence of the cows, the stench of wet wool steaming from his clothes, his tweed, his soaked trousers, his snap-visored cap, and the buttoned cardigan meant to keep out the damp.

So weighted was he with water that he seemed unable to move—stunned, perhaps, to discover that he, like everyone else caught in the path of the demented storm, was subject to inconveniences and discomforts. Surely this was contrary to what had been divinely ordained, that his person, to say nothing of his clothing, was exempt from any effects not within his preference. Immobilized by the affront, he stood there, the growing puddle at his feet threatening even further the survival of his soft leather shoes.

The cows stretched their necks upward, mooing. At the arrival of his lordship, Brid promptly dissolved, taking with her the only calm and resigned presence in the hall. The cows moved restlessly among themselves, brushing against each other's flanks, flicking each other's eyes with their tails, as their hooves scraped and clattered on the flagstone paving. The pig, for its part, had silenced itself and was scraping its brass ring at his lordship's feet, the usual snorting sounds taken up into the tempest's howl.

His lordship was the first to raise his voice above the din. "It was hardly my intention to intrude in this fashion, but it seems to be raining and my vehicle doesn't accommodate flooding with the ease one might expect. I've had to abandon it at the bottom of the road with my architect inside. Is it your experience that it—and he—are in danger of being washed away? My architect persuaded me to come and inquire. I'd intended to show him only the exterior of the castle, to give him some idea of what he'll be taking on when the improvements are decided upon, but do you think you might send one of your menials down to rescue him? Then he could, if you don't mind—and I'm sure you don't—see the interior as well, killing, as it were, two birds with one stone. We promise to be as unintrusive as possible. Except that maybe you could prevail upon one of your staff to provide us with a bit of tea. And a biscuit or two would be quite welcome as well."

With this, Kitty was put at war with herself. The man should be heaved back into the maelstrom whence he'd come, taking the stench of his expensive wools with him and relieving her of the temptation to first chastise him with the valor of her tongue, then treat him to a full dose of her sarcasm—which, she could tell from the still faint impulses given off deep in her stomach, would, by the time they had gained her lips, have gathered enough venom to make even the most impervious among us susceptible to the self-loathing that only self-knowledge can engender. This man had, after all, effected that most feared experience in the life of any member of her race: eviction. And by a landowning lord, no less. The raven itself was hoarse that croaked the entrance of Shaftoe under her battlements.

But this was Ireland, and County Kerry besides. There still flowed in her veins Kerry blood that would rebel at the refusal of hospice on such a day as this. Her ancestry pleaded this drenched man's cause. Tradition formed in the mists of antiquity weighed upon her soul. Instructions voiced by her father and her mother, her uncles and her aunts, her grandparents on her father's side and her grandparents on her mother's side, pierced her heart. Choking with resentment but obedient to her race, she said, "I have no one to send but yourself for your endangered architect, but I'm familiar with the ways of tea and can probably scratch up a biscuit or two, if you require it."

With that, the lights went out. The power was off, probably for miles and miles around. "Ah, Lord Shaftoe," Kitty crowed, "welcome to castle living."

"What's happened to the lights?"

"They're out."

"But the generator . . . ?"

"What generator?"

"You have no generator?"

"Candles. Marvelous invention, A guarantee of independence from the elements, to say nothing of the power authority. And we also have a device called a match. You strike it against a rough surface, and a flame issues forth." As she was saying this she went from wall to wall sconce, lighting candles that sent flickering shadows of cow parts—mostly heads and snouts—jigging up and down the stone walls.

"I must remember to tell Mr. Skiddings, my architect, that a generator comes before all else."

"I should think you might want to look first for the gunpowder."

"There is no gunpowder."

"Smart decision. Conducive to a better night's sleep."

Now all the candles were lit, except for those in the great iron chandelier suspended from the middle of the high-beamed ceiling. Kitty felt she'd done enough to hold off the dark, especially since it was still midafternoon and the possibility of a late sun was still to be considered. She would have to let down the three-tiered ring by means of a pulley and rope, and the noise would further disturb the cows, whose milk was no doubt already curdling, what with lightning, thunder, darkness, and Lord Shaftoe. For a final gesture, in tribute to the gift of Prometheus, Kitty lit a single candle held in a holder shaped like a Persian shoe and decorated at the heel not with a silken embellishment but with a sturdy ring through which she could slip her index finger and light her way—and his lordship's way—to the scullery, where tea and biscuits would be served.

But before she could, in the servile manner of a house-keeper so far superior in status and in worth to any lord, say the words scripted for her from time immemorial—"If you would care to come this way"—there was heard from outside, above the shrieks of the storm, a wounded, frightened cry that could be characterized only as the first baritone banshee ever to give utterance within sound of the Western Sea.

"Ah, good. Mr. Skiddings, my architect. Perhaps you'd be so kind as to let him in. He must be catching his death."

It was at this moment that Kitty decided—a decision that had, for her, the force of an oath—that she would make these moments a time of testing. Now was her chance to measure her endurance, to see how much nonsense she could put up with and not combust. She would lend herself completely to his lordship's requests, demands, remarks, and observings, taking to herself the full burden of his loftiness, allowing herself to have one stupidity after another rammed into her consciousness until at last the fated eruption would come, her volcanic outburst that would reduce the man to ash, then bury him beneath the hot flow of her searing displeasure. She would enjoy that most fragile of her many virtues, patience. She would explore its strengths and discover at last its limits. Out of consideration for her previous adversaries, she had permitted the eruption to take place long before its full force had gathered. For his lordship, no such consideration would be made. He was, all unaware, taking his chances, just as she, all aware, was taking hers. She was now entering uncharted territory. Never before had she given herself this particular license. She felt the gleeful euphoria that only a malevolent daring could provide. She rather enjoyed the sensation. Patience, the first phase of the experiment, descended.

In response, therefore, to his lordship's request that the architect be admitted, Kitty said with a sweetness so foreign to her nature that her stomach threatened rebellion, "Oh, the poor man. Yes, of course. Only too pleased." She drew wide the door, knowing that the slanted rain would drench anyone within a distance of a single meter—which included of course, his lordship—while Kitty herself cunningly stepped aside to make way for the entrance of the drowning architect. "In here, please. You mustn't stay there in the wet," she shouted into the storm.

An anguished cry of relief, not unlike an anguished cry of despair, issued forth from yet another heap of wet wool standing nor far outside the door. Once he'd staggered in past the threshold, he stopped and let loose the cry again, this time in anger and protest.

"You might want to step in a bit farther so I might close the door." Kitty made sure she yelled directly into the man's ear, causing him, in reflex, to raise his hand to protect his tympanic nerve from lasting damage. Obediently he took three more shuffling steps, his waterlogged garments sending a torrent of their own onto the flagstones.

"Much obliged," he screamed, forgetting that he was no longer in competition with the deluge outside. Kitty flinched and managed a small smile that quickly increased to a beaming affability that took possession of her entire face. She let it freeze into position long enough to make sure it had been observed, then reconfigured these seldom-used muscles into her former look of servile superiority. Again she took up her candle. "Tea will be served in the scullery. If you'll be so good as to come this way."

"Oh," said his lordship. "Well." He considered a moment, lengthened the upper part of his body, especially the head and shoulders, and added, "The scullery, then. Why not, eh?"

Whether the intruders knew it or not, they were led to the best-appointed room in the castle. What passed for a sitting room consisted of a well-used couch abandoned by the squatters and an overstuffed chair whose high back was stained with grease that hinted at a predilection for purple hair dye. Except for two ladder-back chairs—also gifts from the scholarly squatters—the rest of the furnishings had come from Kieran's farm: a wing chair set near the fireplace; a low table in front of the couch, crudely made but sturdy; a round table on a pedestal with a lamp, its shade a brown parchment onto which no design had been attempted; and a rug worn thin by generations of Sweeney boots. To give the room a proper baronial claim, the andirons in the fireplace were huge implements resembling giant chess pawns that would have required for their lifting and moving Cuchulain himself. The grate, more suited for burning peat than the metal pawns, was a bed of common metal now undifferentiated in color from the ashes it had created over the years of good and faithful service. The chimney drew perfectly, making this particular room, despite its discolored stone walls of lime and mortar, the most hospitable space in the entire castle—a fair replica of what might be found in a nearby cottage—and far too comforting for his Lordship and his aggrieved associate.

What was called the dining room was furnished with the Ping-Pong table, with seven unmatched chairs—some cushioned, some not—arranged not around the table but along the walls, the table itself reserved for the game for which it had been devised, a diversion often enjoyed by Kitty and Kieran after a day of separation.

But it was in the scullery that communal life was lived in the castle. Here the fireplace could accommodate a pig deemed suitable for roasting—although the roasting planned for the high feast would take place not in the scullery but in a field a kilometer farther west, the castle tower still in sight. (The honored pig had not yet been chosen.)

The table was butcher block, and the four chairs surrounding it were, like more than several of the castle appointments, a set brought by Kieran as a gift to his bride from the family cottage now occupied by his brother, his wife, and their three children. But the scullery's more obvious treasures were the oven, the sink and the culinary equipment no chef worthy of the name would be caught dead—much less alive—without. The refrigerator and a freezer alone probably sent into the surrounding countryside more ozone-killing pollutants than the rest of the village households combined. Vents, a microwave oven, a machine to wash dishes, another to whip, grind, stir, slice, and pummel—all were arrayed around the ample room for the astonishment of visitors and the delight of Kieran Sweeney, who, along with his initiation into connubial bliss, was granted the knowledge, heretofore unsuspected, that he was a cook with great gifts, some of them instinctive, others revealed. This phenomenon can be explained by noting that Lolly—now a McCloud, gave, in a misguided attempt at wit, the wedding gift of a cookbook to her new aunt-in-law. Kitty, embarrassed by the feebleness of the effort at humor, was about to discard the book, along with several Victoria's Secret undergarments and the complete works of Doris Lessing. Kieran, drawn to the cookbook's slick cover picturing a pig roasting on a spit, stayed her hand and wrested the book from her and began, with growing avidity, to scan the possibilities for satisfactions heretofore unknown in his culinary endeavors.

For Lord Shaftoe and Mr. Skiddings, it was to be tea and a few biscuits that had gathered age in the bottom of a tin. While Kitty busied herself with the kettle, the teapot, the pitcher of milk, the sugar bowl, and the plate of hardened biscuits—a breed with a butter base so insufficiently trusted that chips of chocolate rather like bunny droppings had been included for marketing purposes—his lordship and his attending architect felt free, once they had accepted their relegation to the scullery, to express their amazement and approval of what their eyes beheld. Mr. Skiddings was particularly interested in the installations and, without permission, opened and closed doors, flicked on and off several of the machines—to no effect in the absence of a generator—until the power, miraculously restored, set in motion an excitable vegetable chopper and nearly gave the poor man a myocardial infarction. Once recovered, he went on to test the rest of the pots and skillets, the contents of cabinets and drawers, with a skeptical regard.

To lure him to the table, and to end his intrusion into the privacy of Kieran's kitchen, Kitty said, "Help yourselves to the milk and sugar. I never take either, so I'm no good at proper serving. And there are more biscuits, if you like."

"Oh," said his lordship. "I should do it myself?"

"Try," said Kitty. "And see what happens."

"Come, Mr. Skiddings. These biscuits won't wait much longer."

The architect left off his scrutiny of Kieran's knives—a scrutiny that consisted, it would seem, of examining his reflection in the shining blades, including profiles, jutted chin, and, finally, the coating and color of his tongue—and came to the table, but continued glancing back at the wonders he had seen. His lordship also had difficulty concentrating on the repast Kitty had so arduously prepared. He, too, was casting an all-too-appraising eye at the surroundings. To nip in the bud what was being thought by both guests, Kitty said, "You needn't worry. All this will be removed so it won't interfere with your own plans, which I'm sure will shame our own poor efforts."

His lordship, being less experienced in disappointment, said only, "Oh?" Mr. Skiddings, when he had assimilated the import of what had been said, could only add another spoonful of sugar to his tea, stir it, put down the spoon, and stare into his cup. So pleased was Kitty with the moment that she extended it by saying, "We'll be sure to get all this out of your way. As I've said, we're most eager to make the transition as amiable and as easy as possible for everyone concerned. And that, I assume, includes you, Mr. Skiddings."

He picked up his cup, touched it against his lower lip, set it down, and said, "Yes, I suppose it does."

Leaning his head sideways in the architect's direction, Lord Shaftoe said to Skiddings, "We may as well use this opportunity, since we've already been so terribly inconvenienced, for you to make your first survey of the property. Then we can use the journey back for discussion."

Kitty, the perfect hostess, smiled and said, "I'm afraid that won't be possible. I've not prepared the castle for visitors—especially visitors as illustrious as yourselves."

His Lordship, not to be instructed in the ways of affability, said, "But we're hardly visitors."

Kitty's smile stayed, even as her chin was raised. "Considering the recent ruling of the court, you fit the category of visitor until a specified time. More tea?" Without waiting for a reply, she added, "Oh, but the rain has stopped. Or, unless my hearing is defective, it's settled itself into an ordinary drizzle that will hardly discommode men as robust and hearty as yourselves."

His lordship had had two sips, Mr. Skiddings none. Kitty had emptied her cup and enjoyed, to whatever degree possible, one of the biscuits. "It could start up again at any moment, and I doubt that you'd prefer to find your way in the midst of another cloudburst." She held out the plate of biscuits. "Would you care to take one with you? Something to sustain you on your journey?"

Mr. Skiddings's right arm twitched, but seeing an aghast look from his lordship, the architect transformed the gesture in midintent to the placement of his hand on the table next to his undefiled teacup.

Standing, his Lordship touched the declivity between his lips and chin and bowed in the direction of his hostess. "Then you must excuse us. You've been most kind, but we really must be on our way. The storm has reversed itself in our favor, and we would be less than gracious not to accept the consideration. Mr. Skiddings?"

So abruptly did Mr. Skiddings stand that he almost tipped over his chair, and, not to exempt the table from the eagerness of his response to his lordship's summons, he knocked the right hand he'd so cunningly put next to his teacup against the saucer, spilling some of the tea onto the biscuit plate, ruining forever the crispness that only uncounted days and nights shut up in a tin could accomplish. He seemed about to make an apology but apparently decided not to draw further attention to his handiwork and said simply, "Do you think I might be able to use the men's?"

That he was able Kitty had no doubt. If she was willing to give her permission, she was not quite so sure. To give still further use to the smile still pasted onto her face, she was tempted to tell the man that considering the condition he was in, wet to the bone, no notice could possibly be taken if he simply chose to make a contribution of his own to his completely soaked apparel. But, for the first time, she saw an honest need on the poor man's face. She also saw, pretty much for the first time, that the man was inordinately plain. Her phrase to herself was "ugly as an elbow." And indeed the creases and folds in the man's face traced a circular pattern of diminishing circumferences as they neared the nose and mouth, the nose itself providing an acceptable center to the concentrics surrounding it. It helped not at all that the eyes were gray—meaning, to Kitty, that the man was color-blind. For hair, he had been given tufts and clumps randomly placed that would have suggested transplants had the choice of donor not been so immediately discredited. Although his ears were pinned nicely against his head, there sprouted from their whorls and lobes yet more hair. Whether it was his habit or a genetic indisposition, or a combination of the two, his shape was somewhat peculiar and his impeccably tailored cloth-ing—especially in its ruined state—failed to disguise this sad

and obvious truth. It could be said that the man was, in his
own way, perfectly formed, but the perfection was that of a
perfect ripe pear.

In pity, Kitty said, "Come, I'll show you the way. If your
lordship will excuse us."

"Certainly. It will give me time to look around."

"I'll be but a minute."

And, indeed, in a minute she did return, having rushed
Mr. Skiddings up the stair and nosed him in the direction of
the second door on his left. "Fresh towels in the cabinet."

His lordship was running his hand over the stones that
walled the passageway leading to the great hall. "All this will
be covered over, of course." He removed his hand and rubbed
his fingers against his thumb to rid himself of any residue.
After looking around for some object on which to wipe his
hand, he settled for a somewhat ratty velvet drape the squatters had hung in a brave attempt to duplicate the medieval
tapestries that held back some of the seeping damp the walls
could not absorb. "Archival evidence indicates that my
ancestor, had he taken full possession of the castle rather than
been driven off by the notorious plot, would have finished the
task only begun but hardly advanced by the primitives responsible for the original structure. One can't live in a rock pile
and declare oneself civilized. I don't doubt that you yourself
had similar plans, which it was my sad duty to my ancestors to
interrupt."

"It's a castle, not a palace."

"Ah, but it will approach the palatial when I've finished.
I can now complete a task too long delayed. Gives one a
sense of mission, would you say?"

To spare his lordship Kitty's response, Mr. Skiddings

appeared, a good toweling having plastered his tufts onto his skull. He had also taken time to straighten his rain-shriveled tie and make an attempt to revive the delicate but elaborate foldings of the handkerchief stuffed into his jacket pocket. "The plumbing—" he said hesitantly—"the plumbing?"

"Oh," said Kitty, the smile slapped back onto her face, "I forgot to tell you. You must reach inside the water closet and pull up on the mechanism. It works fine if you do it properly."

"I see." The man started back toward the stair.

"No," said Kitty. "It's all right. Nothing I can't tend to later. And I'm sure you gentlemen, now that the rain has stopped—"

"It hasn't stopped." For this, his lordship had adopted a clipped tone common to his kind.

What could Kitty do but intensify her agreeable smile? "Then let's say it's abated."

"One could hardly be wetter that one is now, I suppose."

Kitty approved of his self-referral in the third person, an obvious abjection when his preference no doubt would have been the use of the royal we. To further demonstrate his inbred humility, he had lengthened his neck and thrust out his bit of a chin, locking his jaw and sending forth his words through teeth immobilized by abnegation. If Kitty's smile had extended further, her face would have broken. "If one gets wet, one gets dry," she said, hoping his lordship remembered, as did she, that this was the exact same advice she'd dispensed at the close of his previous visit.

Now, as then, his Lordship summoned the stoical resignation adopted by his ancestors when first confronted by a wisdom to which they were unaccustomed. "Still no umbrella, I assume."

"I keep forgetting." Kitty gave her head a slight bow.

"It's not for myself I'm concerned. It's for Mr. Skiddings, who's subject to pneumonia."

The architect jerked his eyes open wider in surprise at this revelation.

"You have none in the car?" Kitty asked.

"Would we not have availed ourselves of it to come here in the first place?"

"Forgive me. I'm not very bright."

When his lordship offered no contradiction, Kitty lifted her head, the better to display the still beaming smile to which her face was now becoming accustomed. No doubt Lord Shaftoe took it for the grimace of an idiot, and Kitty, so pleased with this interpretation, now smiled with genuine happiness and deep-seated pleasure. "We'll leave this way." Kitty gestured toward the entrance to the great hall. "But mind your step. There are cows in residence." She stepped aside and let the two gentlemen enter first, his lordship preceding the architect.

"There's a pig standing in my way, staring at me." Lord Shaftoe paused, then, with offended astonishment, added, "Oh, and now it's—Well, really!"

Looking past his lordship, Kitty saw the pig planted in the man's path, not only staring up at him, but sending out behind, as is the sow's way, an arc of golden piss that reached, with perfect aim, the center of a steaming cow flop a few feet away.

"*Faugh a Ballagh! Faugh a Ballagh!*" Kitty clapped her hands in the manner of her niece-in-law, Lolly. The pig lowered its snout and swung its pink head to the side, retreated to a corner of the hall, and lay down next to a cow that had been watching the display with all the interest of a lump of lard.

Mr. Skiddings had come to his lordship's side. Kitty waited for them to move on, but George Noel Gordon Lord Shaftoe had begun to gesture with a waving arm. "All this must be tended to. Once it's thoroughly scoured, an admirable room with definite possibilities. The crudities I'm sure can be overcome. And I want fireplaces, at both ends of the hall, and carvings, perhaps with figures emerging from the marble."

It was the word *marble* that roused Kitty from her smiling complacence. Marble? In a castle? Here she was surrounded above and below by stones once hurtled and sent crashing down from the mountain peaks, stubborn reminders that even to grinding glacial ice it had been possible to say, "No farther; here I stay"—a contest hard won against forces elemental in their indifference and implacable in their determination. Never would these stones be civilized. To put them into the company of decadent marble would be an abomination to which her ancestral blood could never give consent. To claim that they were insufficient in themselves was a heresy to which she could never subscribe.

Lord Shaftoe turned to his architect. "I must take you to East Anglia to show you what I have in mind. Can you believe what we see here?" He leaned closer to Mr. Skiddings and lowered his tone. "Fascinating to find out that what's been said of these people is actually true. You have only to look around. I do believe Heaven has sent me—may I say, *us?*—just in time. A moment later and all could be lost, eh, Skiddings?"

So great a pitch had been reached by Kitty's wrath that only complete calm could rescue her from spontaneous com-bustion. To impose it, she had no need. Through natural selection, a strain had developed within her species that would, when threatened with self-destruction through the rise of a righteous wrath, trigger an interior mechanism so that, for the moment at least, a preternatural serenity was substituted for the furies that were already shredding her mind and tearing at her soul. Composed now, she dismissed her smile and decided to answer his lordship's inanities with simple silence and uncaring patience. She would hurry the departures no longer. She would stand where she stood and wait, not ignoring further outrages but setting them aside for future reference, when a conniving rationality could devise a vengeance best suited to the offenses being thrust like poisoned darts at her innocent self. Calm pervaded; patience prevailed.

George Noel Gordon Lord Shaftoe turned his attention to his hostess. "You'll be happy to hear that I intend to bring a celebratory mood to the neighborhood. I am already making plans for entertainments and revels that will no doubt bring considerable joy to the castle, inspiring similar festivities in the countryside around."

"Dances? Parties? And everyone invited?"

"Oh, no. You misunderstand. I'll entertain, bringing to the castle some of those illustrious personages absent too long from the district. It's my belief that my gatherings will inspire a general mood of rejoicing, emanating as it will from no less a prominence than the castle itself. I consider it my responsibility to set a tone, as it were. And the tone I shall set, much to the advantage of the farmers and fisherfolk, and of the cottagers as well, will inspire others to respond with revels of their own devising and consistent with their own customs. I'm sure you see the logic in that."

Kitty's calm stood fast, her patience intact.

"Another benefit," his lordship added, "is the employment I'll bring. One can hardly live on the scale I expect to
achieve without a full staff and, at times, temporary but suffi-
ciently rewarded help. The attendant rise in the common
prosperity will be appreciable, I'm sure."

Kitty was tempted to inform his Lordship that her country
was no longer a prime incubator for a servant class. The common prosperity had arrived, with no help from Lord Shaftoe.
The tide had been reversed. Girls from America were
recruited for the summer tourist season as staff members in
hotels and restaurants throughout the land. Young men from
across the seas were welcomed as waiters and busboys. Perhaps
Lord Shaftoe could scour the student bodies of American col-
leges for his menials, but any hope of finding them among the
"locals" was destined for disappointment. Possessed as Kitty
was by a serenity that had quieted her congenital contentious-
ness, she felt no need to discommode his Lordship with reali-
ties he would encounter soon enough.

As a matter of fact, serenity or no serenity, it was impossible for her not to enjoy her complicity in the man's delusions.
Let him find out the hard way. Glee was threatening to overcome her calm, but tranquility restored and renewed itself
when she heard Mr. Skiddings say, "Are we expected in two
hours' time to dine with her ladyship in Cork?"

"Ah, her ladyship. Yes. And we must tell her of our own
adventure. She will be highly amused, I'm sure."

Relieved as Kitty was by this prompting toward the door,
it surprised her by its reference to her ladyship. George Noel
Gordon was, she knew, unattached as of the moment. He had
neither wife nor family, although he must now, as keeper of a
castle, require an heir. Which would require a wife. It

occurred to Kitty that the ladyship referred to was a candidate for the honor. It further occurred to Kitty that the poor woman was not allowed to see her future home until the necessary desecrations had been effected.

Navigating among the cowpies, skirting both bovine and porcine piss, the two men made for the door with what alacrity their breeding allowed. "You do see possibilities, Mr. Skiddings?"

"Many, I assure you."

"Pity you didn't see the tower. It's cluttered at the moment, as which space is not, but you'll have opportunities undreamed of by any imagining."

"I can readily see them now."

"And, of course, you'll have my generous assistance at every turn."

"I am much obliged to your lordship."

"I admit to a partiality for comfort."

Without waiting for the architect to make the demanded response, his lordship turned to Kitty and said, his voice and his face alive with pleased expectation, "I remember now: 'House of Splendid Isolation.'"

"Sorry," Kitty said. "Edna O'Brien. Again."

"Fancy that. Oh, well." And with that he passed through the door, saying to his accomplice, "I expect to make a suitable offer for the scullery. I wonder who actually did it."

With no words, no gesture of farewell or thanks, the two men continued on, unmindful of the drizzle that was replenishing whatever wet might have dried in their clothing during their time in the castle. Kitty watched them go, her patience and her calm still surviving well beyond the reach of rudeness and other known attributes of aristocracy. His lordship continued to talk; Mr. Skiddings continued to listen, a nod of the head his only contribution to that most civilized of human attainments, conversation.

The rain had relieved itself of the greater part of its generosity, and Kitty could now return the cows and the pig to the well-washed air. When she turned around to coax the cows outside, she stopped on the threshold, then stepped backward, away, outside, into the drizzle and the rising mist. She stared into the great hall, at the milling cows, lowing and moving restlessly on the flagstones, tails swishing, their udders swaying with ponderous dignity beneath them. With determined effort, she forced herself to raise her eyes and look upward, to see again what she had already seen. There, hanging from the iron ring of the candled chandelier, were the young and beautfil bodies of Brid and Taddy, she in her simple brown dress of coarse wool, he wearing the brown tunic cinctured at the waist, the legs of his brown pants reaching to midcalf. Their muddied feet, as sweet as anything Kitty would ever see, bent downward, the toes pointing toward the darkening corners of the hall. There were the raw ropes burning into their slender necks, their eyes bulging in horror at what had been their fate, the swollen tongues strung sideways from their surprised mouths, tongues that would never speak again to tell their tale or speak their woes. Slowly they turned, surveying the hall for one last time, unmindful of the cows and the indifferent pig who went about their shitting and pissing, uncaring that so much splendor had been removed from the face of the earth.

They were, Kitty knew, but shades. Still, they could not be left dangling there, disfigured, mute, blind, their crusted feet brushing against the head of one cow, the ears of another.

She wanted to plead that they would vanish, that they would retreat to shadowed corners of the castle rooms or turn to the harp and the loom in the tower above. She refused to make her plea. She would stand there, the soft rain falling, the mist rising from the earth. She would let her eyes see nothing but these two ghosts. She would keep vigil until they dissolved into nothingness and went from her sight, free of the noose and free to wander again the castle, the pastures, the hills, the stone-pocked fields. If their hanging were to last her lifetime, she would not leave the spot where she was standing now. She would not abandon them to their horror and their final fears. She would be faithful to the last.

The rain, still soft, began to cloud her eyes and the mist to seep into the great hall through the opened door. Kitty made no move. She would let happen what would happen. Softer fell the rain, blurring further her sight. Still she saw the forms, but through the growing mist. She knew whose presence had hanged them there. That they would be condemned to this horror ever again could never be allowed. Peace must come at last. They must be released and set free to join themselves. What must be done would be done. To this she swore, and it would be accomplished, or she was not who she was.

At this, the mists separated, the rain lightened. Brid and Taddy were gone; they were nowhere to be seen. Kitty looked at the iron circle, then began slapping the rumps of the cows. "Move," she said. "Come on. Yes, you, move. Everybody out. Move."

10

In their first days and weeks in the castle Kitty and Kieran were not particularly well matched when it came to Ping-Pong. Neither was practiced in restraint, and Kieran simply had the harder slam, which Kitty was unable to return, the ball's velocity exceeding that of a bullet and its apogee on her side of the net well beyond her reach. Kieran made no effort to conceal his jubilation when the ball smashed against the far wall behind his wife's head.

Kitty minded this not at all. His strength was a source of pride at all other times, and it would be ungracious to single out these moments of humiliation as a goad to resentment. Nor did she resort to the usual antidote prescribed for losers: it's only a game. To play a game (in her view), one played to win. Defeat had nothing to recommend it, and the search for solace would be even more humiliating than the loss already experienced.

Also, she was not a good sport. Her competitive sense was seldom inactive. Had she the strength of the man she loved she wouldn't have hesitated to crack the Ping-Pong ball as if it were nothing more than the shell of a newly laid egg. Still, in seeming contradiction to her nature, she accepted Kieran's accumulation of points, his triumphs at her expense, the undeniable advantage of his good right arm. And while she was sustaining her equilibrium she was also keeping her own counsel.

The relation of the ball to the paddle, the interdependence of the arm and the eye, the role of both as servants to the brain, the coordination of all the elements involved—every aspect of the game was closely observed, minutely analyzed, and subject to constant experiment. Also, it didn't hurt that she had a highly developed habit of concentration. Bit by bit her game—almost imperceptibly—improved. The points her husband earned with his unrepentant slams were conceded. But there came a time when he made fewer and fewer of them. When Kitty won for the first time, Kieran rejoiced. When she began to win two out of five, then three out of five, he, in turn, was proud of his wife—even as he was bewildered by what he thought was an inexplicable diminution of his own powers.

Then Kieran, without full awareness, set out on the path along which his wife had already advanced. He, too, took into account sophistications latent within the game that he, in his brutality, had long ignored: a practiced spin on the ball, a quick flick of the paddle at just the right moment, a twist of the wrist, a judgment of the eye too quickly made for conscious credit, and, most pleasing of all, a heightened sense of the woman opposite him, her skills and her determinations, her cunning response to his every move, her relentless insistence that she give him all she had.

The game had a purpose beyond the heated pleasure it unfailingly aroused. At times in counterpoint, at other times in accompaniment to the rhythms of the game, husband and wife would take advantage of this time together to discuss—with digressions into argument or explanation, reasonings or intractabilities—subjects of common interest. With Kitty at her computer or in her garden and Kieran in his kitchen—to say nothing of his attention to the cows and the orchard and the fields—time together was limited. Conversation was thus all the more welcome when the paddles were taken in hand, the ball put into play, and enterprises of great pith and moment could be addressed without the possibility of one or the other stalking off in a fit of intransigence.

It had been during a game earlier in the summer that Kitty had informed her husband that the castle might well be lost, and he, respecting this method of communication even in so fatal a circumstance, kept the ball moving, as did his wife. Once in a while a serve was postponed briefly for questions, but not for answers. But then, the first half of the first game had threatened to become desultory, its customary verve drained by the possibility of losing the roof over their heads, the ground beneath their feet, and the castle stones they had come so readily to love. At one point, Kieran had seemed deliberately to place a shot so Kitty could make a telling return—an attempt perhaps to cheer her up, to compensate for a tragedy for which no compensation was possible—so Kitty had slashed at the ball, driving it back to Kieran, who, out of habit, responded to the corrective emanations projected by his wife and spun the ball so that it dropped just on Kitty's side of the net, making a return impossible. From then on they proceeded to a five-games-to-three win in Kieran's favor, each game an honorable win for the victor, an honorable loss for the loser.

Also, as the games played themselves out, Kitty, her temperament disciplined by the needs of the contest, was able without advancing into paroxysm to put forth the perfidies of Lord Shaftoe and the law's complicity in their expulsion. Kieran, no less than his wife, took out his disbelief, his execrations, and his oaths, on the demands of the ball that, it seemed, never ceased to require his attention. The shared satisfactions of Kieran's win had helped temper the fury and outrage that would have consumed them both had they gripped the paddles and insisted that nothing—*nothing*—would deny them the full pleasure of their sport or distract them from the exercise of the conjugal exchange and its attendent conversations that the game had become.

The day for the feasting was fast approaching. Kitty took the ball lightly in her left hand, careful not to pinch the celluloid. She must not dent the surface and disqualify the ball from further participation. This was the last undamaged ball; both she and Kieran had forgotten to arrange for a fresh supply. That this should inhibit their game had been considered, then dismissed.

They would play as they had always played, and the ball would have to take its chances. If they had not completed the designated discussion by the time the game was over or the ball broke, they could repair to the scullery, where a chessboard had already been set up in anticipation of any drastic eventuality. Kitty made the serve. Kieran made the return— and the game began.

"Have you given enough thought to the pig?" he asked.

"Enough for what?"

"Enough to agree with me."

Pock-pock, pock, pock-pock-pock went the ball, back and forth over the net, Kieran and Kitty each performing a dance choreographed by the other, stepping backward, moving forward, shifting to the right, to the left, leaning over the table, drawing back, the paddled hand gesturing with a quick grace that seemed at times to be of Hindu origin. After Kieran had accumulated five points to his wife's one, Kitty said, "That we're supposed to eat it?"

"We've certainly fattened it enough."

"Being fat is not the issue."

"We certainly can't give people a skinny pig."

"There are other pigs. Lolly has enough to convince me more often than not that she's really Circe, and Aaron had better watch out. Although to turn my nephew into a pig should be well within anyone's competence."

The score rose to twelve-seven, Kitty's favor. When Kieran started closing in at thirteen-eleven, he said, "Well, she's done the next best thing. More to her advantage I should say."

"Oh?"

"I was driving by yesterday, and there was Aaron in front of me on the road, herding the pigs from here to there, wherever that might be."

"Aaron?"

"Aaron."

"Lolly's changed him into a swineherd? Well, considering his gifts as a writer, he's ascended to a far higher calling." Kitty had backed to the wall, positioning herself for the good whack that sent the ball at the speed of a humming bird over to her husband. Kieran simply leaned forward and, with an expert twist of the paddle, plopped the ball just over the net.

It fell like the droppings of a low-flying gull. "It gets better than that," he said.

"Tell."

Kieran waited until they changed serves. "It's Lolly who's now the writer. She's writing a novel."

Kitty let out an almost triumphant guffaw. This supposedly startling news failed in every way to astonish her, much less affect her game. All during her long "best girl friend" association with Lolly McKeever, Kitty had had to hear the woman's amused disbelief at whatever difficulties Kitty might be confronting with her writing. "What are you talking about?" she'd say. "Who can't write a novel? I'd write one myself if I had the time. Who wouldn't? Who couldn't?"

On occasions such as these, Kitty would draw upon her limited fund of pity and her ample fund of disdain, and choose, for Lolly's sake and for the poor woman's survival on this earth, to simply respond, "Of course. Your swine are far, far more important." And now poor Aaron, promoted to swineherd, had finally given Lolly her longed-for opportunity.

Kitty's only gesture had been to back herself against the wall. And her only words were, "I can hardly wait."

Before she could make the serve, Kieran said, "Aaron admits he's relieved he doesn't have to write anymore. Only too happily has he passed the burden on to his wife."

Kitty made the serve. It went past the table, past her husband, into the wall behind him. While Kieran was retrieving it, she said, "Which means Aaron's the one to pick out the pig for the famous feast observing our loss of the castle."

"I don't see why that will be necessary, to pick out one of theirs." Kieran flicked his wrist and sent the ball to the table's edge. "We have a winning candidate already in residence. It's a way of keeping the event completely within the family."

As if to cry out in protest at the mere suggestion of such a possibility, a piercing scream that modulated into a shriek, then toned back to a scream, came through the open window. Kieran hit a net ball. Kitty let it stay where it was. "The pig," she said.

"Someone must be slaughtering it even as we speak."

Kitty went to the window.

Kieran picked up the ball. "We can't stop every time the pig decides to vocalize." When Kitty said nothing, he asked, "Is someone looking at it cross-eyed? That's all it takes on most occasions."

"One of the cows seems to have its hind legs stuck in a hole."

"That is not a cow's complaint we're hearing." He, too, went to the window.

In a field on the far side of a stone wall was a cow with, indeed, its hind legs down in a hole too narrow for it easily to pull itself out, try as it might. And the pig had taken up its cause. There the animal was, off to the side of the cow, snout raised heavenward, addressing in sounds no deity could ignore its plea for immediate deliverance. The plight of its companion was obviously more wounding than the slaughterer's knife or even the herder's switch or, to note the ultimate provocation and response, impatience when being served its dinner.

The cow, for all its difficulties, had adapted to the inconvenience and, as if performing an exercise at which it was quite adept, kept trying to free its legs at measured intervals, resting between attempts, then taking up again the movements as if it were offering a satisfactory demonstration of its skills. It seemed, even, that all was being done at the pig's insistence. The pig would shriek; the cow would move its hind legs. The two beasts had formed a partnership and devised this cunning entertainment, the cow—to the best of its abilities—dancing, the pig providing the accompaniment.

When Kitty and Kieran arrived at the scene after climbing a somewhat challenging stone wall, nothing had changed. The cow went through the prescribed motions, driven on by the pig's incessant screams and cries, the sounds and movements now set in a series of repetitions that brought to Kitty's mind an opera by Philip Glass and Robert Wilson she'd seen in Brooklyn while studying at Fordham.

"I'll need a spade," Kieran yelled, barely making himself heard over the pig's continuing contribution to the cacophony, "to make the hole larger. So it can get out."

"Does that mean I should go get one?" Kitty unintentionally, but not without some satisfaction, managed to pitch her voice to the key—possibly B-flat—also employed by the pig.

"I'll go. You stay here. Try to calm things down."

"How?"

"A blunt instrument strategically placed between the pigs ears might help."

Kieran climbed back over the stone wall, not without difficulty. He wasn't out of training, but the wall was a bit high and the stones so expertly placed that a toehold was far from easy to find. Twice he slid back down. After the second slide, Kitty yelled, "Maybe I should go."

After a quick glare directed into his wife's eyes, Kieran gained the summit and jumped down on the far side. Kitty remonstrated with the pig, as she felt it her duty to do. When this failed to effect any diminuendo she repeated the phrases, this time in English instead of Irish. This excited the pig to even greater attainments, now surpassing the stratospheric heights any coloratura might envy, and with an increase of power. The animal was obviously equipped with the muscular control, the glottal chords, and the head resonance necessary for vocal feats of this kind. Kitty quickly switched back to Irish, but the pig was beyond placation and bellowed without the least indication of either failing stamina or damaged equipment.

The cow, the better to appreciate fully the pig's display, stopped its futile attempts at freedom and, facing forward, gave its complete attention to the swinish ostentations it had inspired. It seemed no longer to require liberation but was more than content to listen, asking nothing of the world other than this manifestation of unrelenting prayer on its behalf. To demonstrate its approval, it swished its tail and flicked its ears.

Then the screaming stopped. After such a sudden cessation, Kitty's first thought was that the axe had descended and that when she turned from the cow, she would see, bloodied on the ground, the pitiful pig. But when she did turn, the pig had lowered its head and was snouting the grass. There, near a hedge, was Taddy, looking down at the pig, observing closely the twitching and snuffling, then the digging down into the turf and the uprooting of clumps of clotted sod. It was then that Kitty realized that the pig had somehow divested itself of its ring. It had dug the hole the cow was stuck in and could now devastate the world at will.

When Taddy raised his head he looked not at Kitty but at Brid, who was standing in front of the cow. The young man's wounded neck seemed now to have been chewed, as if the noose had not been content to burn into the sweet flesh but had insisted on nibbling at its handiwork, feasting on the welts and reddened nubs. The rope's first purpose had apparently been not to hang or break the neck and choke the throat but to open the skin and make available these meaty morsels to satisfy an appetite that demanded death only so it could then proceed to devour the spoils of its slaughter. Taddy, bewildered and mournful, stared at Brid. Immediately the gaze deepened to the look of a man observing an object of such absolute love that his entire being became suffused with a quiet sorrow that could well be more an ache than a yearning. There he stood and seemed to wait for Brid to possess him, or he to possess her, to take her within himself and hold her gently in his heart, in his soul, Taddy and Brid. Brid and Taddy.

That Kitty could do nothing to assuage his grief brought to her a grief of her own, also quiet and sadly resigned. Brid, more concerned about the cow than about Taddy, watched the beast unprotesting in the hole the pig had no doubt dug for it. The girl was agitated by her helplessness, clasping and unclasping her hands, bringing them up to her chest, then parting them only to clasp them together again and press them even more diligently against her breastbone. First she would look at the captured hooves, then at the swollen udder resting on the ground, then at the cow's head and the soft unquestioning eyes. Finally she saw Taddy. Her agitation ended. Slowly she lowered her hands, rested her arms at her sides, and returned his gaze. She, too, no less than he, became still so that her love and his could join without impediment, her mournful sorrows not for herself, but for him—and his not for himself but for her.

Forever will thou love, and she be fair.

Sorrows of Kitty's own spread slowly but inexorably through her entire being. Whatever her own feelings, how could they take precedence over the eternal and mournful love presented to her now? That Kitty would abandon them to the unseeing, uncaring vassalage of Lord Shaftoe became more impossible than ever. Under his lordship's roof, the two would be not with the loom and the harp, but—as she herself had seen—strung up mercilessly and without end from the iron chandelier of the great hall. The failed confluence that had trapped them here, shades and shadows, appearing, disappearing, grieving, sorrowing, lost, would all be left uncorrected, surrendered into the keeping of George Noel Gordon Lord Shaftoe come at last to claim the castle his forebear had fled in fear—after taking vengeance for a plot substantiated by rumor only.

Still the youthful lovers gazed, a gaze that had its source in their souls. Never would Kitty surrender them. Was she not, like them, possessed? If evil spirits could be exorcised, what rite was possible to give freedom to spirits blessed and filled with grace? Kitty, of course, knew the rite. Peter had told her what must be done. But how? How does one blow up a castle? She could, she supposed, with her vast means, consort with those from whom gunpowder and explosives were readily available, but that would hardly fulfill the original requirement. The explosion had to be a fulfillment of the original plot, the pretext for the hangings. And the gunpowder was still there, somewhere in the castle, ready and waiting. But where? Searches far and wide, deep down and high up, had for almost two centuries yielded nothing. Still, it was Peter she believed more than her own prompting, which had told her the prophecies of the son of a Hag were a fiction even she could not have devised. She might begin the search anew. The gunpowder was there. She would find it.

Kieran, spade in hand, stood atop the dividing wall. After no more than a cursory acknowledgment of Brid and Taddy, he directed his attention to the cow and the pig, both of which had ceased their agitations. "Who took the ring out of the pig's snout? And who got the cow over the wall so it could step into the hole and almost break its legs?"

With that, both Brid and Taddy were consumed by an intensification of light. When the light lessened, no brighter than it had been a few moments before, they were gone.

Kieran threw the spade to the ground in front of him and jumped down. With the spade landing near them, both the cow and the pig renewed their previous actions, the cow struggling, the pig bellowing.

Without expecting Kitty to answer his unanswerable questions, Kieran picked up the spade and, with care, began digging around the cow's entrapped legs, widening the hole so the poor beast could move its hind quarters more freely and get itself up onto level ground—except that the level ground had been unleveled by the snorting pig.

After Kieran shoveled up three loads of turf, he said, his foot shoving down on the spade, "At least now we know for certain which pig is going to be turning on that spit." Kitty said nothing. Now was not the time. Turf is not easy to over-turn, even with a sharpened spade and a digger of Kieran's famous strength. But it was being done. Slowly. Grudgingly.

"Go find," Kieran grunted to Kitty, "go find where the stones fell so I can get the cow back where it belongs before it cripples itself trying to climb the wall."

"I don't see any breaks."

"There has to be one. The cow—and the bloody pig—couldn't have made the climb. There's a breach, and that's the only way we're going to get them both back where they belong."

"Well," said Kitty, not too enthused, "I'll take a look. But I don't see anything."

"It's there. Find it."

Rather than just stand and watch her husband at his labors, Kitty, ever eager to be useful in this world, wandered off, close to the stones, their height sometimes higher than the top of her head. Not hurrying, she walked along the wall, almost hoping there'd be no breach—just to contradict Kieran's certainty. But then, they'd just have to remove the stones themselves, persuade the cow and the pig to pass over, then rebuild the wall.

She could not avoid the thought that the pig had done it.

With its hammer-strong head supported by a bull-like neck and thunderous shoulders, it had easily butted down any number of stones, regardless of their weight or size. Its powers should never be underestimated. Or its stubborn determination. If it wanted to breach a wall, the wall would be breached.

She decided she'd prefer to find where the rocks had simply fallen with help from no one or—thinking of the pig—no thing.

It did little good to renew her longtime obsession with the gunpowder. She could intensify her resolve as much as she wanted, but what good would that be? Maybe she could bring the boy, the seer-elect, to the castle and see if he could, like a divining rod in search of water, detect the explosives' hiding place. She would take him from room to room, from dungeon to turret top. She would walk him through the meadows and the mire, the orchard and the pastures, along the same stone walls where she was walking now, while concentrating all his psychic might on finding the gunpowder. She would try not to show her desperation—to say nothing of her sorrow that, should the gunpowder by found and should the castle be sent skyward, never again would she be visited by Taddy and the mournful eyes, the muddied feet, the rasped neck, the harpist's fingers, and the yearning lover's parted lips.

But it had to be done. And she was the only one on earth—or, it seemed, in heaven—who could do the deed. If the avenging furies could be persuaded to revise their decree, and settle for a dismantling, stone by stone, of the castle, she would beg for the commission. With her bare hands she would do it. Schooled by the pig, she would butt her head, kick her feet; she would do it. Clawing, scratching, tugging, pounding, prying, no resource would be left untried. But the decree, to her knowledge—if such it could be called—had not been revised or rescinded, and if she were to act, she would have to act in accord with the ancient dictates: the castle must go heavenward.

Yellow-flowered gorse tufted the wall, the sweet scent at times overwhelming the salt smell of the stones. The sky was high above, not blue but the white of a thin cloud cover that meant no rain within the next five minutes. A meadow pipit pecked at the gorse for hidden food, and overhead a gull was making its way back to the sea after a foray to the rivers and lakes to the east. The wall had been built as high as the number of stones buried in the earth all those long years before.

More pipits, dipping their beaks in among the stones, accompanied her as she continued her walk that would measure the full perimeter of the enclosed field. And above, the white cloud that had screened the sky began to dissolve, the patient sun following the bend of the earth and lowering now in the west. How pleasant to search a wall for fallen stones.

As she reached the farthest corner of the field, there it was, the breach, the tumbled stones arrayed on the ground, in the grass, among the heather and the gorse. And there among them was the ring that had been put through the snout of the pig, the metal ripped, no doubt, by having been smashed against the unyielding rocks. The pig had done it all.

Before Kitty could give full expression to her exasperation, she turned around. There was the pig and, freed from the dug earth, the cow not far behind, both still inside the enclosed field. Kieran was leaning against the piled stones of the wall, the spade propped at his side. An appreciable amount of earth had been dug up to free the cow, and the hole, even at the considerable distance, seemed to Kitty larger than she would have expected. He was holding a piece of thick paper, tilting it from side to side as if trying to figure out exactly what he had found. He was scowling, which meant that his concentration was absolute and he would not welcome intrusion. At his feet was what she guessed to be a metal chest, muddied, the hinged lid thrown back and the tip of a brown scroll peering at the top.

"The pig butted down the stones," she called. When Kieran paid no attention, she went closer and said, "You found something. A chest, a paper, or a scroll or something."

Kieran made no answer, offered no gesture. He seemed to have distinguished the top of the paper from the bottom and, with moving lips, was reading what the document had to tell him. When Kitty was close enough to break his concentration, he quickly rolled the paper and took on the casual look of someone about to tell a lie.

"What is it?" Kitty asked.

"Nothing."

"Nothing? Then it'll be all right for me to have a look at it."

"Just some old scrawling."

"Was it in that chest?"

"Nothing, I told you."

"I can't wait." She held out her hand.

"It's meaningless. Just a lot of scribbles and some silly drawings. Left behind by some careless workman and covered over in time. Designs, as far as I can make out, for some changes in the castle. That's all."

"Then may I see it?" She reached down, took the remaining scroll from the chest and spread it open. She, too, like Kieran, turned the sheet from side to side, scrunching up her eyes, drawing back her head, crinkling her nose, trying to figure out what she was seeing. Without emphasis, Kieran said, "The gunpowder. It's pressed into the flagstones paving the great hall. We've been walking all over it. And the cows, too."

"And Lord Shaftoe," Kitty added. There were no inflections in her voice. She continued to stare at the opened scroll she held in her hand. The writing was in Irish, but the script was difficult to read, a superseded penmanship that seemed, at first, to require a Rosetta stone before it could be deciphered. Gradually, however, the letters showed themselves to have equivalents to the handwriting strictly imposed by Sister Clothilde in the first grade. Clusters of letters became recognizable words, and an understanding of the words began to seep into the necessary recesses of her brain. The drawings, however, were crude sketches resistant to interpretation. Convinced that if she stared at them long enough they would yield their meaning, Kitty fixed her eyes on the page, trying her best not to blink. Finally she began to comprehend. There were instructions for the laying of the flagstones, telling as well that all precautions must be taken not to bring them into contact with any element that might cause a premature explosion, meaning, of course, fire. Also listed were the names of what must have been the servants attached to the castle. They were to find pretexts—work elsewhere, visits to a sick relative—any excuse not to be present when the gunpowder was scheduled to go off. Only the newly arrived Lord Shaftoe himself was to be present, the man come at the behest of the Crown to inflict the most rigorous "coercions" on the people of the countryside who had demonstrated a decided unwillingness to be evicted or flogged or starved at the Crown's discretion.

Kitty's efforts to make sense of the drawings were interrupted by Kieran. "Of course we needn't worry. With all the damp and all the time gone by, the gunpowder is of no use to anyone now. Except as flagstones for the floor."

Kitty gave up on the squiggles. "Can we be so sure?"

"It's been over two hundred years. And don't forget: after just a few weeks Guy Fawkes's gunpowder was said to be worthless even if he didn't know it. The elements separate in almost no time at all. He couldn't have blown up Parliament no matter what. All we have now are flagstones. Nothing more."

"There were nearly two hundred years between the time of Guy Fawkes and when the flagstones were laid. Have you forgotten? No advances of civilization can keep up with the 'improvements' when it comes to ordinance and the ways of destruction. Surely Mr. Fawkes's difficulties would have been solved in the centuries between."

Kieran shrugged. "We can give it a try, if that will make

you any happier. If we blow ourselves to kingdom come we'll at least know it hasn't lost its zing—"

"No one says we have to set the whole place going. Wouldn't just a piece, a little bit, a chunk tell us what we need to know?"

"I guess we can always give it a try."

"Fine with me."

After getting the cow and the pig through the breach in the wall—a task not without its frustrations—after taking off a small chunk of flagstone from the great hall and taking it across and down the road to a distant rocky pasture, a fire was built, and Kieran, from a distance, tossed the stone chip into the blaze. They stepped farther back. Nothing happened. They waited. Still nothing. Apparently Kitty had been too generous in her appraisal of civilization's advance.

When they'd gone back across the road and were almost to the courtyard sheds a loud sound was heard as if someone were exploding huge kernels of popcorn. They looked first at each other, eye to eye, then looked back at the field. Some of the flaming wood was still falling eastward, accompanied by sparks and embers sifting down through the air. Brid was there, staring up at the falling debris, holding out her hands to catch some piece of shattered stone—as if she were seeing snow for the first time and was dazzled with disbelief at its wonders. Taddy, also stunned with wonder, surveyed the ground around, numbering, it seemed, each fragment of what had been until now an impregnable rock.

Quickly, but not too quickly, Kitty and Kieran went back to the field, and gazed, mouths agape, at the ruined bonfire, at the scattered bits of splintered timber still burning among the sundered stones. Slowly they moved to the fire. It took them both quite a while to stomp out all that was left of the blaze, Kieran ruining his boots, Kitty sacrificing a pair of melting sneakers.

Both Taddy and Brid were watching, with their eyes no longer mournful but wide with what seemed expectation, but worried at the same time that disappointment was possible. To Kieran it seemed a fragile plea, to Kitty a hope tempered by the fear that it was not to be realized.

"Now," Kitty whispered as if the stones had ears, "now we can do what has to be done."

"We can do nothing of the kind. Don't even think it."

"And we just let them be hanged?"

"They've *been* hanged."

"Yes. And they'll be hanged again and again and again until—"

"No! It's not our castle anymore. Or it soon won't be. If you want to blow up a castle, go buy yourself another one and I'll help you send it any direction you say. Up, down, sideways. You name it. But not this one."

"But you see them there, now—"

"Yes, I see them. And I want them gone—" he paused, then said quietly—"even if I don't want them gone."

"What—what does that mean?"

"I don't know what it means. I can't answer. But to be without them—" Kieran stopped.

Peter McCloskey had come into the field. He came close to the extinguished fire and looked down. Kitty managed to take her eyes off her husband. She looked from Peter to Brid, from Peter to Taddy. Peter bent down and picked up a small remnant of the blasted rock. He turned it over in his hand. "I heard a noise," he said. "I hope you don't mind I came to see."

He continued to stare at the fragment, still turning it. As if in response to a sound only he could hear, he raised his head and looked past Taddy and Brid, at the clump of heather not far behind them. Twice he blinked, then turned his attention back to the stone.

"You see them, don't you," said Kitty, her voice again in a whisper.

"See who?" Peter looked up and stared at the heather.

"Brid," said Kitty, "and Taddy. There. Near where you're looking."

"They're here, then?" He, too, whispered.

Kieran shuffled his ruined boots against the newly created pebbles beneath his feet. "And you can't see them?"

"How can I do that? You're the only ones." At that, Taddy raised his hand as if making a pledge or swearing an oath and then was seen no more. Brid stretched out a hand toward Kieran, then she, too, vanished.

"They're gone." Kieran's voice was low, even sad.

"But," said Kitty to Peter, "you didn't see them?"

Peter had resumed turning the stone, twisting his wrist as he held it between his thumb and forefinger. "No one sees them, only you. What reason would I have to see them?"

"What reason do we have?" Kitty still found it difficult to speak above a whisper.

"You'd have to ask my mother."

"I did ask her," said Kitty. "She had only some foolish theory and said she didn't really know."

"Oh. Well. Maybe she knows now."

"What makes you say that?"

"Because she told me just a little while ago that she knew now where the gunpowder is. It had come to her just then."

Kieran glanced first at this wife, then at the boy. "And where did she say it is?"

"Where you got the little chunk you just blew up. The flagstones of the great hall."

"How did she find that out?"

"She doesn't know. Except she mentioned maybe a door opened and there it was. Or maybe the lid lifting from something. And the secret was there. Or else she thought it might have been her great aunt who told her when she was little and she'd forgotten. She said she couldn't be all that sure. And after she said that, she started to make some muffins, but stopped right there in the middle and—" No longer was he turning the stone.

"Yes? And then—" Kitty leaned forward, afraid she might not hear what was about to be said.

"You would have to ask her."

"But she told you something. Tell us," Kieran said, moving the toe of his ruined boot in among the ashes, stirring the blackened wood, the broken stones.

"I can, but I don't want to."

"Why?" Kitty asked.

"Because you won't want to hear it."

"But we do!" Kitty was no longer whispering.

"You think you do. But you don't."

Kieran picked up a stone from among the ashes. It was hot. He let it drop. "Then tell us anyway."

"I wish you'd ask my mother."

"Please," said Kitty. "Tell us."

Head bowed, Peter said, "My mother told me you see Taddy and Brid—and you're the only ones—because it was a Katie McCloud and a Kevin Sweeney who were the ones supposed to set off the gunpowder all that long time ago. And Kevin then looked just like Mr. Sweeney now. And Katie then looked like you, Mrs. Sweeney."

"McCloud." Kitty had returned to her whisperings.

"McCloud," said Peter. "Brid and Taddy recognized you. They think you've finally come to blow up the castle. They don't have the same sense of time we have, my mother said. They're dependent on you to do it. They're waiting."

"It's a Sweeney who—" Kieran brought his right hand up to his chest and from there up further until it disappeared under his beard, possibly to hide the hand but more likely to feel his throat.

Kitty gave her head a slight shake. "A McCloud never—" she turned away, making the sheds of the courtyard her main concern as if her most pressing task were to reach some decision as to their repairs.

With the toe of his shoe, Peter separated a chunk of charred wood from a bit of stone. A chickadee had come into a tree in the orchard nearby and was offering its two-note song in a plaintive minor key. Almost immediately, two notes in the distance answered the call, but at a lower pitch. Without looking up, Peter said, "My mother wondered if she'd heard this from her great-grandfather on her mother's side and only remembered now, or if it's something she never knew before, but knows it now. Then she said it's something she never knew before, but a truth given to her whether she wanted it or not."

Kitty's right hand grabbed her left elbow, immobilizing her arm, unable as she was to decide what she was supposed to do with it. "A McCloud would never have allowed someone to hang, much less not do what she'd sworn to do." Her words were clipped and certain.

Kieran kept shaking his head. "How could a Sweeney—a *Sweeney*—betray—or not confess instead of letting two innocent—" He narrowed his eyes in pain and seemed to be directing his questions to some fuchsia growing among the hedge stones along the road leading to the castle. "It can't be true. It can't possibly be—" He turned to Peter. "With all respect, your mother's up to a mischief, telling you things like that."

Kitty said nothing, but released her elbow and let her hand slide down her arm where it took firm hold of her wrist.

"It's not a mischief." Peter continued to regard the bit of stone as if more curious about its properties than certain of its meanings. "It's a truth. And she never asks anyone to believe her or not believe her. And I'm the same. You needn't believe what I've said. Believing or not believing isn't what makes the truth the truth." He was still staring down at the fragment but not moving it. "If it would make it any better for you, they didn't do it on purpose, Katie and Kevin. They were to be married, and they'd gone off to Tralee to let Katie's uncles and Kevin's cousins living there and along the way know that they must come to the wedding. And they had to walk both there and back because there was no other way in those days. Katie stayed the nights with her uncles and aunts and Kevin with his cousins, but each evening they were together with one family or the other for something to eat and a bit to drink as well. And no one but the man from Cork who'd laid the flagstone floor knew they were the ones to finish the job, and his name was not even known to them. But the rumor about the gunpowder was already started, only it was a rumor that proved to be true—with those who started it not even thinking it was the truth they were telling, but said it only to frighten off Lord Shaftoe already on his way. And when they—Katie and Kevin—had come back home, it was already too late. Taddy and Brid had been hanged and nothing to be done. Katie turned on Kevin and Kevin put the blame on Katie and they never married, too guilty even to look at each other ever again. And so the feud began, but no one was told the cause of it, everyone making up a story, even Katie and Kevin. About priests betrayed long, long ago, she saying it was a Sweeney did it; he saying it was a McCloud. It was betrayal that was on their souls, and it was of that that they must speak, a story with a bit of the truth at the heart of it. The betrayal. The guilt. And each giving the fault to the other."

Kitty, her mouth already open, had to close it and open it again before she could say, "Your mother—did she say who might have told her this so long ago and now—remembered at last—"

"Oh, no." Peter, his eyes still sad from the things he'd said, looked at Kitty. "None of this last part my mother said nor did anyone say it to her. Nor did anyone say it to me. It's only something I know, standing here, and you said you wanted to hear it."

Kieran, too, was looking at the boy. "You made all this up? Just now?"

"None of it did I make up. How could I think of these things and I only seven?"

"You've heard stories all your life."

"This one I never heard. But I know it for a truth, and it doesn't need to be believed to be true. But now you know why you're the only ones see Brid. You're the only ones see Taddy. They show themselves to you because they've been waiting for your coming. And they never blamed you because they knew you didn't do it on purpose. Let them hang, I mean. And now you're here, and they're here, too. And there's no more that I can tell you."

Again the chickadees called and answered, again Kieran could look only at the fuchsia bursting from the hedge. Kitty let go of her wrist and brought both hands, folded as if in prayer, up to her lips. Peter held his bit of stone out over the extinguished fire and let it drop. Then, with his shoe, he covered it with ashes.

11

At Lolly's, the pigs swirled around Kitty, Kieran, and Aaron, each determined to squeal the loudest, with no clear winner apparent. Also undecided was whether their voices were raised in protest at being considered for roasting on a spit or if each was begging to be a candidate for the honor. Objectivity was obviously required of those making the choice. Abilities other than vocal range and interpretive passion would determine which would be elevated from among the chorus and given the starring role. It was not an easy task.

Aaron had, on the evidence, proved himself to be a swineherd of considerable talent. (Kitty preferred to doubt that the same could be said for her lifelong friend's—Lolly's—yet-to-be-demonstrated skills as a writer.) All the pigs were grossly fat, and each seemed to be in excellent health, especially when it came to lung power and the ability to riot, stampede, and trample one another while Aaron and Kieran and Kitty waded among them.

Although the great feast was still some while away, it was advised that the selection be made now since the chosen pig would be taken from the fattened specimens destined for delivery into the slaughterer's hands within the next few days. Kieran had already built a pen for it near the castle sheds to prevent the resident animal from emptying both troughs and reducing the selected hog to an anorexic state unworthy of being roasted on a spit. It would also limit the devastations inflicted on the castle grounds, since it already had been decided not to replace the snout ring of the current pig, letting the damage become a notable part of his lordship's inheritance. And it was further decided that it would be unfair to leave one pig unencumbered and not the other. It was bad enough that the chosen beast would be led to the sacrifice and its companion spared—and even more unfair that its snoutings would be confined to a pen and the other given the full range of the countryside for its inflictions. This minimal attempt to balance the already heavily tipped scales of justice was decreed by both Kitty and Kieran, allowing them their conviction that justice would prevail at the castle for the remainder of their stewardship.

Aaron slapped a few hams, not just to make a show of authority but to see if the favored animal could screech at an even higher pitch than the one already achieved. Lolly had been unable to join them, caught, as she claimed, in the middle of a metaphor. Surely Kitty, as a sister writer, must understand. And Kitty did. She knew only too well a writer's propensity for self-dramatization, self-absorption, and self-pity.

Because the general cacophony made discussion impossible, Aaron would point to a particular pig, Kieran at another, and Kitty at still a third. Each pig, in turn, responded by charging toward the periphery of the herd. Finally, after a protracted dumb show involving pointed fingers, head shakes, waved hands, nods—Aaron, Kieran, and Kitty each contributing his or her share to the confusion—three pigs were nominated for further scrutiny, and Aaron, by means both cruel and consoling, isolated them in another, smaller pen at some distance from the twelve-tone chorale still being lustily sent heavenward by their rejected brethren.

It had not been easy to bring Kitty and Kieran to this present exercise. Throughout the past week two issues had been discussed: one resolved, one not. First, there was the matter of the pig. Would it be the one already in their possession or one selected from Lolly and Aaron's herd? Kieran continued to prefer the pig he already knew, especially since it had been divested of its snout ring and was wreaking havoc throughout the landscape. (A new ring could be inserted or a proper pigpen devised, but Kitty had argued against both proposals since, according to her, she and her husband would soon leave behind them whatever damage the pig might cause. A durable fence around Kitty's garden was the one concession she allowed. The rest of the territory was open and available for any depredations the pig might wish to enjoy. Her reasoning had its source in the issue still unresolved: Kitty's determination to blow up the castle rather than let it fall into the tainted hands of George Noel Gordon Lord Shaftoe.)

By employing negotiating skills uncommon among those experiencing a two-as-one existence, a decision was reached, as regards the pig. During the exchange, each had had the instinctive wisdom to become cool when the other became heated, heated when the other became cool. Also, two competing methods of logic were brought into play, but each with enough flaws and inconsistencies to allow for eventual compromise.

Kitty's first argument had been delivered with some

intensity, since its basis was an accusation of ingratitude on Kieran's part: if it weren't for the pig and its unearthing of the skeleton of Declan Tovey in the garden of Kitty's sea-claimed house, she and her husband would never have been lured into the shenanigans that had led to a mutual dismissal of the ancient enmity between the McClouds and the Sweeneys—which, in turn, had allowed the eruption of a long-gathering passion, her for him, him for her, culminating in their marriage.

To occupy themselves during this exchange in the scullery, Kieran had been dicing homegrown green peppers while Kitty sliced onions for the meatloaf she had asked Kieran to make in place of the tarragon chicken with chili and tomato fondue. It would be from the recipe she had brought back from the Bronx. As they went about their arguments, it was lost on neither of them that each was wielding a well-honed knife.

Along with the meatloaf, Kitty had also requested mashed potatoes and peas, also homegrown. The apples for apple brown betty—for which she'd also pleaded—were from their orchard, which, to their surprise, had flourished and presented them with a bountiful yield. Each was chosen by Kitty's own eye and picked by Kitty's own hand.

That his wife wanted an all-American dinner was easily understood by Kieran. It happened from time to time, an exercise in nostalgia on Kitty's part in tribute to her days at Fordham, when her somewhat intense nationalism was nurtured, if not born, out of simple homesickness for the cliffs and stones of Kerry. Previous to her American sojourn, she had paid little or no attention to her homeland's history beyond an easy subscription to a sense of victimhood whenever she felt herself in need of some pretext for an unfocused wrath that lurked just beneath the surface of her psyche—a wrath that required an airing from time to time, projected during her childhood toward her brothers or her father, her ungainly body, a recalcitrant fire in the fireplace, her hair, her teachers, and boys. The pride of place, of course, had been awarded to Kieran Sweeney, the devil's spawn, the earth's first scourge—and the complete embodiment of all she had ever wanted in a man.

But like so many Irish exiled to American shores, even temporarily, she quickly assumed an Irish nationalism informed by the past perfidies of the English, always available but, until then, in the Bronx, not really nourished to the point of the justifiable wrath she would take with her, along with her B.A. degree (having majored in moral theology), back to Kerry, where there awaited her all the previous instigations to outrage. One exception was the ungainly body, which had now shaped itself into a perfection even Kitty herself had to admit was quite stunning. There still remained, however, her sense of injustices long since inflicted. That most had been remedied during the intervening years did nothing to suggest that she might exorcise these persisting demons from her well-satisfied psyche. Her scalp still tightened with a determined righteousness. Was she or was she not Caitlin Kitty McCloud?

Owning a castle in County Kerry did little to assuage her wrath or lessen her sense of superiority. Losing a castle in County Kerry did much to pitch both wrath and exaltation to an even higher intensity, especially since the past, in the guise of ghosts, had come to dwell not only in her home but, in the case of Taddy, in her heart. And the intrusion of his lordship must be credited with this current instigation to mayhem and to murder.

Her American adventure, with its attendant enticement to patriotism, was inspired as much by the absence of home as by the provable facts that spilled out of any book devoted to the history of the ravaged land to which she had been born. Long had she yearned for a pretext—here called conversion—for mayhem. Long had she awaited a justification for murder. Now both were there for the taking, a consummation perfidiously to be wished.

The onion had brought tears to Kitty's eyes. She ignored them so as not to disrupt her brief on the resident pig's behalf. Since Kieran had offered no rebuttal to his wife's first argument, she continued on to the next. "And didn't it find the gunpowder for us? When the cow put its hoofs right on it, didn't it screech so you could bring the chest to the light of day, and didn't it dig that hole in the first place?"

"I'm not so sure," Kieran said, almost dicing the tip of his thumb into the mound of cut peppers. "I'm not so sure it did us any favors, thank you very much. Except now we can warn Mr. Shaftoe before he puts fireplaces in the great hall and sends with a single spark the whole household over into County Cavan."

"We'll tell Mr. Shaftoe nothing. He can take his chances the same as we did. Except there'll be no castle for him to take his chances in."

"We are not going to blow up the castle."

"*I* am going to blow up the castle."

"*You* are not going to blow up anything. Nor is anyone else."

"Then I'm supposed to hand it over to his Lordship without a fight."

"There's been a fight, and it's over. It was fought in the courts, and you lost."

"I only lost a battle, not the—"

"Not only is the castle not going to be blown up, but the gunpowder is going to be removed and destroyed."

"And let Taddy and Brid hang there and nothing be done about it."

"Taddy and Brid are not hanging. Their ghosts are hanging."

"Their ghosts are part of them. They're hanging."

"Ghosts have no body. You can't feel without a body."

"They feel."

"They don't."

"How do you know?"

"It's common sense."

"We're talking about ghosts—and you mention 'common sense'? God have mercy!" Kitty cried.

"And what makes you so sure blowing up the joint will do whatever it is they want? Whatever it is they need?"

"Peter McCloskey told me."

"A boy of what—nine?"

"Seven. But he knows. And he told me."

"And you believe what a seven-year-old tells you?"

"Peter's different. You know that."

"Everybody's different."

"Lord Shaftoe will never live in this castle."

"Then blow up Lord Shaftoe, why don't you?"

"All right, then, I will. Along with the castle. Both at the same time."

"I give up."

"Good."

"The castle is not—Oh, never mind. And you're chopping the onions too fine."

"I was distracted."

Kieran scraped the knife blade along the chopping block, drawing into the bowl the onion and green peppers. Kitty, with the knuckle of her forefinger, wiped the tears from her eyes. Kieran began adding the other ingredients to the mix, following the Bronx recipe; the ground beef, the eggs, a bit of milk, the Dijon mustard. Kitty started chopping the parsley. The tears returned. Again she wiped them away with her knuckle, careful not to slit her eye with the knife still held in her hand. And again the tears came. And her nose began to run. She sniffed. Then she sniffed again.

"I can't blow up the castle," she said.

Kieran stopped grinding the peppercorns but said nothing.

"How can I do that? Look around. The stones. The walls. The turret. The gallery. The stair, winding. The battlements where you look out toward the sea—"

Kieran handed her a paper towel. She blew her nose, then handed the towel back. Kieran let it drop to the floor. "Those who built it," Kitty said, "How can I—"

Kieran handed her another paper towel. She wiped her eyes and blew her nose.

She let the towel drop to the floor. "Stone on stone. Each lifted, one on the other. On someone's back, held up by someone's hands. Down to the foundations deep in the—Look at the ceiling. The beams. A giant must have put them there. The labor. The sweat. The weariness, the exhaustion. The pain, the aches, the broken bones. The maimings. And still the stones, one on the other." She reached over and touched the wall next to the stove. "A man put this here. Who was he? What was his name? Cold in the night. The heat of the day. Rain. Mist. Wet. The hard earth. Stone upon stone—stone upon—"

Kitty herself ripped a towel away from the roll on the other side of the table. She blew her nose and started toward her eyes, hesitated, then wiped away her tears with the crumpled paper. Again she let it fall to the floor. She sniffed. "The castle was here long before any Shaftoe. And it will stand long after all the Shaftoes in all the history of all the world will have come and gone. Have no fear. Never will any harm come to this place. And Taddy and Brid, they must stay if that's what's been decreed. We can pray. And there's nothing more we can do."

She set down the knife and, with both her fists, dug deep into her eyes and rubbed the remaining tears into her flesh, through to the brain if she could. When she'd finished she turned away so her husband wouldn't see her bloated face. She considered gathering up the crumpled towels but thought the hell with it. She turned back toward Kieran. He was her husband and he had a right to see her red and puffy. "What can I do next? Any more chopping? I'm still in the mood."

Kieran pushed the bowl across the table. "Everything's there. Are your hands clean?"

Kitty held up her hands. Kieran regarded them for a moment. "Squoosh it all together then. Next you can start on the apples. I have to go for the cows."

"We'll do without the apple brown betty I was going to make for dessert," Kitty said quietly. "I'll go with you for the cows."

Kieran nodded. He waited a moment. "Brid will miss them after we take them to my brother's."

Kitty considered this, then she, too, nodded. "And Taddy the pig, all eaten up and gone for good."

Kieran examined the wall to his right, taking particular care to scrutinize the rough surface of the stone slightly above his own height. "The pig will come with us. We'll eat another. If Taddy wants, he can come visit from time to time. If it's allowed."

Kitty gave this some thought. "And Brid to see the cows." Now both gave this their consideration, neither sure exactly what his or her preference might be.

Two of the three pigs in the isolated pen searched with their snouts for some small morsel that might mitigate their removal from the general herd. The third simply stood. Aaron, Kitty, and Kieran made their observations from the other side of the fence, the better to regard the animals with an eye for their succulence rather than whatever other endearing qualities a pig might possess. Since each resembled an enormous sausage stuffed inside a skin close to bursting, the choice was not easy.

"I think that one." Kitty pointed to the one not searching for still more food.

"What about over there?" Kieran's election fell upon one of the snufflers that had now raised its head and pinned back its ears.

Then it was Aaron's turn. For the sake of consistency, he chose the one remaining, possibly so as not to hurt its feelings. "Look at that one's hams" was the best he could do to state his case—a case not supported by any overwhelming bit of evidence: each pig had enviable hams.

All three continued to observe his or her own preference, ignoring the other animals, thinking only of ways to substantiate a claim they were not yet ready to renounce. To complete the impending stalemate it needed only the intrusion of a mischievous god to toss an overripe apple into the pen addressed to "the tastiest."

Lolly came onto the scene, having abandoned her metaphor to offer an opinion. She pushed the sleeves of the black cotton turtleneck above her elbows. (As a writer she now wore black almost exclusively.)

"Are these the first rejects? Someone has a pretty good eye. Let's go take a look at what the possibilities still are."

"These," said Kitty, "are the chosen ones. We're about to make the final selection."

"Oh."

"They look pretty good to me." Aaron made slits of his eyes, demonstrating his method of scrutiny.

"They're all pigs," Kitty said. She pointed again at her preference. "Why don't we just take that one and forget the rest?"

Lolly, the writer, without reference to the subject at hand, directed the conversation to more crucial matters. "I need your help," she said to Kitty. "No, not your help. Just your advice. I didn't want to tell you until I'd finished, but my novel is about this couple—he's very handsome, she's a real knockout—and they marry and—can you believe this?—they move into this castle."

Kitty stiffened. Kieran relaxed every muscle in his face, the better to lower his head and look directly at Lolly. "And to make it interesting, the castle has ghosts—I guess you can tell where I got that idea from—the way everyone always said the castle there had these ghosts." She smiled nervously, her cheeks twitching slightly. "Write what you know. Isn't that what you're supposed to do? Anyway, what has to be done to—and I really like this part—what has to be done to get rid of the ghosts and lift the curse from the castle is to blow it up. How's that for a surprise bit of plotting?"

Now Kitty, too, relaxed her face and cast a gaze of determined indifference at her friend. "How can you say you lifted a curse from a castle that no longer exists?"

"But it does exist. Until it blows up. And when it does, well, the curse is ended. The ghosts will be gone. And they'll stop terrorizing the neighborhood. And blowing up a castle will make a good ending, don't you think?"

"I don't know," said Kitty. "Sounds a bit far-fetched to me."

"You mean blowing up the castle?"

"I mean the whole thing."

"Well, it's too late now. I'm on page five hundred and eighty-two."

"It would seem, then, that you don't need advice from anyone."

"But how do I blow up a castle?"

"That's hardly within my competence," said Kitty.

"Oh, but I forgot to tell you. You know that part of the story, the same as everyone does: there's gunpowder already planted in the castle."

Kieran spoke, a slight drawl having come into his voice. "Then that's the way you blow up the castle. With the gunpowder. Simple. End of novel."

"But no one is sure there's really gunpowder. It's never been found."

"Then have someone find it," said Aaron, his impatience

becoming more and more evident. Somehow, since his defection from the art of fiction, his interest in the subject had noticeably diminished. "It's a ghost story. The ghosts find it."

"I thought of that, but—"

"Well," said Kitty, "keep thinking. You'll come up with something that will amaze us all, I'm sure."

"You think so?"

Never had Kitty seen her lifelong friend so undecided. A want of certainty was not one of Lolly's prominent characteristics, any more than it had ever been one of Kitty's.

For her, the art of writing was a simple extension of her inborn trust in herself. Her gifts, her skills, were apparent to her without the need of validation. Those unable to see them and appreciate them were blind—and never once did Kitty feel the least bit of sympathy for their inability to discern self-evident truths. (Her usual impulse was to gouge out the vile jelly of their unseeing eyes.)

The one consolation Kitty could summon was that Lolly's lack of self-confidence must be the proof she'd been waiting for, expecting—nay, *demanding*—that poor Lolly, for all of Kitty's love for her, for all her good wishes and thoughts on her friend's behalf, was not a true artist. For Kitty, in the bright lexicon of art, there was no such word as *fear*. Too many risks had to be taken, too many doubts resolved. And *that* was yet one more of Kitty's certainties.

For now, she must devise ways to console her friend's disappointment without revealing the soul-felt glee with which she greeted this calamity so deservedly befallen her niece-in-law. A way must be found to say the obvious without saying it: Aaron must reclaim his computer. Lolly must accept again the fate for which she had been destined from the beginning of time: to be a simple swineherd. It was decreed by forces beyond anyone's control, and Kitty must help her friend in this acceptance. She—Kitty—would think of ways. Was she or was she not an artist, a creator of startling imagination? How fortunate was Lolly to have so faithful a friend.

Kitty relaxed. She was prepared to say whatever she felt Lolly needed to hear.

But her insincerities were postponed when Kieran said, "To find a way to blow up the castle, the woman is digging in her garden—"

"Not another skeleton!" cried Aaron in great alarm.

"No, not a skeleton," said Kitty. "That's been done to death—so to speak."

Kieran ignored the interruption. "The woman is digging, and her spade hits a metal box. Inside—"

Before Kieran could continue, Lolly said, "Sounds awfully contrived. A bit too 'convenient,' wouldn't you say?"

"All right then," Kieran said, "an animal—maybe even a pig—a pig digs it up—"

"Who would ever believe that?" Lolly sneered.

"You must *make* them believe it, by believing it yourself." Kitty pressed her lips together, parting them only so she could say, "And if you can't believe it, don't write it. Do you believe "The Three Little Pigs"? No? Well, I do. Because the writer believed it."

"Me? I should *believe* what I'm writing?"

"Lolly, either you're a writer or you're not a writer."

"But I *am* a writer. I'm on page five hundred and eighty-two."

Kieran charged ahead. "The gunpowder is compacted into the flagstones of the castle's great hall."

"Oh, I like that." Lolly looked off to the side as if to see whether or not she should believe what she'd just said.

Kitty licked her lips. "Darling," she said to Kieran, bringing into use a word absent until now from their connubial vocabulary, "I think we should let Lolly write her own novel. After all, she *is* a writer. And she *is* on page five hundred and eighty-two. As we all know, any writer worthy of the name can figure things out for herself."

"Is that true?" asked Lolly.

"As true as any word I've ever spoken." (Not for nothing had Kitty been schooled by Jesuits.)

"I have to do it all myself?" Lolly almost whined the words and drew her head back a little, believing perhaps she could still escape the blow about to fall.

Kitty felt it was now time to be unctuous. "You've heard of the loneliness of the writer. Well, then—" Kitty said no more. She wanted to give herself fully to the absurdity, the sentimentality of what she'd just quoted, the self-pity, the implied dramatization all too evident. If anything, writing was all too crowded, all those characters flinging themselves at her, screaming like pigs, both stuck and unstuck, demanding their deserved portion of the plot Kitty was preparing.

And then there were all those ideas, all those possibilities, each to be sorted out, some to be given more consideration than others, the competition fierce and unyielding, with Kitty the ultimate arbiter. Sooner or later, an infallibility beyond the aspirations of the most misguided pope was imposed, decisions made, judgments of life and death enforced, and, when all was finished, after all the crowding elements had been treated according to their deserts and the last page completed, then the true loneliness would come again. Her close and faithful companion, her book, would leave her. The one colleague who had gone with her everywhere, available for colloquy at any time of day or night—gone. And until she would invite into her imagination yet another clamoring mob, she would be subjected to the bereavements that justly mourned the loss of a true and most intimate friend who had given her the intensified life available only to a writer. Agonizing the writing might have been, despairing, sickening, and conducive to complaint, but *lonely?* Never. Never. Never.

"Well," said Lolly, "it does get rather lonesome. It's not like always having the pigs about."

"Ah," said Kitty. "The sacrifice!"

"You can say that again."

Kieran, to put the conversation back on track, said, "The gunpowder is in the flagstones. All you have to do is set it off."

"But how do I do that? And I mean, who sets it off? And how?"

"Kieran," Kitty said, smiling the smile of one whose patience is nearing its end, "aren't we here to pick up the pig?"

"Right!" Aaron thrust out his arm and pointed first to one pig, then another, no longer sure of his original choice. Lolly, however—Lolly the writer—was not yet prepared to let the priorities of the day reassert themselves. It was too soon for her to abandon her writer's prerogative of monopolizing an entire event and directing it toward whichever subject might, at the time, suit the writer's needs. "I know," she said, her voice gaining assurance. "I'll have the ghosts set it off. That should be interesting."

She paused. Kitty parted her lips, but the words were too

slow in coming. "Except," Lolly continued, "the ghosts, they can't make things move. I mean, how can a ghost, when he doesn't have a real body, make something go from here to there?"

Kitty closed her lips. She would let her husband say what he wanted to say. Was she not his good and amiable wife? And then the day's business of picking one bloody pig for a bloody roast on a bloody spit for their bloody party for their bloody neighbors could be resumed.

Now Kieran would have his say. "Then forget the ghosts," Kieran said. "The man and the woman set it off."

"Their own castle?"

"Don't they have any feelings about the ghosts wandering around for all eternity?" Kieran asked.

"Well, maybe sort of. But it *is* their castle. And I know, Kitty, you've lost yours to you-know-who. In that case, you could blow it up if you had ghosts. Except it would be a crime and you'd have to go to jail, I guess. But then, too, if I had someone like you-know-who—expect I don't have room to bring in anyone new like what's-his-name."

"Shaftoe," Kitty intoned, her voice flat, as if she were removing from the word the least trace of life, making of it a husk of a word, not a word itself.

"Right," said Lolly. "But I don't have any more room for new characters. Of course, I could cut the part where it turns out the woman, the wife, murders a former lover and buries him in her garden. Or maybe the flashback where the ancestors of the man—the husband—where they save their own skins by helping a priest get captured before he can get away to the Great Blasket. But I rather like those parts. And they help explain that the two newlyweds are really bloodthirsty beasts. No writer would give up material like that. What do you think?"

Kitty's answer was "I think I've stopped thinking."

Lolly shifted her gaze toward Aaron. "And what do you think? You were a writer."

"I think we should pick a pig. That one there, okay?"

"Well, I see I have to decide for myself. No help from anyone. Left alone. I have to get used to it. The loneliness. But that's the way it is. Don't trouble yourself about me. I'll do all right. Alone."

She started toward the dooryard but stopped, frozen in her tracks. She turned back. "I've got it! The man blows up the castle because his wicked wife has fallen in love with the young man, with the ghost. What do you think?"

She was greeted with stares from Kitty and Kieran. Only Aaron had an answer: "Yes. Yes. Fine. Do it that way. Now, that pig there—"

"Or maybe," said Lolly, "the wife does it because the selfish man has fallen in love with the girl ghost. Which do you think is better? Kitty? What do you think? Kieran? What do you—"

Aaron interrupted. "Lolly, my sweetheart, if you want to convince the reader that your main characters are idiots and morons instead of intelligent adults, go ahead. Fine. Falling in love with a ghost! Really! You should have a little more respect for your characters than that. But *you're* the writer. I'm just a swineherd. So do what you want, but don't say you weren't warned. If you want to reduce your characters to imbecility—"

"Aren't we here to pick a pig?" It was Kitty who interrupted, retaining the drained tone of voice she had decided would serve her best for the remainder of her visit. Kieran said nothing.

Grateful for the needed cue, Aaron said, "The pig! The pig! Yes, the pig!"

"But," said Lolly, "the castle—"

"No. The pig. The pig. Bring your truck round, Kieran," said Aaron. "We'll load this one. It's a little cross-eyed, but no one's going to eat the eyes. Your truck, Kieran, and you're on your way." He slapped the pig's rump to validate his selection. The pig made no sound, and neither did Kitty nor Kieran.

"All right, then," said Lolly. "Forget the novel. I'll figure it out for myself." She continued across the yard and slammed the door behind her.

For a long moment Kitty looked at Kieran, and Kieran looked at Kitty. Kitty lowered her head and studied the rough texture of the ground beneath her feet. When she looked up, Kieran's head was tilted to one side. He was still gazing at his wife. For another moment they looked only at each other, saying nothing. Aaron looked from Kitty to Kieran, from Kieran to Kitty, puzzled but still impatient. "Thank God, I never have to write another word."

Kieran drove the truck to the pig area, and, with no difficulty, he and Aaron persuaded the chosen pig to climb up the ramp and onto the bed of the truck. Kieran got behind the wheel. Kitty hoisted herself into the passenger side. The truck drove off. The pig, unaware of its privileged destiny, head and snout raised, sniffed the late afternoon air and found it sweet.

That evening, dinner was a bouillabaisse, asparagus vinaigrette, and an apricot tart washed down with several glasses of fresh milk. Kieran, after some exchange with Kitty about the chosen pig, finally said, "What about Lolly's novel?"

"Please," said Kitty, "not while I'm eating."

"That's not very helpful."

"Lolly should not be encouraged. Or discouraged. She has every right to disgrace herself, if that's what she wants. Let her do what she has to do. That's the first thing she has to learn. Write what you really want to write—and then take the consequences. There's no other way." She pressed the side of her fork through the tart, then speared a fair-sized piece and put it into her mouth.

With uncharacteristic reticence, Kieran took only small mouthfuls. Kitty finally asked, "What did you think?"

While he was giving undue regard to the morsel on his half-raised fork, Kieran said, "What do I know about writing?" He brought the fork closer to his mouth, then returned it to its previous position. "I—I'm inclined to agree with Aaron, though." He continued to concentrate on the tart. "Don't you?" He completed the gesture and began chewing.

"Agree about what?" Kitty, too, began to give more intimate attention to what she was about to eat. She was also taking smaller and smaller bits, chewing slower and slower.

"About the man and the woman. Loving the ghosts," said Kieran.

"Oh. That." Kitty's chewing allowed her not to elaborate.

"Yes. That."

After she'd swallowed, Kitty said, "I guess Aaron was right. The—the woman—and the man—they'd certainly be close to demented if they—if they—" She put another bit of tart into her mouth and again began the measured chewing, during which she was excused from further speech.

"—fell in love with ghosts." Kieran completed the sentence.

Without swallowing, Kitty, in midchew, said, but rather quietly, "Yes. Demented."

"Of course," said Kieran, "demented. They'd have to be to be." He put his fork down. "And for either of them to blow up the castle out of jealousy—"

"It makes no sense," said Kitty. "They . . . they'd have to be mad. Totally insane."

"Right. Crazy. Completely crazy."

After one quick glance at each other, they drained their glasses of the last of the milk. Dinner was over.

Kitty retreated to her computer so that her husband could do the washing up in a solitude similar to the one she sought in her turret room. Too unsettled by their discussion—and the quick glance—she would give the Tullivers, both Maggie and Tom, an evening free of her corrections and, instead, simply check her e-mail and, perhaps, ascend to the landing above and sit silently at the loom and think her thoughts.

Given the knowledge that she, Kitty McCloud, and her husband, Kieran Sweeney, were descended from the rightful candidates for the hanging, she hadn't been sure she wanted to show her face to either Brid or Taddy ever again. Still, since the time of that unwelcome revelation from Peter, she'd been anxious to see how she'd fare in their presence—and what form her responses to her newly found complicity in their fates might take. Would she even be able to bear the sight of them? Would she finally know the horror, the terror a ghostly presence was supposed to inspire? Would she plead for pardon? Would she debase herself in ways as yet unimagined? When the rending of garments had made a slight peep into her consciousness, she rallied herself and came to the only possible conclusion. *She* had not betrayed them, nor had her husband. They were guiltless. It was an accident of history that required neither from her nor from Kieran any accounting whatsoever. And if either Brid or Taddy made the slightest gesture or gave an accusing glance suggesting the opposite, she— And here Kitty stopped.

But now she had this new knowledge to contend with— or, rather, knowledge she already knew and now had been confirmed. She was in love with Taddy. Kieran was in love with Brid. And with a glance, each had let the other know. For the first time, Kitty considered that it was possibly their good fortune that they'd be leaving the castle, as devastating as that would be—a love lost—love for a ghost not least among their sorrows. Or their madness.

Her e-mail, usually an annoyance, would help her find some composure. These banal and irrelevant retrievals would possibly return to her the equanimity she had once possessed—before her ascendance into the glories and curses of Castle Kissane.

Kieran was spooning up the last of the bouillabaisse from the bottom of the cooking pot. Kitty came into the scullery with what looked like a computer printout in her hand. Never had she shared with him her work; never had she sought his advice, reaction, or response. But then, the events of the day might have had some adverse effect on her sense of being in control of her deeds and of her works. He would help her if he could.

Wordlessly, she handed him the page. Unmoving, she

waited while he read it. When he'd finished, he looked back at the sink a moment, then handed her the page. Each looked directly at the other, but again the glance was quick. Kitty turned and left the room. Kieran, after she had gone, ran his finger along the bottom of the pot and licked the last of the bouillabaisse. He shoved the pot down into the warm soapy water. The printout from Kitty's lawyer in Cork had informed them that the Shaftoe papers had been declared forgeries. The taxes had never been paid. His lordship had no claim to Castle Kissane. It belonged by decree of the court to Kieran Sweeney and his wife, Caitlin McCloud. Kieran released the pot. When it bobbed to the surface, he pushed it back down into the sudsy deep and held it there, the warm water wetting the rolled cuffs of his sleeves.

12

Fair was the day for the feasting. The field, a kilometer to the west of the castle, out of the shadow of Crohan Mountain, had been handsomely prepared. The chosen pig was spitted above the embered coals. The musicians' instruments were already in place at the far side of the wooden dance platform, the boards raised so that the slap and stomp of the dancers' feet would resonate and thrum beyond the percussive sounds that characterized the Kerry dances.

Guinness in kegs was at the ready and Tullamore Dew in abundance for those whose thirst was as much for rejoicing as for drink. Hot dogs and hamburgers had been suggested by Lolly, but the idea rejected for fear that, given such irresistible temptations, no one would eat the pig. Pizza, too, for the same reason, had been overruled. All the cabbages and all the potatoes in Kitty's garden were joined in pots of colcannon, the entire mess a product of Kieran's wizardry. Nettle soup—a specialty of Kitty's—was kept simmering, since the cold could come unannounced at any minute. Bread and butter were there in plenty, both of Kieran's devising—the butter, of course, from his very own herd before it had been carted off the day before yesterday to his brother Jack's near Blarney, as contracted before it was known the castle would not, after all, pass into the hands of Lord Shaftoe.

Apple brown betty, for which the orchard had been stripped, and tarts made from berries foraged from the road-sides—all were in readiness, eager to celebrate the castle's retention in Kerry hands. Coca-Cola had been included to placate the immature, after Lolly's suggestion of milk had been dismissed as too salubrious for the occasion.

Kieran would see to the pig. Kitty's job would be to mingle graciously and encourage one and all to further indulgence. Since the prosperous young Irish no longer took service jobs, to tend the food and drink young Americans had been hired—three men, one from Yale, one from Columbia, and one from Marquette—and three women—two from Bard and one from Barnard. As part of their recompense, they were encouraged to eat and drink their fill and consider themselves guests of the nation.

Kitty, not without effort, moved among her guests. She was determined no act of hers, no glance, no gesture, would betray the apprehension she felt about the climax she had prepared for the celebratory event. A certain unease had come over her earlier when she seemed to detect a certain distraction in Kieran's behavior. At first she suspected that he had suspicions regarding his wife's plottings. It then occurred to her that he, too, might have made plans not dissimilar to her own, but she dismissed the very idea. Never would he plot so drastic an act without first consulting and informing his beloved wife. The idea that she herself was capable of anything so unfair and he be exempt from an extravagance to rival her own began to formulate itself in her brain, but she dismissed the notion as an absurdity unworthy of her consid-

eration. Kieran could never—she refused to complete the
thought. Twice it reasserted itself. Twice it was forbidden
completion—each time with greater vehemence.

She'd given a particular welcome to Maude McCloskey
and thanked her again for the service her son, Peter, had performed the night before, working the spit, adding more fuel to
the fire when needed, and making sure no one came early to
sample the roasting animal. It hadn't eased Kitty's discomfort
that the Hag herself had seemed a bit agitated and had kept
looking off into the distance, in the direction of the castle.
The afternoon sun was achieving its usual alchemy, changing
the blackened castle stones to a ruddy gold—a revelation of
the castle's true glory that, even as it thrilled her, had sent a
pervading sorrow deep into the recesses of her heart.

Maude, too, had taken note of the castle's transformation,
her gaze impassive, indifferent to the sun-revealed splendors
but somehow interested nevertheless. Kitty refrained from
comment and decided as well to ask no questions. It wasn't
that she had no interest in the Hag's thoughts and possible
knowledge. Far from it: she was most interested but was particularly eager that she, Kitty, not be told what she already
knew—that the castle would blow up before the feast was
over.

Whether the Hag knew it or not, Kitty couldn't tell. But
the woman knew something, and Kitty preferred for once not
to know what it might be. The words must never be spoken.
No one, not even Kitty, must hear articulated the devastation
and liberation that would soon make the earth shudder and
tremble, the air to rain ashes and the sky to brighten as if the
sun itself had burst in one last display of power and majesty.

Only with a great and almost unbearable effort could

Kitty keep herself from reviewing in her mind the device she'd employed, its intricacies, its placement, the minute details so cleverly worked out to guarantee that all that she had decreed would come to pass. The Hag, she suspected, would know her thoughts—and, quite possibly, she already did. But so far she'd made no reference to the castle or its fate or to Kitty's part in the fulfillment of its destiny. And Kitty had managed, as far as she knew, to empty her head of any and all thoughts as to what would soon be accomplished.

Now, however, seeing the great gilded stones rising beyond the hill, she felt her resolve failing, her adamant pro-scription of all thoughts concerning the castle being sub-verted by the glory of what she saw. How could she let this resplendence be no more? Her answer had been rehearsed over and over, her reasonings, her motives, examined from any and every angle she could possibly imagine.

She had found a motive of her own. She must set Taddy free. She loved him. That he had no flesh, no body that she could touch had long since ceased to matter. Her yearning was enough.

It was not to free herself from this madness that the castle must be sacrificed. Kitty had other reasons, and she must stop—now—looking at the turret and the transfigured battle-ment. It was none of the Hag's business to know so much. And Kitty must not take the risk of communicating, by what-ever means, the true and irreversible motive for her action by thinking it in the Hag's presence.

To reinforce her resolve she deliberately turned away from the castle and took in a view of the gathering crowd. She would excuse herself from Maude, graciously reminding the Seer that her duties required her to give her attentions to as many of her guests as possible. And besides, Maude, now reviewing the crowd herself, seemed ready to move on to other concerns and considerations. It did nothing, however, for Kitty's redirected concentration to hear the woman say, "You mustn't neglect your other guests, enjoyable as I do find your company. *Most* enjoyable, I assure you."

"Too kind," said Kitty, smiling her sculpted smile. The woman knew every thought that had gone through Kitty's head. Maude was aware of the entire plot. What she would do about it was anyone's guess. Kitty considered asking her outright: Do you know what's going to happen? And then, more disconcerted still, the other question: Do you know why? But she needed to persuade herself that the woman knew nothing, that her most secret thought—made in response to her most secret need—was still a secret and would remain one forever.

Thoughts, almost as much as words, could be dangerous. They could migrate, unspoken, from one person to the next. The Hag merely represented an intensification of a known phenomenon; by some synaptic idiosyncrasy, some impulse of an as-yet unexplained charge could jump from skull to skull—a thought let loose, eager, even insistent on effecting further connections, a kind of mating—all achieved without the knowledge or consent of either the transmitter or the recipient. With this privileged knowledge wandering around inside the Hag's head, the entire gathering could be made aware of Kitty's innermost secrets without a word spoken. The danger might be remote, but it was real. And Kitty could think of no defense against it this side of accusing the woman of thievery and demanding the return of her plans and her most intimate motives.

But, of course, no return was possible. By thinking her thoughts, Kitty herself had given them life, and whether they could grow and prosper and inseminate other minds was beyond her control. She had done what she had done; she was doing what she was doing; and she must be prepared to accept whatever penalties might be imposed.

The musicians—two fiddles, a pennywhistle, a bodhran, and a guitar—were playing, and the dancing had started, the steps choreographed generations before and lustily performed now by couples ranging from preteens through octogenarians, from the unbearably beautiful to the inordinately plain. Hair coloring went from black to white with in-between stops for blond, brown, carrot, tawny, and one purple. All shapes and sizes were represented, each made in God's image, suggesting that the deity, like his human brothers and sisters, preferred to offer more than one version of himself to the rest of the world. The continuing exchange of partners guaranteed that the plain would in turn dance with the handsome, the ample would hook arms with the scrawny, the stompings made in unison with the entire people gathered to celebrate the castle—Kitty's and Kieran's reassured gain of it proof, if proof were needed, that the town and the countryside around were flexible enough to find both gain and loss as sufficient cause for communal rejoicing. A christening or a funeral would do nicely; the arrival of a returned relative, the imminent departure of an emigrant son—each would bring together with equal ease, if not the fatted pig on a spit, at least enough musicians (one could be enough) to rouse the blood and render the feet helpless after the first two notes had been sounded.

Kitty, paired with Tim Tyson, accountant, wheeled and stomped and clapped her way through "Maggie in the

Wood"—Tim stern in his determination to prove his knowledge of all the age-old intricacies; Kitty near-forgetful more than once but quickly recovering so that no major collision took place.

When Kitty decided against the next dance, the polka "Bonnet Trimmed with Blue," Tim was handed over to Peg Fitzgerald, who had been waiting with some impatience for a defection so she could exercise her feet before they did a jig all their own on the periphery of the dance floor. From then on it was up to Kitty's nephew, Aaron, to uphold the McCloud reputation for being as superior at dancing as the McClouds invariably were at any other undertaking they might choose to favor with their prowess and skill.

Aaron, in preparation for the event, had been initiated by Lolly in the ways of the Kerry dances and had proved a pupil of stunning receptivity. Lolly suspected some genetic memory but wondered as well if her husband was yet another example of that breed that had flourished among the Danes and the Normans who, once arrived on Irish shores, became more Irish than the Irish—a historical phenomenon from which the English had exempted themselves in a somewhat ornery fashion.

The one moment, so far, of apprehension as to the success of the festivities came when both Kitty and Kieran, tending to the now perfectly roasted and unspitted pig, its full porcine length stretched out on a wide plank table, saw clambering over the stone wall at the far side of the field their very own resident pig, the one they had spared.

She realized immediately that pandemonium was at hand. The pig would disrupt the dancing, interfere with the storytelling, and create general havoc among the guests, begging for food, rooting up the turf, and doing whatever mischief was potential to its nature. Most likely the entire project would now become a pig-catching contest. No one Kitty knew would exempt himself or herself from the sport. This would be the remembered event, an addition to local lore, the day we all tried to capture the pig. The winner would be numbered among the great heroes of Kerry. The goat of Puck Fair at Killorglin would be replaced by a pig; the triumphs of Wolfe Tone, the feats of Cuchulain would now be diminished when compared to whoever would finally take hold of the pig and wrestle it to submission.

By rights, the job should be done by Aaron, now the designated pig person of the family, and, no doubt, he would give it a try. But who would be content to stand by and simply watch? Nor man nor woman, nor boy nor girl worthy of his or her birthright would forswear the chance to participate in the general chaos about to be unleashed by the pig. What Kitty and Kieran had to do—and without delay—was to deploy their forces to protect the tables of food and drink. They must not be overturned, upended, their contents sprawled onto the ground and mashed into the soil, the full energy of the feast now appropriated by the pig.

The first sign of what lay ahead was the pig's approach to the dancers, deflected by a boy of about ten, Bryan Kerwin, who jumped in front of it, clapped his hands, and yelled, "Suuueee! Suuueee!" Responding to this enticement, the pig galloped toward the *seanchaí* (the storyteller), its head lowered, preparing itself for a charge directly into the enthralled listeners. Now it was three boys slapping and shouting and stomping. "Suuueee! Suuueee!" Great cries of glee were interspersed among the shouts and assaults. Attracted by the promise of a riot, the four Tyson brothers set aside their Tullamore Dew and skipped and danced their merry way into the growing tumult.

Now even the dancers were defecting, rushing into the fray with all the energy the dancing had excited. The pig, no doubt to make sure the sport would be prolonged, began a zigzag race across the field in the direction of the roasted pig. Immediately a phalanx formed in front of the table, not to protect Kieran's greatest triumph, but to greet the animal and embroil themselves in what was quickly becoming the riot that everyone had hoped for, the mob further inflamed by its own yells, its own shoves and pushes, its own determination that no satisfaction this side of complete anarchy would be considered acceptable.

The pig had not yet reached the waiting contestants when a strange thing happened. The pig stopped. Three boys in hot pursuit went flying headfirst over the pig's now stilled body. Two more, plus a girl, stumbled and fell partly onto the pig and partly onto the first group of boys.

After a few more tumblings onto the heap, the mob, too, began to quiet down, with only a few random shouts insisting that the contest be resumed. But what was the triumph in capturing a quiescent pig?

With murmuring disappointment, the heap disentangled itself and completed the circle forming around the object of its bewilderment. Solidly the pig stood its ground, its head slightly raised, its ears strained backward. It was staring at the carcass, whose hams had already disappeared. When one of the Tysons slapped the staring pig on the rump, determined not to be deprived of the expected disorder, the pig made no response, neither a blink nor a twitch of the tail or the flick of the ears.

A few more shouts, a clap of the hands, a feeble "suuee," but to no avail. The chase was over. The pig had become completely uncooperative, just standing there, transfixed by the sight before it. It raised its head higher and let out a few small snorting sounds, taking from the air the scent of the roasted flesh of its own species. One more slap was tried. The pig remained intent. The festivities threatened to become a disappointment of major proportions, the participants without exception surly at this neutral outcome of the game in which they'd invested their full energies, their lifelong propensity for cacophony, and their congenital yearning for chaos—now all come to naught by an uncooperative pig. Low murmurings began; threats against the animal were being formulated. Soon the festivities would deteriorate into a sullen dissatisfaction far worse than the debacle threatened by the pig's arrival. Future chronicles of the present age would record a day of thwarted expectations, eviscerated hopes; a day when promised anarchy was left unfulfilled.

Kitty knew that a simple suggestion that the crowd disperse to its previous revels would do no good. She could dispense Tullamore Dew by the bucketful, but to no effect beyond an intensification of general complaint. She was tempted to offer a guarantee of rewards yet to come—without being in any way explicit—but thought it better not to invite speculation, much less a questioning she was most anxious to avoid.

Then was heard the beat of the bodhran accompanied soon by the pennywhistle, with the fiddles not far behind. The tune of the polka "I Know What Mary Wants" was readily discerned, and, led by Aaron and Lolly, the dancers made their way back to the wooden flooring provided for their slappings and stompings. The music grew more assertive, the notes themselves now dancing in the air. One of the Tysons—Tim, or was it Ted?—began singing in a tenor voice pure and clear as the water of a mountain stream. Other voices caught up the words and sent them out toward the hills and into the heavens above. Tullamore Dew was brought back into action and the nettle soup was served. Sean O'Sullivan took up again the recitation of his story and quickly lured to his hearing even more ears than he'd commanded before.

The first to disregard the pig's transfixion at the edge of the glowing pit was Peter, just arrived, having missed the revels that had, so far, provided a defining distinction to the day's doing. He held out a thick slice of gold-crusted bread onto which Kieran, with an attempt to renew the jollity enjoyed earlier, placed a juicy slab and said, "Tell me if you've ever tasted better, and I'll slay myself on the spot." The boy, in appreciation of his host's wit, giggled and said, "No need to do that, I'm sure."

Kieran laughed in this throat, giving Peter his own appreciation of the boy's highly sophisticated riposte. Immediately Peter bit off a chunk far in excess of his mouth's capacity and, while chewing and shoving in the overhanging meat, made some pleased murmurs that were accepted by Kieran as the honest statement that was his only true reward. Unable not to challenge his luck, he said, "Good, eh?"

"The greatest, I'll have to say."

Kieran contented himself with a nod, at which the boy smiled, managing at the same time to further swell his cheeks with an additional push of the meat that had as yet refused to enter his mouth. It was then that the *seanchaí* got his attention, and he wandered off to find out which story was being told. Kieran had slapped a chunk of sizzling pork between two pieces of his best bread and now began to chew with a gusto consistent with his own generous response to all the good things of this world, and a tribute to his own contribution to roasted pork's excellence. Never had he tasted better.

After a second chew, the motion of his jaw began to slow. Kitty had come to his side and was helping herself to an extravagant ration. Just as she was about to clamp down on her first bite, Kieran's hand stayed hers.

"What?" She made another attempt, but again her husband forced down her arm. "What?" she repeated.

"Look—the pig," he said.

"Look at it? I'm trying to eat it."

"No. The pig looking at the pig. See? It's cross-eyed." Kitty had taken advantage of Kieran's pointing off to the left and had taken a generous bite of her sandwich. Dutifully she looked at the pig looking at the pig. It was, indeed, cross-eyed. Her chewing slowed and then stopped completely. She was unable to swallow what she had already taken into her mouth, which, when she could speak, gave her words the garbled sound of someone with a mouthful of roasted pig. But Kieran understood them.

"That—that's the pig from Lolly and Aaron, the one we picked for the roasting." She had mumbled so no one could hear. She looked down at the sandwich in her hand, then slowly placed it on the planks near the carving knife. The food in her mouth was moved from one cheek to the other, her eyes making the same motion, appealing first to her left, then to her right, for a solution to a somewhat disturbing bit of information. She knew now which pig she was eating.

Accepting defeat she forced the passage of the food through her throat.

"The butcher from Killarney took the wrong pig," Kieran whispered. He, too, placed the remains of his sandwich on the plank, too stunned for his body to give a more demonstrative response. "I told them the pig in the pen." His voice was unable to rise above a hoarse whisper.

At this, Kitty almost succeeded in straightening herself from the crouch into which she had retreated. "The pig in—in the pen?"

"Of course, the pig in the pen."

"Oh."

Kieran scrutinized his wife, who had decided to search among the revelers for someone who might help her in her present predicament. "What do you mean, 'Oh'?"

"Nothing. Nothing."

"Nothing means nothing. Everything means something. And I want to know what it is." He was finding his voice. Her perplexity was fading; his suspicions were rising. When Kitty did no more than lick her lips, he said, "I definitely told them the pig in the pen. And now we see before us, live, the pig that was in the pen. Is there any explanation you might want to offer? If so, I would like very much to hear it."

"The—the pig in the pen was so restless—the one—the one in the pen, the one from Lolly's. And any minute it was going to be taken away and—" Kitty sounded as if she were pleading, a tone and pitch so seldom used she had to struggle to release the words—"and you know. . . ."

"I do know. And I want to know more."

"It kept pacing, like in the zoo. Back and forth. Back and forth. Like a panther. Except it's a pig. And—and the other pig—" she made the slightest nod in the direction of the diminishing pig on the table—"the other pig—our pig—was just standing there, watching. And this—this made the pig in the pen pace even faster. And it—it was going to—well, you know. So it was all going to be over with and done. For the pig in the pen. And I—I—I decided—I decided—"

"You decided to give the pig in the pen a few moments of freedom before the slaughter. And so there'd be no hassle between the two, the spectator pig—our pig—was put in the pen and the pig in the pen was allowed out. Am I right?"

"For—for just a little bit. Allowed out, I mean."

"How much of a little bit?"

"Well, I—I did get an idea, you know—about Tom in my novel. Tom Tulliver? It wouldn't take more than a minute to write it out before I'd forget. But—but—well, you know how it is. You get yourself involved and—"

"And they take the wrong pig. They take the pig in the pen. Our pig."

Before saying anything more, Kitty, trying to be lofty and casual at the same time, then elegant and dismissive, then straightforward and defiant, said, "Yes. They took the wrong pig. They took the pig in the pen." She returned her gaze to her guests. She looked out over their heads as if nothing in the whole wide world would ever again be of any concern to her, immune as she was to all things that might bring shame or blame onto her singular head.

After she'd satisfied herself that nothing within view required her attention, she looked at her husband with a bland stare that dared and, at the same time, begged him to say something. Anything. But before the hoped-for response was made, Peter came back, empty handed and wiping his mouth on the sleeve of his shirt. "You were right. That was the best pig I ever ate. It tasted like none I've ever had. Was it you, Mrs. Swee—I mean, was it you, Miss McCloud, did it?"

Kitty waved her right hand away, dismissing the very thought and demonstrating that any repentance was clearly not to be considered. "No, my husband. All the credit is his."

"Not *quite* all of it," Kieran said, his voice as dry as dust. "My wife deserves *some* of the credit." Kitty, with a slight movement of her shoulders that seemed to shake off her husband's words, returned to her previous examination of the air about six inches above the heads of her guests.

"Is it all right I have some more?" asked Peter.

Not without much difficulty, Kieran steeled himself and, not without hesitation, picked up the finely honed knife, the blade catching the quick glint from the embers in the pit.

He waved it near where the most recent slice had been cut, as if reluctant to make an incision. "Maybe," he said to Peter; "maybe you'd like to do it yourself. You *are* seven, you said."

Peter, thrilled at the idea of taking on an adult responsibility, took the knife and, with an expertise Kieran—even in his present condition—had to admire, quickly relieved the carcass of a considerable portion of its flank. Peter giggled as he placed the meat between the two pieces of bread, as if he had tickled the pig and was now providing the laughter unavailable to the animal itself. Still chewing his first bite, he asked, "Is Mr. Shaftoe coming here or just stopping at the castle?"

It was Kieran who answered. "I doubt if Mr. Shaftoe will put in an appearance either here or at the castle."

"But he should be there by now."

It was Kitty who spoke. "Now?"

"Unless he was just driving around." Peter took in another fair-sized chunk of his sandwich, too big to fit into his mouth. He pulled part of it free, held it in his hand and looked down at it, giving it the same degree of attention he had given the mucus chip and the bit of shattered stone. "I don't think he should go into the castle," Peter said between munchings. "I yelled after him about the gunpowder and the ghosts, but maybe he didn't hear. Should someone go tell him?" With that, he put the scrutinized bit of meat into his mouth.

Kitty had already waded in among the guests before Kieran, who had stopped at the dance floor and told Aaron to take care of the carving, caught up with her. He didn't bother looking at his wife. "Are you going to the castle?"

"Nothing for you to worry about. It—it's just he's not supposed to be there. He—he's trespassing. And I won't have it. I'll be right back."

"No, it's all right. I'll go too. He might—he might be more—cooperative if I'm there as well."

Now they were pushing their way through the guests, returning quick nods and fake smiles as they were showered with comments about the food, the music, the dancing, whatever polite things they could quickly summon and offer to their speeding hosts. "It's all right," Kitty said to Kieran. "You're needed here. I'll go."

"Aaron's with the pig. I'll go."

"I told you. It's all right. *I'll* go."

They were at the pickup they'd parked just over the wall on the far side of the field. Kitty had her hand on the door first, but Kieran's was quickly clamped onto it.

"Please," said Kitty, "I'll only be a minute."

Their hands still on the unopened door, Kitty found herself staring into Kieran's eyes, and Kieran found himself staring into the eyes of Kitty. As they held their gaze, Kitty let her mouth open slightly, and Kieran widened his eyes. For one more moment neither moved, each reading what could be seen in the eyes of the other, each allowing comprehension to make its way through whatever labyrinth that twisted and turned its way between an eye locked upon an eye and a consciousness not readily roused by the information being offered for its consideration. The connection was completed. Each knew what the other had done.

"Then we should both go," Kieran said quietly.

"It would seem so."

Kieran opened the door. Kitty ran around to the other side and got in. Her door was slammed before his.

"How long do you have before—before it happens?" Kieran asked.

"Until Brid begins to work on the loom. How long do you have?"

They were on the narrow road, the dust rising behind them. Twice they steered in and out of a ditch to avoid neighbors on their way to the feast. "Until Taddy picks up the harp."

Two more neighbors had to flatten themselves against the hedge as the pickup sped by. Both Kieran and Kitty sat in silence, their eyes on the road. A great calm had come over them. Imperceptibly, or so it might seem, the truck began to move not quite so fast. But that could surely not be the case. The clouds of dust rising behind them contradicted the very notion.

It was Kitty who spoke first. "It would be what he deserves."

"And Peter *did* warn him."

"And he's so bloody arrogant. You never saw him there, the way he strutted around the place, like the lord of the manor." She paused, then added, "Which, of course, he almost was, damn him to—" She stopped and let a quick exhaltaion complete the sentence.

After another moment, Kieran said, "We could turn around."

Kitty pursed, then unpursed her lips. "Yes, we could do that, couldn't we?"

"He *is* trespassing."

"Yes. Trespassing."

For whatever reason, they continued on until, up ahead, they saw Brendan Malloy and his cows moving leisurely along the road. It would do no good to honk the horn. There was nowhere for either the cows or Brendan to go. At his age— more than eighty—Brendan could hardly climb over the hedge that bordered the road, and the cows were far less agile than he. The pickup stopped. "Is this a sign we're allowed to go no farther?" Kieran asked.

"I don't believe in signs."

Kieran looked at the sky. Kitty, too, was searching just above the western horizon. Without one referring to the other, each got out and began making the climb over the stones and into the pasture to their left.

"Damn!" Kitty said. "Why can't we just leave him there?"

"We've got enough ghosts for one lifetime."

"Now I suppose we're going to get there just in time to fly sky high along with him."

"How much time do you have?"

"Brid comes to the loom not long before sunset. When Taddy picks up the harp."

They made a quick twist of their heads toward the west. The sun was a fair distance from the horizon but lowering fast. Without looking at his wife, Kieran said, "Don't talk."

They began to run, Kieran pacing himself so that he stayed two feet behind his wife. Whatever might prevail, he had no intention of leaving her behind.

But then again, if he out-ran her, he might dismantle her device before the fatal moment arrived. Trying to keep the urgency out of his voice, he asked, "How'd you find out how to do it?"

"The Internet. You?"

"A catalogue from Texas. Tells you how to blow up a whole town."

They ran toward the castle. His lordship's SUV was at the doors to the great hall. "When we see him, what do we tell him?" Kitty asked.

"To get out."

Kieran's breath was shortening, but Kitty seemed to be having no difficulty. Kieran explained to himself the difference in stamina by noting that the efforts not to overtake his wife had cost him more energy than an unfettered run would have required. Restraint, as always, exacted the larger toll.

Now they were nearing the shadow of the castle. Still they kept running. Perhaps Brendan and his cows had acted in their favor. Cutting across the fields at a diagonal from the road, the distance to the castle was geometrically diminished. The main road was at least a quarter kilometer from the castle, thereby guaranteeing that no airborne debris would inconvenience some unsuspecting wayfarer, including Brendan and his cows, when the plotted event would take place.

Past the hedge and across the courtyard they ran, both panting. Kitty flung back the door to the great hall and stepped over the threshold. Immediately she took a step back, her stiffened body slamming into her husband.

"What?" Kieran had hardly enough breath to gasp out the word.

Kitty stepped back into the great hall. "Don't you see?"

Kieran looked around the hall, then repeated the one word he seemed capable of speaking. "What?"

"You don't see? There?" She was looking upward, at the huge iron ring of the chandelier.

Kieran tilted his head toward the ceiling. He said nothing.

There, as before, effected by his lordship's presence in the castle, were the hanged bodies of Brid and Taddy, limp, their horrified faces—so fair and fine in life—now twisted and distorted by the quick pull of the searing rope, which thrusted their bulging eyes from their heads and their swollen blackened tongues from between their lovely lips.

"We have to cut them down," Kitty whispered.

Kieran shook his head. "They're ghosts. Even the rope is a ghost."

"But"—she touched her husband's shoulder—"should we just leave? Go back to the feast?"

Kieran slowly shook his head. "No time. We'd never get clear of the explosion."

"How can we leave them like this? With *him* here along with them? It's his being here has done this."

Kieran turned his head aside, away from the slowly turning bodies. "If he's responsible, then aren't we responsible, too?"

"We didn't do the hanging. It was his people did it."

"And it was our people should be in their place. If he's still guilty, so are we." He looked directly at his wife. "We can leave and let it happen—and Shaftoe be killed—or we can—"

Kitty quickly moved through the door opposite, Kieran following. Along the narrow passageway they went, up the stairs to the gallery, then to the steps that led to the turret, neither able to avoid glancing through the window toward the lowering sun.

"Maybe as long as Shaftoe's here," Kitty said, "they won't come to the loom or to the harp. Maybe we have until he leaves to do what we have to do."

"We can't be sure. Let's take not chances. They can be wherever they want to be when they want to be there. Keep moving."

They began their climb up the steep rise of the winding stair, Kieran leading. Kitty wanted to reach out and touch her husband to let him know she was near, that should there be some miscalculation that might bring a sudden end to all they were ever to know of each other, she was with him and she wanted no parting. As they passed through Kitty's room on the first landing, she refused to glance at the emptied desk, the space from which she'd removed the computer and the work she'd been doing. She could surrender her castle but not her manuscript.

By the time she had reached the next landing, Kieran was kneeling at the stool where the harp lay, reaching under and pulling apart what looked like a clumsy device a boy might have concocted to wake himself to serve at morning mass. The task achieved in seconds, he let his arms fall to his sides, each hand still holding its share of the disconnected circuitry. His panting breaths came more slowly.

Kitty hurried to the loom and bent down toward the treadle, where she wrestled with a device attached to its side. Quickly she began untwisting the bare wires that connected the apparatus to the wires leading down under the flagstones below. Some confusion, however, set in. She couldn't tell if she was separating the two wires or winding them more thoroughly together. Or was she doing both at the same time, twisting and untwisting? The two had to be torn apart. She was on her knees, fumbling. She needed more light. Kieran had been lucky. His work was done away from the loom, having the benefit of the slanting rays of the westering sun.

The wires continued to resist, no matter how hard she tried. She pulled to no avail. She considered trying to bite through with her teeth but knew she might lay bare the wires beneath their insulation, allowing them to connect with, to put it mildly, a devastating effect that would not be confined to the castle alone.

"You need some help?" Kieran had crouched down next to her and was watching over her shoulder.

"All I have to do is get the two wires apart."

"You don't seem to be having much luck. Here. Let me." He reached down, and Kitty, with a resigned snort, surrendered her handiwork to her husband. With very little effort, the two recalcitrant wires were bent to his will and promptly flew apart. He offered the remains to his wife. "You need glasses."

"I don't need glasses."

"I know the type. Rather blow up than wear them."

"Not true." Kitty grabbed the device from her husband's hands. Kieran returned to the harp and retrieved his own implement. He looked at it a moment, then set it down underneath the stool. Taking her cue from her husband, Kitty, after straightening one of the wires, placed her contraption between the loom and the wall.

"You were doing it to get rid of Brid?" asked Kieran quietly.

Kitty dropped the wire still held in her hand. "Sometimes I thought it was to give them both peace. How can I forget they died instead of my ancestor? And please, don't tell me I shouldn't feel any guilt, that it wasn't my doing. It was a McCloud's doing and I am a McCloud and nothing can change that." After she had run her hand along the breast beam of the loom, her voice low, she said, "Other times it's to get even with Taddy. Because I'm jealous. His love for Brid." She paused, then added, "I wanted to kill him. And this was the only way I have to do it." She took her hand away and scratched her elbow. "And there could be more, but that's as much as I'm going to say."

Kieran sat on the stool and put the harp on his lap. "I want Taddy to be gone and I'd do what I had to do to send him away." He touched the harp with the tips of his fingers. "But I can't forget, seeing him hanging now in the great hall—I can't forget that my forebears were, even if unwittingly, culpable in their deaths. Maybe I have no right to feel this guilt, but what difference does that make? Right or not right, I feel it. The least I, a Sweeney, can do is send them to themselves where they can find rest." He placed his hand on the harp as if it were to the instrument itself that he was imparting his wish for peace. "Maybe there's more, but I've said enough."

A voice, unmistakably Peter's, was heard shouting outside. "Mr. Shaftoe! Up there! There on the turret! Listen to me! You have to leave! The sun is almost set. You have only minutes. And I can't stay here to tell you any more. Come down. Come away! You have nothing to do with what they've planned. Mr. Shaftoe—please!"

After a swift wide-eyed glance at each other, both Kitty and Kieran were on the stair leading to the battlement above. The trap door was hoisted by Kitty with no difficulty at all. There, standing near the parapet, was Lord Shaftoe, his tweed jacket removed and his tie thrown next to it. The top button of his shirt had been undone. With the appearance of Kitty and Kieran, he backed against the parapet wall. Kitty leaned out over the battlement. Peter was still looking upward. In the distance was the feasting, faint sounds of the music and laughter reaching her ears.

"It's all right, Peter. No danger. For the time being." Peter stared up at her, then turned and began to run toward the courtyard, toward the entrance to the great hall. Kieran was looking first at his Lordship, then at the clothing he had taken off. Kitty turned around, equally puzzled, letting her eyes trace the same path as her husband's.

His lordship stood erect, his arms at his sides, his face blank, as if he'd shed all feeling along with his jacket and his tie. A breeze flapped the open collar at his neck. "I didn't mean for this to disrupt your festivities. And I apologize. I am also not appareled for receiving company. For that I apologize as well. If you could just leave me here, I promise I'll be here no more when you return."

Kieran shook his head, trying to clear it. "And what are you doing here now?"

"Since you ask, I assume I'm obliged to answer." He waited, then went on: "I am going to jump. I'll be found—or, rather, my remains—will be found at the foot of the tower. To be disposed of in accordance with a letter to be found in my pocket there." He nodded toward the jacket. "And if you would excuse me, I would like very much to complete the task I've set myself."

"You—you're planning to jump?" Kitty, too, shook her head, an attempt, like her husband's, to rid it of its confusions.

"Perhaps I didn't make myself clear. Yes, I am going to jump. But, if you don't mind, I'd like it to be a private affair."

"Why jump?" Kieran brought his forehead lower, an attempt to better focus his eyes.

"The purpose would seem to be quite obvious."

"But why? I mean, you—you must have a reason." Kitty had to shake her head again.

"I assure you. Yes, I have a reason. But that, too, if you'll allow me, is privileged information."

Peter popped his head through the opening, then climbed the last few steps onto the parapet. His chest, so skinny and frail, kept heaving up and down as he fought to take in air. "He—he—"

Kieran put his hand on Peter's back. He could feel the shoulder blades poking against the lean flesh. "Easy, easy."

"He—he"—Peter made no attempt to continue with what he wanted to say—"he—"

Kitty went to the boy's side. "You'll tell us, but give yourself a chance to breathe first. Slowly. Breathe."

Peter let out a yell. His lordship had lifted one leg to the top of the battlement wall and was grabbing at the stones, trying to get some hold that would help raise the other leg. Kieran, after one swift stride, circled his lordship's waist and pulled him down and away from the wall, ripping away two buttons from the front of the man's shirt. His lordship made no effort to resist. He stood quite still, his head bowed, his arms straight at this sides.

Peter had picked up one of the popped buttons that had landed at his right foot. Instead of looking down at the button, he gazed off into the distance, toward the sea. "All his life," Peter said, "away there in Australia, Mr. Shaftoe—or, I guess, Lord Shaftoe—all his life he dreamed of coming to live in the castle his ancestors had held. Word of the castle had been passed down from generation to generation and—"

"Nonsense! The poor child's—" Lord Shaftoe had stiffened at the sound of Peter's words. "Why do you let the boy babble on like this?"

Peter, as if he hadn't heard, continued. "—and to reclaim the castle and live here himself was what he wanted more than anything in the whole world. He'd heard about the gunpowder and the ghosts, too. It didn't matter. All that mattered—"

"Stop. Make him stop. Please, I . . ." His lordship then spoke more quietly, even despairingly, as if knowing his plea would never be heard, "I beg you."

"Is he telling the truth?" Kitty asked.

His lordship let his own gaze reach out toward the darkening hills to the north. With a simplicity that seemed foreign to his nature, he said, "I am not a criminal by habit. For all my faults—and I've been told they are many—forgery, bribery are not among them. But there are times when one feels compelled to—enlarge—the range of one's natural inclinations."

He seemed to have seen something in the distance that held his gaze, unmoving, almost entranced. "This castle was to become my own true home, the home won by my ancestors by means I know too well but have chosen to dismiss. It had been the lordly seat of my family for centuries, no matter what history has to say. All my youthful yearning reached out toward these stones, this turret, these lands around. And the sea besides. The boy spoke the truth. What is gunpowder to me? Or ghosts? Or ancient perfidies? Let it all be on my head. But it is here that I must live. Or not live at all. And if the boy has more to tell, I'll listen to him now."

"No," said Peter. "I have no more to tell."

"Then," said George Noel Gordon Lord Shaftoe, "by your leave." He picked up his tweeds, his tie, and the other button Peter had decided not to retrieve. Again erect, he smiled wanly. "And for my crimes, for trespassing beyond the bounds of my nature, I must to prison go. Where I doubt I'll take upon myself the mystery of things. And now, I wish you good evening."

Head high, with only the stately step his words had earned him, he made his measured descent down the winding stair, disappearing little by little until he could be seen no more.

Peter looked down at his hand. "He forgot his button." He started toward the stair, but Kieran stopped him. "Let him go. He'll get himself another."

Peter considered this, nodded, then contemplated the button. Kitty looked at Kieran, Kieran at Kitty. Peter obviously had more to say. "And so no one knows if the castle will blow up or not," he said. He thought this over, then shrugged his shoulders. "I was eating my sandwich and I found myself looking into the eyes of the pig there on the plank. They were open. And so I came here to warn his Lordship. Because at that time, the castle was going to blow up. And he wasn't meant to get blown up with it. That's all I knew then. The rest I knew here. About him and all his life. But now I can tell you this. No one knows if the castle will blow up or not. And I want to know, is it all right if I go back and eat some more of the pig?"

"Yes," said Kitty, still quiet. "Of course."

"Thanks." He started toward the stair but stopped. Without turning around, he said, "What you don't know, either of you, about why you were setting off the gunpowder is this. Mr. Sweeney, you love Brid. But you love your wife more. And so Brid, a ghost, must be let free, only this time not to her death, but to her rest. For love of your wife."

Peter seemed about to take another step but said instead, "And Mrs. Swee—Miss McCloud, you love your handsome Taddy, and there's no one should blame you, the same as no one should blame Mr. Sweeney. Brid's that beautiful and Taddy the most handsome. And they have all their sorrows, too. You shouldn't even blame each other. These are things people sometimes can't decide for themselves. But much as you love Taddy, you love your husband more. And that's why Taddy's ghost must also be freed. For love of your husband."

Kitty raised her head. "You've told me what I'd never intended to tell. It was in my thoughts at the feast when I was with your mother. She knew what I was thinking. And so she told you."

"Oh, no," said Peter. "I know this only now, here, with the two of you." Again he seemed about to move but chose to speak again. "And if there's more I ever know, would you want me to tell it?"

Kieran, his voice kind and quiet, said, "No. You've said

what had to be said. For both of us. We need hear no more."
Peter nodded, then continued toward the stairs.

His foot on the top step, he stopped once more. "Your
truck is down there across the pasture and beyond the next
field. If you're going back to the feasting, may I have a ride? I
really would like more of that pig. I don't know how, but it's
the best ever."

At that the harp was sounded and, above its thrumming
sound, the creak of the treadle and the whisperings of the
loom. When Peter received no answer to his question, he
waited as both Kitty and Kieran raised their heads to listen.
Plaintive was the melody rising into the evening air, steady
and measured the sound of the loom. They listened, then
Kieran nodded, letting Peter know they would follow.

Down the stairs they went. Peter passed the loom, the
harp, seeing nothing, and continued on his way. Kieran and
Kitty stopped to watch, to listen again. Streaks of red and
gold slashed across the western sky, seen through the window,
the hills darkening and the sound of the sea and the revelers'
cries coming more clearly through the evening air.

Kitty retrieved her device, wrapping the wires around it.
Kieran lifted his from under the stool and put it into the
crook of his arm. They both looked toward Brid. There, as
she worked the treadle and moved the shuttle through the
taut threads, a rich cloth of many colors appeared, spreading
itself out along the length of the frame. They could do no
more than stare. To them both it was as if Brid were weaving
a great cloak, the patterns of which would hold, in their warp
and in their woof, the long story of the land and all the souls
gone on before, their sorrows and their griefs. And it was
given to Taddy to set the harp to singing, the plucked,

strummed strings sending forth the plangent song that told of love and loss and the sad yearnings that reach out past the ends of the bent world.

And it came to Kitty and to Kieran that here they would live out their lives—here in the castle—haunted, each of them, by the ghost of a lost and impossible love. Sorrow would be with them always, and with it the remnant of an ancient guilt. And this would be companion to their love for each other.

Clutching the devices that were to have brought the castle down, they followed after Peter, crossing the great hall, treading on gunpowder, holding even closer to themselves the means to set it alight. Out in the courtyard, they went to the farthest shed and thrust deep into the pile of accumulated discards left behind by the departed squatters the implements for which they had no further use, planting even deeper the Internet text and the Texas catalogue with their deadly but now unneeded knowledge.

Kitty and Kieran danced the night away, and their guests danced, too. "Dingle Regatta," "I Wish I had a Kerry Cow," and, of course, "Sweeney Polka." They wheeled around, they changed partners, then went from one figure to another, clapping, slapping their feet, whirling and twirling until it seemed no combination had been left untried. They had journeyed through the labyrinth and emerged exhilarated.

Inspired by the rising moon, the musicians excited each other to greater and greater energy. The Guinness was gone, but enough Tullamore Dew remained for one final sip before the night was over. The spitted pig was left with only its head, which Kieran spirited away for decent burial. Even the pot of nettle soup had been emptied and the bread eaten to the last crumb.

To the battlements Kitty and Kieran went to watch the sun come over the eastern hills. Silver, then golden came the light. The dark pastures could now be seen, the green beginning to show itself little by little as they watched. The sea was already awake, slurping against the indifferent scree.

Brid was seen in the distance with Taddy behind, moving toward the orchard through the morning mist, and after them, the pig, unjustly slain, its presence no more, no less ghostly than theirs, trotting, snuffling, lifting its snout to catch the first breeze of the new morning. "The pig," Kieran whispered. Kitty, her own voice hushed, repeated the words, "The pig." She paused, then said, "Will we ever know where it really came from? And what it meant?"

"No," said Kieran. "We won't. Nor should we. Not everything has to be explained. Some things are better left to the unknown."

Kitty gave a single nod of agreement. With no more words spoken, and no prior agreement needed, wife and husband lay down alongside the crude battlements, each in the other's arms. Before the sun had fully risen they had become—not for the first time and not for the last—the envy of angels.

ACKNOWLEDGMENTS

First, the author must thank Noelle Campbell-Sharpe and her Cill Rialaig Project, in County Kerry, for his cottage stays on the cliffs above Ballinskeligs that gave added inspiration to this work.

Both Yaddo and the MacDowell Colony also provided the author with generous hospitality, and he is most grateful. He also thanks Catherine, Mary, and Eileen Clarke, as well as their friends Doreen and Harry Naughton, for the much-needed information about their native Ireland. David Smyth an Irish bartender, also contributed.

His thanks to Margot Mensing for her shared expertise in the ways of weaving and to Martha Witt for her welcome help and encouragement. A special thanks to Beth Leanza, of the Saratoga Springs Public Library, for her assistance in the complexities of research.

The Luddite author's final draft, in typescript, was transformed to digital format by his nephew Jim Smith and carefully copyedited by his sister Helen Smith. Daniel D'Arezzo made the corrections in the document submitted to the author's agent and publisher. To them all he is deeply grateful for this helpful accomplishment.

For the dedicated and gifted expertise of his editors, Barbara Ascher and Christopher Lehmann-Haupt, he is grateful beyond measure.